IN YOUR DREAMS

LEAGUE OF THE MOON - BOOK 1

ROBERT SANBORN

Copyright © 2020 by Robert Sanborn

Cover Art and Design by OliviaProDesign

Contact:RobertSanborn@robsanbornauthor.com

CONTENTS

To my wife Diana and my sister Susan—who believe and believed.

"All human beings are also dream beings. Dreaming ties all mankind together." - Jack Kerouac

The universe is full of magical things patiently waiting for our wits to grow sharper - Eden Phillpotts from 'A Shadow Passes'

CHAPTER ONE

HENRY'S DREAM

THEY'RE COMING FOR ME. I can hear the voices echoing through the dark woods ... closer. I can see the faint orange glow of the torches when I glance behind me. My heart feels like it will explode from my chest, and my throat is raw from gulping in the harsh winter air. Snow crunches under my feet, and it's the loudest sound in the world. I want to stop, try to reason with them, but I know it's futile. The madness they all suffer from isn't born of reason. Innuendo and superstition are the parents of the mania that consumes them. They will not stop. They will not reason. They will kill me.

This is the dream I've been having, night after night, for over two months now. As I lay in bed, I try to reel myself back toward shore from an ethereal river of insanity. I grasp the everyday items in my room like life preservers—TV remote, alarm clock, iPhone on the dresser.

My heartbeat is returning to some rate approaching normal. I get out of bed and feel my way across the dark room. Reaching around the frame of the door, I slap blindly at the cool tiles (they feel mercifully solid and real) until my flattened hand trips the bathroom light switch. Fumbling toward the sink, I slap the faucet on and splash cool water on my face, then fill a glass for myself and take a few swallows. I place the glass down on the counter, reach up, and run my hands through my hair. Something falls into the sink. Pine needles. What the fuck? Am I still dreaming?

I trace my steps back through the day, trying to figure out if there is any logical explanation for this. Nothing comes to mind. "You are seriously losing your shit," I say out loud. The dull echo of the bathroom walls offers confirmation. But am I? I mean, I'm staring at actual physical evidence that, apparently, just came from a dream. I shut off the bathroom light and head back to bed. The clock on the dresser reads 3:13 a.m. Wonderful! I can look forward to moving through another day like some mindless zombie.

I run the dream back through my mind, trying to make sense of the fading images consciousness is claiming back. I can see myself in an old-fashioned, white nightie and weatherbeaten leather boots. I'm falling in the snow. A pile of branches breaks my fall. I try to pull my exhausted body up, and it's useless. I look down at my feet. My ankle is twisted at an ungodly angle. The mob in the distance is closing fast. Hopelessness and resignation are all I can feel as the dream fades. The last thing I remember is being covered in branches, snow, and pine needles. And then … nothing.

Chapter Two

The Morning After

Harsh morning light streams through the bedroom window, waking me up a lot earlier than the six a.m. alarm I'd set the night before. Gotta remember to close those damned curtains before I hit the sheets at night. I'm still getting used to the quirks of this new apartment.

I moved to Salem, Massachusetts, a little over two months ago from Portland, Maine, where I worked in the ER department. I loved my job there but couldn't pass up a chance to work in the ER department at Massachusetts General Hospital. The bump in pay had absolutely nothing to do with it. Really. No bullshit. Okay, maybe a little.

My name is Henry Trank. Yes, Hank Trank, haha, hilarious. What the hell were my parents thinking? Just call me Henry, and we'll get along fine.

Any-who, I've been having this terrifying and confusing dream almost since the moment I arrived in Salem. I don't remember why I decided to move to Salem. There are plenty of places a lot closer to MGH I could have picked. I don't even remember making a conscious decision to live here. But ever since, oddly enough, I've had the feeling I *belong* here. I'm not talking about the feeling you get when you live in a place for a while and start to feel you fit in. I'm talking about the feeling of being ... home, for lack of a better term.

I'm not the most superstitious person in the world. I'm not the kind of guy you would say is a big believer in religious or spiritual things. That being said, I'm also not *so* married to science and cold reality that I would outright deny there are things out there that can't be explained. *"Pine needles in my hair for $200, Alex!"* But I just can't shake the feeling I'm here for a reason. What it is, I haven't clue one. And I've felt *nothing* like this until I arrived in this town. It's like a long-dormant, mud-covered beacon in my head got accidentally uncovered and is shining its ass off.

Anyway, back to the dream. Sorry, I ramble sometimes.

Every time this dream happens, it always seems the angry mob following me is getting just a little bit closer. And the weird thing is, until last night, I had never actually seen myself—in the dream, anyway—from the perspective of another person looking *at* me. It was always me, seeing out of my own eyes, the snow and the trees and my freezing breath. Something changed this time. I could see myself through the eyes of my pursuers. Well, at least what seemed to be the head pursuer. The leader of the pack. He was pissed-off and scared shitless all at once. He was aware of some special knowledge in my possession, and he was desperate to know what it was. And the strangest part of it all was (aside from pine needles in my bathroom sink) in the dream, I'm a woman. How's that for a twist?

I don't really understand how I could be feeling what he's feeling, but if I had to describe it, it would be akin to telepathy. It seems strange to me I would be conscious of this in a dream. It's like some weird mental tennis back and forth between me and whoever this crazy bastard is. I don't know what he looks like, and I don't understand why he leads these people to come after me. But I can feel his anger and fear like they are my own. Last night was the first time I had viewed the dream from this new perspective. The feelings were so raw and powerful that the more I dwell on them, the more it affects me in my waking hours.

I need to get out of here for a while.

Thank God I took some vacation time, and I don't have to deal with the ER's craziness today. I grabbed my keys and my cell phone and headed out the door and into the chilly October morning.

The feelings of the dream are falling away like the dried skin of an onion. I'm feeling more like my usual upbeat self again. Time for a nice, tall, iced coffee. I headed over to The Cracked Cauldron on Essex St. I discovered this little hole-in-the-wall not too long after I got here in July. And they just so happen to make the best iced coffee on God's green earth.

I pulled open the black, broad-plank door, dinging the bell that hangs from the ceiling inside. Joanne, the barista, looks up at me with her usual thousand-watt smile, and I can't help but return it with my own crooked grin. I've gotten to know her since I've been coming here on my weekend mornings (okay, I've kinda made a point of it ... fine). Aside from being drop-dead gorgeous, she's got the kind of sarcastic, biting-but-not-cruel humor I find sexy as hell.

"What's your pleasure this morning, Band-aid boy?

Band-aid boy! I love it! See what I mean? "I think I'll go with the iced coffee, half-decaf, milk, two sugars, and a side of haha, Band-aid boy!"

She gave me a little smirk and then whipped around. Her straight black hair fanned out and dropped back to her shoulders. She got to work on my order.

She looked great, as always. She was wearing an above-the-knee black leather skirt, fishnet stockings that complimented her toned calves, black heels, and a red Cracked Cauldron apron draped over a black polo. It may be a work uniform, but she looked almost ready for a night on the town. She caught me watching her, ahem, working. Her sharp green eyes miss little. She cracked a wicked grin of her own.

"So what's new in your life lately, Henry?"

I gave her a raised eyebrow, pursed my lips, and tried to decide how to let her in on the news about the dream. We've known each other a while now, but I'm unsure just how far down *"Intimacy Road"* we actually are. So far,

I was the only customer in there at this early hour. So I didn't have to worry all that much about speaking my mind.

"Well, now that you've asked, there's something that's been happening to me ever since I've moved here, and I'd like your take on it."

"Fire away," she said.

"Okay. This is gonna sound strange, but ... here it is. I've been having this really vivid dream almost every night since I've moved here. It's not something I've dreamt about, ever, in my life before I got here. In the dream, at least when it first started out, I'm being chased by an angry mob through a snowy forest. I don't know how, but I intuitively know they mean to catch me and kill me."

She put the iced coffee down in front of me and leaned over the counter on her elbows. "You've got my attention."

"Okay ... it went on like this for a while, at least a couple weeks, with them gradually getting closer and closer on each occasion. Last night, though, things changed. Instead of being pursued, I became the pursuer. And what's strange about it is there is this kind of weird telepathy thing between us. It's not like reading someone's mind. It's more like being able to feel their emotions, their fears."

I didn't really feel all that comfortable about telling her I was a woman in the dream. I didn't think it would enhance my chances with her. But then again—Nah, moving on.

"Do you think maybe it might have something to do with moving down here? You know, like, the change in lifestyle and location could be a little more unsettling than you may have given it credit for?"

"Normally, I'd be inclined to agree with you on that, but there's more to the story. After the dream last night, it took me a little while to get my bearings. Once I did, I got up and went into the bathroom to splash some cold water on my face and get a drink. I kinda ran my hands over my face and hair, and when I brought them back down, they came with some strange cargo. A few pine needles landed in the sink."

She looked at me, her left eyebrow raised like Spock's in the old Star Trek shows.

"Come again?"

"I shit you not."

"And how, exactly, would there be pine needles in your hair from a dream? Do you think maybe you could have been sleepwalking during the dream? Or maybe you brought it in with you after a walk? Had it in your hoodie and didn't realize it?"

"None of that occurred to me. All of that's possible, I guess. I've never sleepwalked in my life before," I said, "but I think I would have noticed if I'd been outside during a dream. There would have been other evidence, like some needles, maybe on my feet, or some dirt dragged into the apartment or into my bed, but there was none of that stuff.

She started twirling her jet-black hair between her fingers and stared unfocused down at the bar. I got lost in my own train of thought when the bell over the door dinged, and in walked another customer. She came out of her reverie and got down to business with the new customer, and I was left to my own thoughts.

What could all of this possibly mean? Does it even mean anything? Am I overreacting to this? I didn't think it was an overreaction, though, for two excellent reasons. The first: night after night, the same dream since I got to Salem. And physical evidence, maybe, but not for sure, being the second.

Another ding. In walked another customer. It was looking like we were gonna have to leave this little meeting of the minds for another time. I headed for the door when Joanne piped up.

"Henry, don't leave yet. I got one more thing to ask you before you go."

I sat back down on the black leather barstool and waited out customer number three.

When she finished, she came over to where I sat and asked, "What are you doing later on tonight? I thought maybe we could get together and, you know, talk some more about this. And maybe a few other things?"

Again with the crooked smile. This ... is getting good.

Okay, be cool, Henry. "Um, I'm gonna go with ... Yes!" So cool.

Amused, she motioned at me with her hand to continue.

"Um, when do you get off?"

Again with the Spock eyebrow ...

"From work! What time do you get off from work?"

I wondered if my face looked as beet-red as it felt. Could I possibly look like more of a geek at this moment?

"So smooth. I, ahem, *get off* from work at around four. Why don't you call me around five and we can decide where we want to go for dinner? Sound good?"

Dinner? I like her style!

"Sounds great!"

We each pulled out our cell phones and exchanged numbers. I grabbed my iced coffee and was getting ready to head out the door when she said, "Oh, and Henry, you should really get something for that sunburn."

She winked me out the door with a laugh. I shot her a sheepish smile and got out while the getting was good.

)☆(

Across the street, the man in the dark suit watched as Henry exited from the coffee shop. He noticed Henry appeared to be in fine spirits. This puzzled him. He knew what Mr. Trank had been dreaming about lately. They all did.

Chapter Three
Leonard and Delilah

I walked away from the coffee shop in my own little world. I couldn't believe *she* had actually asked *me* out! Feeling pretty good about myself, I decided I would take a pleasant stroll around town. It was a beautiful late October day, after all.

There is nothing like New England in the fall. Sixty-five degrees and sunny, with just a hint of a chill in the air. Bright orange and red leaves were strewn across faded green lawns. Houses decorated with monsters and ghouls. Bales of hay and cornstalks lining the walks of some homes, while others were adorned with faux spider webs, witches on brooms, and jack-o'-lanterns sporting a million different expressions.

I turned the corner onto Essex Street and saw Samantha's statue from "Bewitched" across the way. I made a finger gun at Samantha and winked. I know, total geek move, but I was feeling it! I hooked a left and made my way into my new favorite restaurant I'd discovered since moving to

Salem—Rockafellas. The thought of those steak tips here tonight already has my mouth watering. And I know Joanne will love them.

I set up a reservation for two at one of the window booths for 8:30 pm. I made small talk with the guy at the counter—the usual stuff. How do you think the Sox and Pats are doing? Is this Brady's last year with them, or is he gonna stay and play till he's forty-five, maybe fifty, if we're lucky?

The man behind the counter launched into his opinion on the Pats when a strange tingle started in the middle of my head. I don't know how to describe it, exactly. It felt like when you eat a piece of cake, and the frosting is way too sweet. The sensation lasted about ten seconds—and this probably has a lot to do with how this dream had me feeling lately—but when that odd tingling faded, I couldn't shake the feeling I was being watched. I snapped my head around and looked out of the massive glass windows at the restaurant's side facing Essex Street. Still, I noticed nothing out of the ordinary. I couldn't swear to it, but there seemed to be a spot my eyes settled on that essentially looked like the outline of someone. As if they'd been standing there only moments before—almost like a weird photo-negative effect. This dream is fucking with my head.

I thanked the guy at the counter and left for home. It's a good hike up Lafayette Street to my place, but I had plenty of time to kill until tonight. I love my street. Everyone takes excellent care of their homes here. Nicely manicured front lawns. Lots of wonderful landscaping. The houses are set back from the sidewalk and not leaning out over it like rude spectators at a baseball game. Beautiful.

I noticed a couple and their Rottweiler strolling along on the same side of the street. They were coming my way. As I got closer, I saw the dog's ears perk. He turned his head in my direction. He started a low growl and I moved slightly to my right, keeping a safe distance. As we passed, I said to the man holding the leash, "I wouldn't want to get on the wrong side of that puppy."

He stopped, tilted his head, and said, "I would hope it never comes to that, Henry."

How the hell does this guy know my name?

"I'm sorry, have we met?" I asked.

"No, sir. Not yet, anyway."

He sported a crooked grin, bordering on a smirk.

"Then how do you know my name?"

"It says 'for Henry, aka Band-aid boy' on your coffee cup."

Duh!! I never noticed Joanne had put that there. I still felt like a guilty asshole for being suspicious, however.

I let loose a nervous laugh. "Ah! That's my friend Joanne. She likes to embarrass me for sport." Then, "I'm sorry, your name is?"

"I'm Leonard. Leonard Shrumm. And this is my fiancée, Delilah."

Leonard is lean, about six-two, six-three. He's got slicked-back, iron-grey hair and is well dressed in a grey sport coat, black mock turtle-neck, black slacks, and black loafers. He smells mildly of expensive—would cost me a week's salary—cologne. I don't know what it is about him, but there is an aura of high and mighty there. One of those guys who looks like he knows a secret about you. Like maybe he saw you spanking your monkey when you thought no one was looking.

Delilah is about five-six, pretty—in a Kim Basinger kind of way—with long, wavy blonde hair. She's wearing faded jeans, tan calf-height boots, and a white sweater with one of those big, floppy collars. I think they call it a cowl-neck. She's wearing perfume that would probably cost me the *next* week's salary.

You can always tell when a scent is expensive. I don't know how, it's just an innate thing people who don't come from money can sense.

"Nice to meet you both. I would shake hands, but I'm afraid Cujo here would probably eat mine."

Polite laughter from both. Not exactly a denial.

"Are you new to the neighborhood, Henry?" Delilah asked. "I don't recall ever seeing you around here before today."

"Yes. I just moved here right after the fourth of July weekend from Portland, Maine. Still getting used to the area, but I really love it."

"It is beautiful. And gets even more so the deeper into fall we go," said Delilah.

"Do you work in Salem, Henry?" Leonard asked.

"No, I just started working in the ER at Mass General."

"That's a great hospital," said Delilah. "They took excellent care of my mother after her stroke. You wouldn't even know she had one to see her today."

"I'm glad to hear that. I've only heard good things about the place, and so far, it's lived up to the reputation. What do you both do for work? If you don't mind me asking," I said.

"Not at all, Henry. I have a real estate company right here in Salem, and Delilah works there with me. I'm the one who does all the glad-handing and selling, and Delilah is ridiculously good with numbers, so she keeps the books ship-shape."

"That sounds like an ideal setup."

"We think so," said Delilah.

"Are you considering buying any real estate now that you've settled in for a bit, Henry?" Leonard asked.

"I haven't actually given it much thought. The temptation is there, though. The more and more I walk around town, the more I feel I would like to put down roots and stay here. I don't know how to describe it, but I feel like I belong here."

"Well, if you ever feel the urge to take the plunge," said Leonard, "we would be more than happy to help you out."

"Thank you. I just may take you up on that. Well, it was very nice meeting you both. And you too, Fido.

"I'm sorry. We never introduced you to Hercules. He's not so intimidating once you get to know him. But that intimidation *does* comes in handy ... just in case there is someone you'd *rather not* get to know," Leonard said, winking.

"He really is a sweet dog," Delilah said, leaning toward Henry, an odd look on her face. "I know *I sleep well at night*, my dreams protected by Herc. And there is nothing more important than that. Wouldn't you agree, Henry?"

"Um, absolutely."

I was feeling a bit freaked out. They were both a bit on the creepy side.

"You two have a nice day now. Nice meeting you both."

They smiled and strolled along the way they had been heading, and I did the same. But something nagged at the back of my mind about the end of that conversation. Most people would say, 'I sleep better at night knowing my dog is protecting the house. Not, *'I sleep well at night, my dreams protected.'* Kinda weird. And I couldn't swear to it, but when she said it, the faintest look of ... I don't know ... agitation crossed Leonard's face. Or maybe I'm just imagining shit. Like I said, the dream is fucking with my head ... a lot.

Overthinking (a nasty habit of mine) as I walk along Lafayette, I realized I'd walked right past my apartment and had to double back the way I came. As

I looked back in the direction Leonard and Delilah were headed, I saw them getting into a red Jaguar. They seemed none too happy with each other.

Oh well, not my business. Time to head upstairs for a quick power nap and then a shower. I got me a date with the lovely and wise-cracking Joanne tonight. "Alright, alright,"... apologies to Matthew McConaughey.

"Why the hell would you say something like that to him, Delilah?"

"Like what?"

"I know," (Leonard made quotes with his fingers), "I sleep well at night, my dreams protected. Why would you say something like that? Why even take the risk of giving him a clue as to who he is ... or was?"

Delilah rolled her eyes.

"He's not gonna figure anything out. Don't worry about it. I just like to have a little fun now and then. You know," (quote fingers), "live on the edge."

"And what do you think Solomon would think?" Leonard asked.

She said nothing.

"We need to keep this under wraps for now. There's no point in taking stupid risks and tipping Henry off before the time comes."

She put up both hands in mock surrender. "Okay, okay. No more playing with him like that anymore. I just like to have a bit of fun now and then. And I like to tweak you a little bit, too ... spice things up, you know?"

He relaxed a little. He couldn't stay mad at her for long. And, truth be told, when she did shit like that, it kinda turned him on.

Chapter Four

Need to Know

As I HEADED UP the stairs to my apartment, I was getting a bit tired. Not ready for a nap just yet, but close.

Fragments of the dream kept popping to the surface of my consciousness like dead fish in a polluted pond, and it had me curious. I grabbed my laptop and headed out to the back balcony for a little research session.

The first thing I checked out was anything I could find on the subject of sleepwalking. Well, new word for the day learned. Somnambulism—aka sleepwalking. It also stated between one percent to fifteen percent of the population sleepwalks. Common causes for sleepwalking are sleep deprivation, sedatives and alcohol, and certain medications—none of which applied to me. It's more common in children than in adults. Interesting.

I thought back over my childhood and couldn't ever recall sleepwalking—or my parents ever bringing up the subject. The web page also stated sleepwalkers remain in deep sleep as the event occurs and usually have no recollection of it happening. So I suppose it is possible I might have sleepwalked. I need proof.

What if I could catch myself in the act?

I headed back inside to the bedroom and grabbed my GoPro camera out of the closet. I set it up on the dresser across from the foot of the bed, facing diagonally, making sure the shot included the balcony's sliding glass doors. With that done, I headed back out to the balcony and the laptop for more investigation.

Apparently, some bizarre shit can happen during sleepwalking events. There was an account of one guy creating masterpieces of art during his episodes. Another where a guy drove ten miles in his sleep and killed an in-law. Yikes. There is the case of a woman who left her bedroom at night to have sex with complete strangers. No bullshit, it happened in Australia ... *'Lucy, you got some splainin' to do!'* Yet another where a wife woke up at two o'clock in the morning to find her husband mowing the lawn, naked. Actually, that one didn't sound like too much of a problem, save the nakedness.

Okay, I guess Joanne might be on to something with the sleepwalking angle. It would explain the pine needles being in my hair when I woke up. Still, it doesn't explain the lack of any other evidence I was actually outside.

After a couple of hours researching out on the balcony, I finally felt ready for a power nap. I kicked off my shoes, hopped on top of the blankets covering the bed, and closed my eyes. Drifting towards a pleasant doze, I snapped out of it and realized I hadn't turned on the alarm or the GoPro, and set about doing just that. Wouldn't want to miss my date with Joanne ... or anything I might do in my sleep without my expressed written consent.

)●(

This was the last day of my old life. Looking back on all of it now, I'm still not sure how I ever really came to believe that what happened to me was possible—it took *a lot* to convince me. But it was. Every last bit of it. You'll see. I have to leave you now, but you're in good hands. This is just the beginning of a long and magical journey. Where it all ends? Who knows? I'll pop back in from time to time in later volumes—give you a birds-eye view of the situation. As for the rest of this particular story—well, hang on tight.

CHAPTER FIVE

UNWANTED GUEST

As DUSK APPROACHED, LEONARD Shrumm pulled into the neatly paved driveway of his large, brick-faced, Cape Cod-style home, and waited for the garage door to open so it could gobble up him and the Jag.

He'd dropped Delilah at the office with the premise she needed to finish up this week's paperwork. He told her he would grab something for them to eat and pick her up later. He left out the part about coming home and doing what he was about to do.

He entered the dimly lit living room and assumed the lotus position. Dropping into a meditative trance came easily to him. He'd been doing it for well over three centuries now.

Across town, Henry had started to dream. Leonard sensed the exhaustion coming from Henry in waves during their conversation on Lafayette Street. Just being in proximity to Henry now, he could feel all the old connections coming back. Connections that had formed in a different time and place.

Now, alone in his living room, deep in meditation, he could take a peek into Henry's dreams. It wasn't hard for him. He'd learned to travel the astral planes back in the late 1600s. He'd learned at the foot of a master who'd been doing it long before Leonard (as he called himself now) had been born.

There was a tingling sensation, and then a high-pitched whine only Leonard could hear as he slipped from his earthly body and into the astral plane. He could see the astral cord trailing out behind him. It kept him tethered to his flesh form like the lifeline of an astronaut.

Most newcomers to the astral plane would have to worry about the various different entities trying to feed off your energy when you first get there. Leonard had no such worries now. He'd established himself there as one not to fool with, given the reputation of his master, of course.

Time and space differed greatly from where Leonard was now. He merely had to think himself into Henry's dream, and he was center stage. He was careful not to allow Henry knowledge of his presence in the dream realm. He waited patiently as Henry cycled into REM sleep, and then the usual churn of images commenced.

Random snippets of Henry's subconscious streamed by him like movie clips blurred at the edges. Mostly mundane stuff. Henry brushing pine needles out of his hair. A scene from a Little League baseball game. On a date as a young man, Henry clumsily removes a young lady's bra while a woman with straight black hair and wearing a red apron stands on the hood of the car, looking in.

Now the field in front of Leonard turned black for a few moments. Then, distant but instantly noticeable, the light of several torches painted the trees and snow in a shimmer of dark orange and yellow light. Directly in front of the space Leonard covertly occupied, a frightened woman staggered through the snow—panting, exhausted, and crying. She looked back in horror at the approaching mob and, despite her exhaustion, summoned the will to keep running. Leonard concentrated with all he had to discern the emotions and thoughts running through the frightened woman's mind.

They know I've discovered his secret. I must escape! If I don't, they will kill me, and the others will never know the truth. It is not us who are the evil ones. It's him ...

Henry awoke with a scream and tumbled out of bed. As he got up off the floor, he noticed a quick shimmer of light in the room's corner. It vanished almost as fast as he laid eyes on it.

Leonard snapped back to this realm—hard! He tumbled backward out of the meditative position he'd been in for roughly an hour, hitting his head on the antique coffee table. He was startled and confused. Nothing like this had happened to him before. He had been a master of the astral realms he'd patrolled for centuries—until today.

Shaken badly, he heaved himself from the floor and headed into the kitchen to use the phone. With the receiver still in his hand, he considered the situation. He asked himself how he was going to explain this failure to Solomon, and couldn't. At least, not yet. He put the phone back in its cradle after a few moments and wondered about his next move, then grabbed his keys from the marble counter and headed for the garage.

)☆(

Henry snatched the GoPro from the dresser and hooked it up to the laptop to download the video recorded from the last forty-five minutes. He brought up the recording on the laptop screen and watched himself at triple speed to save time.

Not much happened in the first twenty-seven minutes. Then he smiled and made motions with his hands, like he was trying to untie a complicated knot. Or a bra, perhaps? Video Henry rested his hands, and nothing much happened for the next ten minutes. Then, to his shock and amazement, his legs shot straight up at the ceiling, and he started to mock run like a cartoon character. It would have been funny but for the look of absolute terror on his face. His legs came to rest, finally, and he cried. He talked aloud in the shot, but it was hard to make out what he was saying through the tears. Turning the volume up on the laptop, he clicked back to where he started talking. The only words he could make out were, *"...escape! If I don't ... the others ... truth. It is not us ..."* He was dumbfounded.

Chapter Six

The Date

"Henry? ... Oh, Henry?"

"I'm sorry. Just kinda zoning out there for a minute."

"I noticed. You've kinda zoned out a lot tonight. And your steak tips look cold and lonely. Is there something wrong? You're not your usual upbeat self. You seem ... preoccupied." She said this with a genuine look of concern on her face. It both scared and warmed him.

"You remember the dream I was telling you about earlier today?"

"Of course."

"After I left you this morning, I took a long walk around town. I came here to book the reservations for tonight, and then I went home to relax ... only I couldn't relax. The dream kept popping up in my thoughts, and I couldn't shake what you said about sleepwalking. So I grabbed my laptop and headed out to the deck with a cold one, and I did some research on sleepwalking." Henry then filled her in on all the different incidents he'd looked up.

"Sex with the neighbors without knowing it?" She looked a tad skeptical about that one. "Anyway, did you find out anything that might point you in the right direction?"

"No, not exactly."

Jo tilted her head, confused. Henry continued.

"Don't get me wrong. I learned a lot about something I know nothing about. But it led me to do a little ... how should I put this ... detective work."

She leaned in. "What do you mean by detective work, exactly?"

"While I was doing my research, I kinda got the idea maybe I should set up a camera and see if I actually was sleepwalking. I grabbed my GoPro outta the closet and set it up on my dresser for later. I went back to reading about, hold on to your hat ... new word for the day ... somnambulism."

She licked her thumb and pressed it to Henry's forehead.

"Why d'you do that?"

"It's your imaginary gold star for getting the synonym for sleepwalking correct on the first try, Einstein."

Henry took a modest bow, and she winked at him. "Anyway, after about two hours of reading, I was getting a little sleepy. After almost *forgetting* to start the recording, I set it and went to bed for a bit of a power nap. And I probably should have stayed awake because I got a *lot* more than I bargained for."

"And by that, you mean?" She gestured with her hand for him to continue.

"I can't really explain it as well as what the video will show you."

"Did you bring the video with you?"

"It's on my laptop. I didn't want to carry it to dinner. Kinda cumbersome to carry with me for a night on the town."

She tilted her head and looked at him like he was slow and in need of some encouragement.

"What?" he said.

"You have a cell phone, right? I mean, I could have sworn we exchanged numbers at the coffee shop this morning. Or is my memory failing me?"

"I, um ... didn't think of that. Don't give me that look. I was traumatized."

"Uh-huh. You know what *I* think, Henry?"

He was getting a little nervous now. "What?"

"I think you leaving your laptop at home with the video on it ... and then pretending you didn't know or couldn't remember you could have just downloaded it to your phone ... I think it's all part of a little scheme to get me to leave here with you and come back to your apartment."

Holy shit, she looked furious. "Nonononono! I swear I just had a complete brain fart. I wouldn't do something like that. I swear!"

My God, he thought, I've already screwed things up with her and ...

She held up her hand to stop his rambling.

"No! No more bullshit, Henry. What are you really trying to pull here?"

He just looked at her helplessly while she glared at him, waiting for an answer, and finally (she couldn't hold it any longer) she broke into a huge grin and laughed. The relief Henry felt was like a solid block of ice melting from his shoulders in about two seconds.

After she stopped laughing, she said, "I was just fucking with you, Henry. It's my way of saying I think I'd like to keep the night going. If that's alright with you?"

CHAPTER SEVEN
KISSES AND TELLS

SLAM! THAT'S THE SOUND they made as she backed him hard into the front door to his apartment. She pressed up against him and tilted her pretty face up toward his with a mischievous grin. Her green eyes twinkled in the blueish-white LEDs that lit the hallway. He leaned down and put his hand gently behind her head and into that silky, jet-black hair and kissed her. Slowly at first. And then she made it clear right up front slowly wasn't gonna cut it.

"Get a room!"

It was Mrs. Greenblatt from down the hall. Neither of them noticed her coming up the stairs at the other end of the hallway.

Joanne looked up at him. "Keys would be a good thing right now, Henry."

Henry was still a little dazed and really in the moment, so it took a second or two for him to snap to it.

"Oh, right, right." He fumbled the keys out of his pocket, looked down to open the door, and realized he may need to turn slightly to the right so Mrs. Greenblatt didn't notice *how much* he was enjoying the night so far.

They headed into the apartment and closed the door on the ever-so-nosy Mrs. Greenblatt. Joanne took her coat off and tossed it onto the couch. She looked over at Henry and pointed, then turned her hand upside down and crooked her index finger back and forth in a come-hither gesture. A wicked grin crossed her face. Henry did as he was told. When you see a beautiful brunette in a strapless black dress and killer heels, really, what chance in hell do you have of saying no?

He couldn't say what perfume she was wearing, but it suited her perfectly. It's said the sense of smell is most responsible for the triggering of memories, and tonight would be no exception.

He put his hands on her shoulders and slid them down her arms. She raised hers up around his back, one high, one low, and his arms mimicked hers. They were tightly wound together now, and his lips gently met hers with a soft flick of tongues. After a few moments, she leaned back in his arms and looked at him with half-closed eyes, and said, "Well ... my judgment never fails me. I knew just by looking at you, you'd be an excellent kisser."

Taking a page from her book of smartassery, Henry looked her straight in the eyes and did his best Han Solo impersonation. "I know."

She leaned her head back and laughed.

"I love a guy that can quote Star Wars. And from Empire, the best movie, no less!"

Henry was impressed. Star Wars knowledge *and* gorgeous! We're definitely on the right path.

Henry liked surprises, so when she took both hands and shoved him backward really hard onto the bed, so hard he bounced, he burst out laughing, and so did she. Then she crawled on top of him, slowly and deliberately, until she was face to face with him ... hair hanging down all around his face. They kissed and tangled, tangled and kissed for who knew or cared how long. It was one of those moments that slips through time unnoticed by the clock or the universe. It was just two people so into the moment neither realizes they've crossed into the next level. From meeting to friendship, from friendship to intimacy, and then something more that's felt in the soul. And you know it without a word being spoken. It's the kind of moment you never want to end. But when it does, it leaves you with a longing for more. Not in a junkie-fix kind of way, but something akin to joyful expectation. And not just the physical more. There's no doubt he definitely wanted the physical more. Looking at Jo, what guy wouldn't? He wanted to get to know her. All of her. He'd not felt this way in ages about any woman. He found himself, more and more lately, caring about what she thought and felt. He looked forward to his times at The Cracked Cauldron just to share what was on his mind with her. But there was only so far they were going to go tonight, and she'd made it sublimely clear. And he gained another level of respect for her.

Spent, panting, and laying side-by-side in comfortable silence, they held hands for several minutes. Joanne then turned to him and said, "Let's get something cold to drink, and you can fire up the laptop you conveniently forgot to bring to dinner tonight, and we can watch your home movies."

"Ha. Home movies. I know how to party, right?"

She smiled and got up off the bed, smoothing out her knee-length black dress. But not before he caught sight of the tattoo on her upper left thigh.

"What's that tattoo mean?"

"This," (she pointed her index finger at it), "is the triple goddess symbol."

"Okay. But what does it mean?" he asked.

"It has a couple meanings, actually. It represents the waxing, full, and waning moons. They're symbolic for the three phases of womanhood—maiden, mother, and crone." She then pointed to the left-facing crescent of the symbol, "They also represent something else. This one symbolizes new life, rejuvenation, and new beginnings. The middle part, or the full moon, represents when magic is at its most powerful, and the right facing one, the waning moon, represents the best time to send things away, get things out of your life, or to finish things."

"I hope I fall under the waxing category." He clasped his hands together in prayer. A beseeching look on his face.

She laughed, "Most definitely, Mr. Trank!" She returned his prayer by putting both hands together in front of her and bowing. They laughed.

Henry then asked, "So, why do you have the tattoo?"

"It's just something I liked and also something, when I get to know you better, I'll tell you more about. But let's keep a minor mystery around it for now." She wiggled her eyebrows and flashed him a wicked grin.

"Fair enough. Okay, let me set up the laptop so you can see what's been occupying my mind most of the night."

He set up the computer on the coffee table in front of the couch. They sat side by side as he started the video.

Henry didn't bother to watch the video again. He watched her instead—more interested in her reaction. She studied the images flashing before her intently, revealing nothing. The video ended, and he was about to ask her what she thought about it, when she raised a hand to stop him.

"Rewind to about the thirty-seven-minute mark."

He did as told and asked her, "Did you notice something?"

"Oh, yeah."

"What?" He asked.

"Start it up, and I'll show you."

He resumed play. She took control of the laptop mouse and stopped the video.

"Look here, Henry, to the right of the bed."

"I don't see anything."

"You don't notice how it gets slightly darker on the right side of the bed? In front of the door?"

"Rewind it a little further back, like ten seconds," he said.

She did as he asked, and he focused like a laser on the door to the bathroom. And ever so slightly, the door darkened. "Holy shit!" he said.

She nodded. "Hold on to your hat, Henry. I'm just getting started."

She tapped the right arrow on the keyboard to move it frame by frame, then stopped, took the mouse, and circled the pointer around an area higher on the door.

"Do you see what I see?" she asked.

Squinting, Henry tried to make something out, but all he saw were lighter and darker shades in the place where she'd indicated.

"I don't see anything out of the ordinary. Just some lighter splotches in the dark."

She went into the settings and adjusted a couple of colors. And then he saw it. It was a face! Its features were not distinguishable, but surer than shit, it was a face!

"Oh, my God! This house is fucking haunted!" he whispered.

She looked at him and tilted her hand back and forth.

"Maybe, maybe not. There's more you need to see."

Joanne fast-forwarded the video. The black mass was still there, all the way to the end. Then there was a flash of white light that appeared near the camera, at the foot of the bed. When the light entered, the black mass didn't just disappear. It zipped upward like it was escaping through the ceiling. Like it was scared.

Henry sat in stunned silence. He'd noticed the white light before, had seen it with his own eyes, and then on the video. He just thought little of it. He'd chalked it up to maybe headlights reflecting off of something from the street. Not now.

"What do you think is going on here?" he asked.

"I don't know. But I do know someone we can talk to. Maybe get a better grasp on what we just saw."

Jo took out her cell phone.

"Wanda, it's Jo. I'm at a friend's house right now, and we have something we need your expertise on. Are you still at the shop, or are you at home?" A brief pause, then "are you sure it's no trouble? I know it's kinda late. Okay, thank you so much. We'll be there in about twenty minutes. Thanks a ton, Wanda." Click. "Okay Henry, let's hit the road."

Chapter Eight

Wanda

Henry thought Wanda's Wicca'd Emporium was ... interesting ... to put it mildly. The exterior of the building was comprised of black wood shingles. There was a large multi-paned picture window trimmed blood-red, and a door painted to match. The sign above the door was the establishment title in reflective gold paint. On the sign's right was a fingernail moon facing left and a black cat sitting on the moon's bottom edge. The other end of the sign had a handcrafted witch's broom pointing up and to the right. The bristles on the broom were tree branches bound with twine, and the shaft was the same reflective gold as the lettering.

In the large storefront window were various items for the practicing witch. There were cauldrons, sage bundles, thousands of crystals of different sizes, shapes, and colors, and several books on wooden stands. Henry noticed one stand was empty and wondered what book belonged there. Being close to Halloween, the inside of the window was trimmed with strands of plastic, autumn-colored leaves, and all the items in the window rested on straw. The border of the display case was ringed with small pumpkins.

Henry and Joanne stepped through the door, and a strong but pleasant smell immediately struck Henry. It had an instant calming effect on him. "What's that smell, Jo?"

"Dragon's blood. Do you like it?"

"Yeah, it seems to mellow out the entire atmosphere in here. At least, that's the way it's making me feel at the moment."

"It can have that effect on people."

The room was classic old-style New England. The floor was comprised of broad-plank hardwood, complete with wood knots, and glazed to a high-gloss finish. The walls were ringed with wood shelving holding an impressive array of items Henry was mostly clueless about. The wall to the left held candles bearing titles of spells, cauldrons of various sizes, tarot card decks, herb concoctions, spell kits, and more. The wall to his right was filled top to bottom with books about witchcraft, wizardry, spell-casting, and various old world and new age religious titles. Some he actually recognized. Others, not so much. In the center of the room was a large display stand lined in black velvet with insets slotted at different intervals for crystals and gems. Hanging above that stand were chains bearing pendulums of various sizes and necklaces with a vast array of charms and gemstones. The pendulums reflected the display case's soft light and sent tiny sparks of prismatic light lazily around the room. The rest of the area was filled with glass display cases containing jewelry and charms, most of which Henry hadn't a clue about.

They headed toward the back of the room where the cash register sat next to a break in the counter. Jo pushed through the black swinging door, its hinges squealed in protest, and into the back.

"Wanda, it's Jo!"

"I'm back here, sweetie!" Wanda said in a sing-song voice.

They walked down a narrow hallway painted black on both sides with reflective gold and silver witchcraft symbols. They were arranged in random (or so, at the time, they appeared random) patterns on both walls. At the end of the hallway was a beaded door straight out of the nineteen-seventies. Jo parted the beads, and they rattled their arrival into the room that held Wanda.

She was a sight to behold as she stood from the black vinyl beanbag chair positioned in the middle of the room. Standing about four-foot-ten, she was dressed head-to-toe in a dark-purple velvet cloak. The sleeves came down her arms about halfway, there were about four inches of arm showing on each side, and the rest of her forearms were covered by bracelets, bangles, and charms, left and right. Her fingers were covered with rings of various shapes and sizes. Some rings were silver, some gold, others a mix of both precious metals. Some had stones, others didn't. Her hair was about shoulder length with kinky curls and was a mix of dirty-blond and some grey. She had a round face with a small chin, button nose, and eyes that were slightly turned down—giving her a sympathetic look—with light wrinkles at the outer edges. Her eyes were a radiant blue, and the whites were without blemish. They made him feel both welcomed and intimidated. Her face was kind, and Henry immediately took a liking to her.

"And who is this tall, handsome stranger, Jo?" Wanda said.

"Wanda Heinze, meet Henry Trank."

"Henry Trank? Hank Trank? Hahahahahaha! Now isn't that the cutest thing I've ever heard!" She was doubled over in laughter. It was infectious, and he laughed despite himself. Jo just looked at him with a grin and shrugged her shoulders as if to say, *'that's Wanda.'*

"I'm sorry, honey, that just struck me as funny. No offense."

"None taken. I've actually gotten that reaction quite a bit. There are worse things in the world," he said with a smile.

"So, what brings you to my little shop of horrors at this hour on a rainy night?"

"We have a video capture we'd like you to look at. It's something Henry caught on his camera earlier today. He's been having really strange dreams lately, and when he wakes up, he's finding things in his apartment that shouldn't really be there. He was worried he may be sleepwalking and bringing things in from the outside, which would explain a lot."

"What kinds of things are showing up after these dreams, Henry?" Wanda asked.

"Stuff you would usually find in the forest. Pine needles, grass, dirt ... sometimes little puddles of water on the floor, and sometimes my clothes or the mattress are damp. And I don't think it's from sweating."

Wanda cupped her right elbow in her left hand and unconsciously tugged on her lower lip as she pondered this information. Her jewelry rattled softly as she did this. "Let's look at the video. It might help me get a better grip on the situation."

She motioned them over to her little Dell laptop set up on the bar in the back of the room. The bar was well stocked. She took position behind the counter and asked them if they wanted a drink. Henry told her he'd have a Diet Coke, if she had one. She frowned at that until he told her he was driving. She nodded her approval and said, "That was a test, my young friend. That girl you are driving around tonight means the world to me ... and you just went up a few notches." She reached into the fridge and made a production of placing the Diet Coke in front of him like it was a magic trick.

Joanne looked up at Henry from behind the bar. She was downloading the video from his phone onto the laptop—a little embarrassed yet pleased at Wanda's protectiveness. The affection between the two was obvious.

"I know what you'll have, Miss Jo." And she set about making a pot of herbal tea for both of them.

Jo finished setting up the video and motioned Henry behind the bar so they could all watch it together. Henry stood off to the side to watch Wanda's reaction as he'd watched Jo's earlier.

When it got to the thirty-seven-minute mark, Joanne stopped the video and said to Wanda, "This is where it gets really interesting." She resumed the video and pointed out to Wanda all the same things she'd discovered in her first run-through. Wanda asked her to rewind and replay things several times. Each time she reviewed something, she made no comment. Wanda studied the video like it was the Zapruder film. After about forty-five minutes of intense study, she finally pulled her eyes away from the screen and rubbed them with the backs of her hands.

"How long have you been having these dreams, Henry?" Wanda asked.

"Ever since I moved to Salem."

"Nothing like this before you got here? No pine needles? No dirt? No puddles?"

"No. Never."

"Did you ever see or hear anything unusual in the apartment? A fleeting shadow? Footsteps? Ever feel unusually cold? Even in the summer with the A/C turned on?" She asked.

"Nada."

"What else happens in this dream of yours, Henry?"

He filled her in on the details of the dream. How it had been going on continuously and exclusively since he'd arrived in Salem.

She did the elbow-lip thing again for a few moments. Joanne kept silent.

"Henry, do you know what the word *"apport"* means?"

"Um. No. Unless you're talking about the left side of a boat. But I have a feeling that's not what you mean."

"It's not. An apport is an object that appears, by supernatural means, into our world from another realm. Usually, it happens at a seance conducted by a spiritualist. But I have known it to happen in other ways. I'm not saying that's what is happening here, but I'm not ruling it out either."

He stood there, silent for several seconds. Jo and Wanda did the same, letting him process what he'd just heard from Wanda.

"I ... um ... are you telling me you think things are coming into my house, through my dreams? That I'm carrying things back with me from another ... how did you put it ... realm?"

Jo and Wanda looked at each other—communicating, it seemed—never saying a word, and then Wanda looked at him and said, "I know this is a lot for you to swallow, Henry. And I'm not saying I think this is definitely what's happening, but let's take a few facts into account. First, (she ticked off a finger with each point) nothing like this has ever happened to you before. Second, you have video evidence now that you are *not* sleepwalking. Third, you are on this video reacting, very dramatically, to some event you are obviously terrified by. Fourth, we have, on tape, at least one, possibly two entities, that have taken an interest in your dream activities. And most important of all, and this is something we've all overlooked until this point, you live on the second floor."

"How do you know I live on the second floor?" he asked, a tad suspicious.

She pointed to the computer screen, "The camera is facing the sliding glass doors in the bottom right-hand corner of the monitor. You can see the top of a wooden picket fence. Either that's the shortest picket fence on record, or you live high enough to see the tips of the pickets on the fence. Hence, the second floor."

He had to hand it to her. She was really freakin' observant. "Okay, but what does that have to do with whether or not I've actually been sleepwalking?"

Jo handled this one, "It's kind of obvious Henry. It *is* possible you brought in pine needles from the porch outside, even though it's screened in. But it's *highly unlikely* you would bring in dirt on your clothes and shoes from that same porch. And in order to do *that*, you would have had to get up—in a sound sleep, mind you—unlock the door, walk down two flights of stairs, go around the back of the building, roll around in the yard, headfirst, because that's where you told me you found the pine needles, in your hair, come back into the building, lock the door again, and get into bed. Oh, and all without the lovely and not-nosy-at-all Mrs. Greenblatt ever asking you what the heck you were doing? Now, does that sound like a likely scenario to you?"

He cleared his throat and croaked out a weak, "Um, no."

Wanda took over again, "Now for your apparent visitor, or visitors. In my opinion, the shape in front of the door appears to be watching not only you, but if you really study the tape, the entity actually appears to be looking over the bed and beyond it. Almost as if it's tracking something. From what you've told me about the dream you are in some sort of danger, and you are being pursued. Has the dream always gone this way? Is it the same every night, or is it a progression from one point to the next?"

"It's steadily gotten worse. In the beginning, I saw it from the perspective of someone being chased by an angry mob. I have no idea why they're chasing me. The last couple of times, it's been different. I see myself but through the eyes of the man leading the mob. I can feel his emotions. He's a tangle of anger and fear. And the thing that really knocked me for a loop ... through his eyes, I came to realize that in the dream, I'm actually a woman. But not only *that*! Through this guy who's following me, I've got the feeling I know a terrible secret about him and his followers. The only way they can handle this problem is for me to die. And they aren't in the mood to talk nicely about it."

Wanda took all this in silently and with razor intensity. She took her cup in both hands and sipped what had to be now tepid tea. She was silent for several moments and then said, "Well, the good news, if you could call it that, honey, is I don't think your apartment is haunted. However I do think, going by what you've told me so far, whatever it is you are dreaming about ... it's a matter of importance to someone or something. And the sooner we find out what they want, the better."

He looked over at Jo. She looked back at him, worry written all over her face. *That* scared him more than anything.

Wanda said, "There is a silver lining, Henry."

"And what's that?" he asked.

"The last shot of that video, when you hit the floor. Whatever that bright light was, I can tell you this—it wasn't car headlights shining through the window. It wasn't a reflection. It wasn't a lens flare. That was someone or something protecting you. That dark entity, whatever it was, wanted no part of that white light. It shot up through the ceiling like shit through a goose!" She leaned toward him, locking eyes. A knowing smile crossed her face. "It was scared!"

CHAPTER NINE

SOLOMON

LEONARD SHRUMM KILLED THE headlights on his Jaguar two blocks before he pulled into the vacant lot behind the funeral home located on mostly deserted Maven Street. He saw the muted reflection of the black Cadillac Escalade's headlights before they briefly flashed twice to acknowledge his arrival. He pulled up next to the big Caddy and hit the button to roll down his driver's side window, thankful he had vent shades equipped above his windows on this cool, rainy night. It seemed to Leonard it was raining all the time lately.

Staring up at the Escalade, he suffered an anxious few moments waiting for the back window to roll down, not sure if the next thing he would hear was the start of a conversation or the bang of a bullet, making this his last night on earth. Being alive for almost four hundred years was no guarantee of immortality if you fucked things up. Solomon did not suffer fools gladly.

"Good evening, Leonard," Solomon said. His voice, as always, hoarse and scratchy.

"Good evening, Mr. Dobson."

"What brings you out on this beautiful, October evening?"

Leonard gulped, here goes nothing. "Sir, it seems we have a ... situation ... involving Salem's newest resident. I did as instructed and monitored the progress of his latest revelations. He is awakening since he, unfortunately, has come home. Thankfully, he is not yet aware of who he really is, and I think that's to our advantage. However, as I observed his dreams, something quite unexpected happened to me. Nothing like this has ever happened to me before, and hopefully will not again."

"Do tell."

"I observed the usual pre-REM onslaught of images that come before the main event. Of note, in the opening previews before the feature film, it seems Mr. Trank has an interest in a certain coffee shop owner in town. A woman named Joanne. She was in the dream, on the hood of his car, as he attempted the removal of a young woman's bra. Probably not all that important, but she bears watching—given the history of events over the ages. Now, back to the feature film. As much as I was able to work out, it seems Henry has ascertained an understanding not only that he is in danger—at least as far as he knows, it's just in a dream—but he somehow has worked out an understanding of the intentions and emotions of his pursuers. Though it appears he doesn't, at least for now, understand the reasoning behind them.

He was close to getting to that point when something very unexpected and unnerving happened. There was an intruder, sir."

"Interesting. And you know this how, Leonard?"

"I was expelled from the astral plane ... rather violently, sir."

"Come again?"

"As unlikely as it sounds, sir, another entered the realm and forced me out before I could garner any more information. It was a force I've never experienced before, and hope to never encounter again."

Leonard could feel his ass cheeks puckering from the withering gaze Solomon shot down from above.

"This is extremely disappointing, Leonard. I expected better results from one I have trained so thoroughly and carefully. I'm wondering if maybe I need to start the search for a successor? It would be a setback, but I've had to do it before, as you well know. Is this something I need to consider, Leonard?"

"No, sir. I'll figure out what or who the problem is and take care of it with utmost speed and certainty. You have my word."

"Your word? I don't need your word. I need results!" Solomon slammed his cane down on the window well to punctuate his anger. The gold lion's head atop the cane reflected the muted glow from the dome light within the SUV.

"I'll get it taken care of, sir."

Solomon eased back in his seat and out of Leonard's view. "That's more like it. Good night, Leonard."

The window of Solomon's Caddy was already halfway up, and the chauffeur already pulling out of the spot as Leonard said his goodnight.

Chapter Ten
Truth, God, and Video

"I don't understand something, Wanda," Henry said. "Why would someone, or something, give a rat's ass about my dreams?"

"I haven't the foggiest idea yet, Henry, but I know this—that is not a ghost on your video. I've seen a million different videos of ghosts and hauntings and any number of paranormal activities. Many of them credible. A lot of them, total bullshit. I've seen nothing like what you've shown me tonight."

"Do you have any idea what the white-light entity may be, Wanda?" Jo asked.

"Hard to say dear, hard to say. But I've no doubt it's aware of something potentially evil keeping an eye on Henry, and it's apparently duty-bound to protect him. And, so far, it's doing a pretty good job," she said with a nod. "Henry, you said you recently moved to Salem in July, right?"

"Yes, right before the fourth."

"Do you have any family around here? Any relatives in Salem at all?"

"As far as I know, most of my family is mainly from the Portland area. No pun intended. Why do you ask?"

"Call it intuition, a hunch, or just a RAG?"

"A RAG?" Henry asked.

"Random-assed guess," she winked.

"Okay. I'll definitely check into it tomorrow."

"Do you believe in God, Henry?" Wanda asked.

That was out of the blue, he thought. Where was this going? "I believe it's possible there is a power greater than myself, absolutely. I'm not religious, if that's what you're asking me. And I don't hold it *against* those who are. I would probably describe myself as a healthy skeptic. Being an ER nurse, I think I tend to be more reliant on what I can see, feel, touch, and physically prove, versus what others would call "faith". I sometimes wish I had that kind of faith. I guess when I see some people come into the ER battered and bruised by others ... when I see some of the heinous things people do to one another, it makes it really hard to believe there is a God who would allow any of it to happen.

"And then, once in a great while, you meet a kid like Timmy Allen. Timmy was brought into the ER in Portland one day, about a year ago. A car hit him while skateboarding. The guy driving the car never saw him, never really had a chance to see him because Timmy and his friends were taking crazy risks! They were daring each other to skate, as fast as they could, down a hill and across the street, without looking for cars. They called it Froggerboarding. Named after some old video game, I guess.

"Anyway, the inevitable happened. Timmy took his turn and got nailed by a big, white SUV. It hit him so hard his shoes were later found in two separate backyards. Of course, he wasn't wearing a helmet, and he came down on his head. I'll spare you the gory details, but suffice to say he was in terrible shape. They brought him into the ER and he was sent straight to surgery. I was one of the attending nurses to the surgeon. We worked on that kid for eleven hours and didn't hold out much hope he was gonna make it. And even if he did, he would probably be in a vegetative state for the rest of his life. We actually lost him—that is to say, he flat-lined—twice during the surgery. He was, for all intents and purposes, dead. Twice! The first time, he was gone for about thirty-five seconds. The second time, a minute and a half. It was dicey for sure, but he pulled through. Tough kid.

"So, after that marathon surgery, I went home. It was about six o'clock in the morning and I went straight to bed. My shift would start at about seven p.m. that evening, so I just slept the entire day. When I got into work that night, the first thing I did when I got there was visit Timmy. I expected him to be out like a light from sedatives at the very least, vegetative at the worst. Neither were true. When I walked through the door, he was sitting up and watching TV. It blew me away. So I went through the usual questioning I would go through for any patient. I checked his vitals, had him follow my finger with his eyes to check on the progress of his concussion—the usual stuff. After all that was over, we got to talking. Just shooting the shit, you know? And out of the blue he said to me, *'Hey doc, do you know anyone that may have lost a gold chain?'*

"Kind of a strange question, but I figured maybe it had something to do with having his brain bounced around a little bit. So I humored him. I said, *'No, not off the top of my head, why do you ask?'*

"And he said, and I'll never forget it, *'I saw one up on the roof last night. I think it belongs to that hot nurse ... Rebecca. She didn't realize it but, when she took her jacket off to get her cigarettes out, the jacket snagged the chain she was wearing. It fell behind the door to the roof. It's right next to the Folger's can they throw their cigarettes into.'*

"I played it off, thinking the kid really *did* hit his head too hard. But what he said kept nagging at the back of my mind and, at first, I couldn't figure out why. And then it hit me! Rebecca works the same shift I do, only she wasn't on the day I talked to Timmy. She was on the night before, when Timmy was in surgery. So I went and checked the time stamps on her time card. I checked when Rebecca punched out for lunch. It was at 11:30 p.m. And then I checked the logs on the surgery. 11:33 p.m. Timmy was flat-lined for one and a half minutes. Rebecca went for a smoke on the roof. I saw it in the security video. I went up on the roof and found the chain, exactly where he said it was. I have no explanation for it. So when you ask me, do I believe in

God? I still can't say yes. Do I believe there is something more to life than just cradle to grave? After Timmy Allen, I can't rule it out. What about you, Wanda? Do you believe in God?"

"Yes, Henry. I was fortunate though."

"How so?"

"I'm an alcoholic."

"Um, okay. I'm not sure I follow."

Wanda extended her right arm straight out, fingers pointing up. She studied her rings and appeared to mull over how she wanted to proceed.

"When I was a young girl, Henry, I never felt like I fit in anywhere. I could go to a party and be in a room full of people and I would be polite and nod and give quick, one-word answers to questions, make fleeting eye contact with people, but I never felt a connection to anyone except a few close friends.

"Then one night, when I was around seventeen, I went to a party with my best friend, DeeDee. It was a party being thrown by a bunch of freshman college guys at one of the frat houses at the University. The guy hosting the party—handsome bastard, I think his name was Bobby, but it's been a while—came over to us with a friend of his, and offered us each one of those red plastic party cups filled with God knows what. We politely accepted it and we each took a sip and it was disgusting, but neither of us wanted to be the one who threw it in the trash and insulted our host. So I continued sipping mine bit by bit as I chatted with Bobby, and as I *kept* sipping, I felt fantastic. Mind you, I had a bit of a buzz going when we got there, so the skids were greased. Bobby didn't seem so intimidating to talk to the more and more I sipped. DeeDee, meanwhile, had slipped away with the other guy, and it was just Bobby and I, talking and talking away. So, Bobby got two more red cups, and about an hour-and-a-half later we were in the back seat of someone's car. To this day I have very fond memories of the song, 'Waiting For A Girl Like You.'"

Henry smiled and said nothing. He wanted to see where this was going.

"From that night on, I thought I had found the answer to all my problems. Alcohol was my god now. I relied on it to take away all the fear and shyness and awkwardness I had always felt on the inside. I depended on it to allow me to show what I *thought* was my true self. It gave me permission to be what I didn't have the courage to be sober. At least, that's what I thought *then*.

"And then, a few years later, I woke up in my little one-bedroom apartment, by myself, and realized to my utter horror, I hadn't the slightest idea how I'd gotten home the night before. I'd blacked out. That was the first time I had ever had a panic attack. Terrible things, those are. You feel your heart pounding. You get short of breath, feel like the walls are closing in, and you're not sure if you'll die right there on the spot! Well, several minutes later, my mind and body calmed down, and I got the courage up to get off the floor and try to figure out how I'd gotten home. I looked out the front window to see if my car was still out there. It was. It also had damage to the right front bumper, a shattered headlight, spider web crack on the right side of the windshield, and a streak of crimson on the hood and lower part of the windshield."

Uh-oh, Henry thought.

"Turns out I had hit someone or something on the way home." She paused, looking ashamed.

"You don't have to do this, Wanda. It's none of my business," Henry said.

"But I do, honey. You'll understand why, soon. So I went out to the car, terrified the whole time, and looked over the damage. That was the first time I can ever remember praying to a God of any kind. The whole trip out to the car I prayed, *'Please, dear God, if you are there, please do not let it be I killed someone. I will never touch another drop again if you'll just let it not be that!'*

"Well, I got out to the car and my prayer was heard. On the ground, next to the car, was a can of red paint the landlord had been using to do the trim on the front porch. He'd left it out front, on the sidewalk, the night before. In the side yard were two mangled lawn chairs and a plank he'd rested the can on. I can only tell you I lost all control of my legs and fell flat on my ass I was so relieved. Then I cried. They were the most wonderful tears of joy and relief you could ever imagine. Finally, I got up off my sorry ass and cleaned up the mess. That's when my landlord, Mr. Stillings, God rest his soul, pulled up in his pickup truck and saw what happened. I thought to myself, *'You're in the shit now, Wanda.'* So, big Jim Stillings, who was about sixty-five years old at the time—handsome guy, thin as a rail, bout six-two, six-three, dead ringer for Jimmy Stewart, by the way—asks me what the hell happened here? And, I shit you not, I told him the stone-cold truth. I said to him I had too much to drink, I must've blacked out, and then I waved my hand at the mess before both of us. And in that moment, without saying the words out loud, I'd realized and admitted to myself, for the first time in my life, I had trouble with booze. I was an alcoholic."

Henry shook his head in disbelief, "He must have been pissed!"

"No." Wanda said.

"No?!" Henry was incredulous.

"Big Jim walked over to me and gave me the warmest, kindest, most compassionate look I'd ever seen. He gave me a hug and said, *'That took guts, Wanda. I can help you, if you want it.'* I looked at him like he'd just arrived from another planet. After all I'd done, he wasn't mad. Wasn't even angry in the slightest. I asked him why he would do anything at all for me after what I'd done. He looked me dead in the eyes and said, *'There but for the grace of God go I.'* That confused the hell out of me, so I asked him what he meant. He said it was an expression he'd learned from his group, and it meant he thanked God he was not in my shoes, but he understood he *could* have been. It was his way of telling me he wasn't there to judge me, but to help me.

"Okay, so now I was more confused. So I asked him what group he was talking about, and he says it's his AA group that meets in the church on Tuesday nights at St. Theresa's. I don't mind telling you, I was absolutely astounded! Big Jim had the same problem as me, only you'd never know it because that man was as straight an arrow as they come. So I told him I would. He smiled, and said, *'Great, see you tonight!'* I was so clueless at that moment, and so grateful I'd not killed anyone, I'd totally forgotten it was Tuesday!"

"So, did you go?" Henry asked.

"You bet your sweet ass I did! And it was the single most important night of my life. When I got there, big Jim was up front, holding a cup of coffee, and talking to a small group of people. Did you know the reason they have coffee at AA meetings is actually for the sugar? Alkies need their sugar, it's kind of a stand-in for some of the sugar they're missing from the booze. Anyway, I'd be lying if I didn't admit I was a nervous wreck walking up to the front of the hall to meet with Jim and all those people. He saw me and waved me over and introduced me to his friends. They were so friendly and willing to help! We chitchatted for a while and then the meeting started. I have to admit, the whole *'Hi, my name is blank and I'm an alcoholic'* thing, at first, seemed kinda corny, but over time it just became part of the entire experience and I never thought much about it.

"So this young girl gets up there and introduces herself—Marybeth was her name, I'll never, ever forget her—and she tells her story. This is where it gets interesting. She started talking, and it was like I was the only person in the room. The feelings she described were, to a *tee*, all the things I had felt over all those years. The loneliness, the isolation, the feeling you can be in a room full of people and still feel alone. The self-loathing and the eventual desperation you feel when you know you can't live with the booze or the drugs—her thing was both—or without them. And then she got to the part where she explained how she got sober and stayed sober. She said she had accepted a power greater than herself could restore her to sanity, and that she was the problem, not the solution. But the most important thing, at least for me, was she said it wasn't a religious thing for her. That she was not a believer in God and she wasn't a churchgoer at all. All she had to do was be humble enough to ask ... whatever ... to keep her away from a drink or a drug for *that* day. And she let everyone know whatever you chose for your higher power was *your* choice and no one else's."

"So that's how you came to believe in God?" he asked.

"I'm getting there, Henry." She winked. "So she finished up her story to lots of applause and took her seat. To this day I couldn't tell you if it was a guy or a girl who spoke next because I was so lost in my own thoughts. Before I knew it, the meeting was coming to a close. Everyone stood up and said the *'Our Father'* prayer. After the prayer, all the people got up and started chatting, and I must have had some kind of strange look on my face because big Jim came over to me and asked me if I was alright. I told him I was, and I was amazed by that girl Marybeth and her story. So then he offers to introduce me to her, and I was, at first, a little shy about it, and he just looks at me and says not to be silly. Big Jim brings her back to my table and introduces us to each other, and we just hit it off like that!" She said with a finger snap.

"Me and that girl talked until they started breaking down the hall and cleaning up, and she invites me to Dunkin' Donuts after the meeting with her and her friends. So, we head over to Dunkin's and start shooting the shit for a little while longer, and by the end of the night, I ask her to be my sponsor."

"Your what?" Henry asked.

"A sponsor is someone who kinda shows you the ropes. Guides you along and kinda keeps you in line a little bit. She gladly accepted. That girl helped me so much in the beginning. I will always be grateful to her. Now, here's the part I wanted to get through to you, Henry. The part where I know there is a God, or a Higher Power, or a Spirit of the Universe, or Divine Energy ... whatever you choose to call it. That morning when I prayed to God I hadn't killed anyone, I thought my prayer had been answered when I'd discovered it was just a can of paint that died on the hood of my car. But after the meeting, having talked to Marybeth, she'd mentioned in an off-hand way she believed her higher power worked through people. I didn't give it much thought at the time she'd said it, but the next day it hit me like a bolt outta the blue. God hadn't "let me off the hook" by allowing it to be a can of paint I'd murdered.

God had allowed me to fall, to come to my lowest point, to seek him out, and then he answered my prayer by putting Big Jim in my life. He hadn't answered my prayer by giving me what I *wanted*, He'd answered it by giving me what I *needed*! And from that day to this, from Marybeth to Joanne, and a thousand other people, he just keeps on helping as long as I'm humble and allow it to happen. And it always does! Not maybe."

Henry sat there for a few moments, absorbing the story he'd just been told. To look at this woman, you would never think she had been through anything like what she'd just told him. Never, ever judge a book by its cover. He asked her, "So how'd you become involved in this business you're in? I don't mean just the store, I mean your spiritual beliefs, too"

"That's the other half of the equation, my young friend," she winked, continued, "a large part of the reason I felt different from other people—that I couldn't communicate with others unless I was a bit tipsy or outright drunk—was ever since I was old enough to remember, I could see things others couldn't. I would be in a room, alone, and out of the blue there would be some random person who would just appear out of nowhere. I don't have to tell you it scared the hell out of me. They would never say anything. At least, not at first. It would suddenly get freezing in the room, I'd see whatever spirit decided to show up that day, and I would bury myself under my blankets and pillows and wait until the room warmed up. That's how I knew it was safe to come out. But you could imagine how I'd felt when, as a young girl, I would tell my mother or my father what I'd seen, and they would dismiss it out of hand. They would say something like *'Isn't that cute, Wanda has a new imaginary friend.'* Or, *'Wanda, enough with the pretend people, it's not funny anymore.'* So I learned to shut up about it and to grin and bear it."

"That's horrible," he said. "How'd you finally come to grips with what was going on?"

"I didn't. I drank. But remember what I said before. God answers your prayers. Not all. Sometimes, for good reason, he says no. But the day I prayed to Him to not let it be I'd killed someone, He was very busy lining up the people in my life He would work through. I believe He really does know what you need long before you ask Him. He just needs you to ask, because He will not interfere with free will.

"Anyway, that girl, Marybeth, when she agreed to become my sponsor, it wasn't out of pure altruism. She's also sensitive to the dead. That night after the meeting, when we were getting ready to leave Dunkin' Donuts, she said she saw me surrounded by several people who were not necessarily there to get sober. She said she thought they were relatives of mine who had passed away because they were pleading with her to help me. My mom and dad, who didn't believe or understand what was going on with me when I was a kid, were the ones doing the pleading. For some reason, I couldn't see them, but she could. Maybe I was too close to it emotionally, I don't know. But you could imagine the absolute joy I felt when she told me she could see my parents! And then to know, after all this time, they finally acknowledged the truth about what I *now* consider *gifts*! That was the night I started to heal. I wasn't a freak! I wasn't alone anymore! And the best thing of all ... I had a friend who understood. She understood it all! She wasn't a witch, like myself or Joanne. She was a lapsed Catholic who told me to follow my heart, and it would lead me to my beliefs. And it did. That's how I got here. And I fear nothing!"

"That's an amazing story. I don't know if it convinces me of the existence of God, but it swings me more towards believing than not," Henry said.

"That's fine, honey. I just thought you should hear it and know what I believe and where I'm coming from. If anything, I hope it gives you confidence I can help you. And judging by what I've seen on that video, in my opinion, you're gonna need a lot."

She paused, and Henry waited her out.

"I want to send a copy of this video to a friend of mine over at the University and get his opinion on this. Is that okay with you, Henry?"

"Sure. What does this friend do at the U that would help in this situation?"

"He's an expert in the occult and past-life hypnosis and regression. He's sharp as a tack and has just the right amount of skepticism tempered with belief to smell out the fakes from the real deal."

"I hate to be the party-pooper here, you two, but I have to get up at six a.m. and run a coffee shop in the morning," Joanne chimed in.

"Can't you just tell your boss you need a day off?" Henry asked.

"The bitch won't let me. She says she needs me there and the place just can't run without me."

"Wow," he said. "Sounds like a real asshole. What's this boss of your's name?"

Wanda started howling with laughter, and Henry stared at her like she'd lost her mind.

Joanne looked at Henry, dumbfounded.

"What?" He asked, feeling like he may have missed something. A big something.

"Henry," Jo started, "how the hell do they let you work on the sick and the lame and yet be so utterly clueless?"

"Sorry, I don't follow," he said.

"I own the coffee shop, numb-nuts," she said.

At this point, Wanda walked over to her beanbag chair, doubled over with laughter. Tears rolled down her cheeks. "You two have a good night!"

"Come on, Einstein. Take me home."

CHAPTER ELEVEN
A SIMPLE RIDE HOME

THEY HOPPED IN HENRY'S car without saying a word to each other. Henry's ears were beet-red from embarrassment at having basically just called this woman, who he was starting to care a lot about, an asshole. He resolved not to say a fucking word. He'd already tasted his toenails once tonight. It wasn't gonna happening again.

They drove on for a few minutes and Henry chanced a look over at her. She was staring straight ahead. The rain from the windshield and the glow from the streetlights painted grey smears down the front of her face. So it was hard to get a read on what she was feeling or thinking. Finally, she looked over at him with a big, shit-eating grin on her face.

"What?" He asked.

"I'm not mad at you, Henry. You'd have no idea I owned the shop. I never told you. But I soooo enjoy messing with your mind." She started laughing, and the relief he felt was overwhelming.

Henry pulled the car over to the side of the road and put it in park. He looked her straight in the eyes and said, "Come here."

She leaned over the center console. He pulled her close and kissed her. The only sounds were their breathing and the steady beat of the rain on the roof of the car. They were so lost in the moment Henry almost shit his pants when he noticed a man standing in the shadows behind Joanne, about three feet from her door. When the dark figure saw Henry notice him, it moved with surprising speed as it ripped open Joanne's door, grabbed the back of her jacket, and tried to yank her from the car. She reacted quickly, grabbing the top of the door frame and Henry's arm, hanging half-in, half-out of the passenger side, and holding on for all she was worth. Rain poured down on the half of her hanging out of the car, and Henry held on to her with all the strength he had. This psycho son-of-a-bitch was strong! The man leaned down into the car, grunting with the effort of trying to wrest Jo from her seat. Then, in one quick flash, Joanne leaned her head forward and slammed it back into the fucker's nose. Henry heard an audible *crunch!* It sounded like a celery stalk being snapped in half. The psycho let go and staggered back, falling on his ass into a puddle. Henry pulled her back into the car and she reached back and slammed the door shut, locking it. He leaned into the back seat, fumbling for the baseball bat he kept there, thanking God he was still a wannabe jock, and brought it forward while simultaneously opening his door, and bolted over to Joanne's side of the car. He was ready to put this guy's head over the Green Monster, but when Henry got to where the attacker had been, he'd vanished. No blood. No footprints. Henry looked both ways down the street and saw no sign of him running away. The only sign of any life at all was a huge Rottweiler standing behind a gate and watching him from across the sidewalk next to Joanne's side of the car. Two Rotties in one day. If he never saw another one, he'd be good with it.

Soaked and keeping an eye out in every direction at once, Henry went around the back of the car and got in on his side. He locked the door and looked over at Jo, expecting her to be nervous or afraid. Wrong. The look she had on her face only made him feel sorry for the bastard when she found him.

"Are you alright, Jo?"

"I'm fine. I'm fuckin' pissed right now, but I'm fine." She ran her fingers through her hair, combing it back. "I don't know what's happening in this town. It used to be a safe place at night, but now you can't even go parking with your guy without some asshole trying to steal you out of a car."

"What the hell is that smell?" Henry asked. "It's disgusting!"

"I don't know. Whoever that guy was, hygiene wasn't his strong suit. It smells like rotten eggs and burnt matches," said Joanne.

"I can't believe he got away so fast. It didn't take me more than five seconds to get to your side of the car. And even then you'd think I'd have been able to see which direction he ran off in."

"Wait," Jo said. "You didn't see where he went? How is it possible he could get away that fast?"

"Beats the hell out of me. But with all the shit that's gone down since this morning, I'm surprised by less and less."

"I don't think I want to be alone tonight, Henry."

"What do you want to do?"

"I hope this doesn't seem too forward ... but could I stay with you tonight?"

He put his arm behind his back and made a show of being in pain. "Stop! Stop twisting my arm! I'll do it! I'll do it!"

"Ha! You are learning the ways of smartassery, young Padawan!"

He started the car back up and headed back to his apartment. Despite all that just happened, he was in a pretty good mood.

Walking up the stairs to his second-floor man cave, they ran into Mrs. Greenblatt again. Did this woman ever sleep?

"Good evening, Henry," she said.

"Hi Mrs. G. How are you tonight?"

"Fine. Except some stupid dog got into the building. I shooed him away, but the bastard must have taken offense ... he left a gigantic pile of shit right in front of my door after I went back inside."

Henry looked down at the floor so she couldn't see the smile he had on his face. Joanne started looking at the ceiling, the floor, her nails, her shoes ... anywhere but at Henry to keep from bursting out laughing.

Finally, he regained some composure, and with the straightest face he could muster, wished the lovely Mrs. G goodnight. When they finally got into the apartment they were giggling their asses off.

Chapter Twelve

The Talking Dog

Back home, after his tense meeting with Solomon, Leonard poured himself a healthy dose of Johnny Walker Blue. Nothing but the best JW would do for now. Leonard belted down some Blue and felt the warm sting of the fine scotch make its way down his throat and into his belly ... seconds later smoothing out the frayed ends of his nerves. He lit up a Cuban cigar and was just about to settle down in his favorite leather chair when he heard scratching at the door. Irritated, he walked down the hall to let the Rotty in. Hercules followed him into the library and climbed up onto the matching couch directly across from Leonard and stared at him, waiting.

"I trust you were able to establish whether the coffee girl is one of them?"

Leonard watched, ever fascinated, as Hercules went through the transformation. It always looked rather painful. Probably why it chose to stay as long as it could in its current form. It could not talk as a dog, however—the rules of the physical world weren't to be ignored—so it had to shift into the dark spirit form of its true self in order to converse. It always creeped the hell out of Leonard to see it this way, but after dealing with Solomon tonight, he decided there were worse things to worry about.

In a voice part whisper, part gravel, part mucous, and sounding like several voices in distinct tones wrapping themselves around each other like snakes, the entity that was Hercules said, "I smelled her. She is one of them. *And she loves him!*" He spat the last sentence out as if it were poison. To him, it was.

"How did you find them?" Leonard asked.

"I followed the scent from where he lives. Followed to the place where their leader makes her business. But I dared not go too close. The light around the dwelling forbids it. She is strong with the light."

"You were wise not to go near. She probably would have sensed you."

"What do you require of me now?"

"Nothing more at the moment."

The dark one morphed back into its canine form and padded down the hall, through the open door in the kitchen, and into the night.

CHAPTER THIRTEEN

MATCHMAKER

WANDA HEINZE WAITED FOR her friends to leave. She was overjoyed Joanne and Henry—Hank! Ha ha—had finally become a couple. And not surprised at all they had hit it off almost immediately.

She smiled to herself as she thought about how she had managed to get Henry to go into the coffee shop way back in July. She had dressed for the occasion and had played it just right. After all, she'd known almost to the second when Henry had arrived in town. All the bells and whistles in her soul were set off like some spiritual tripwire. It had been a long time coming.

On that Saturday morning, back in July, she sat outside the coffee shop waiting for Henry to make his usual morning trip to Dunkin' Donuts. Like clockwork, he came around the corner at six and started down the street toward her. Wanda was dressed in a green jogging outfit. She had kept the hood up, just in case Joanne looked out the window. Jo might notice her distinctive hairdo. She made a show of fanning herself as if she'd just run a marathon. As Henry went by, she hailed him and asked if he could do an old lady a favor and grab her a cup of ice. Henry told her it was no problem. He came back outside with the cup of ice and a faraway look on his face.

"Are you alright, dear?" she asked.

"Hmm?"

"I asked if you're alright. You look like you forgot where you are and why you're here. And my ice is melting."

"Oh! I'm sorry. Just thinking. Here you go."

"Thank you. These workouts are a killer. Even in the morning. So hot this summer." She made another show of fanning herself. Henry never noticed she wasn't sweating. In fact, to Wanda, Henry looked like he was on another planet. Inside, Wanda was jumping for joy.

"Well, have a nice day ma'am," Henry said. And then he turned right back around and into the coffee shop. Wanda sat there for the next half hour, pretend-fanning herself, waiting to see how Henry looked when he came back out. The bell over the door rang, and she pretended not to notice. Henry walked right past her, whistling something catchy. A big smile on his face. Meeting your soul mate again in this life will do that for a guy! Mission accomplished.

Chapter Fourteen
They Call Me Doctor Love

Henry woke up the next morning after the best night's sleep he'd had since arriving in Salem. He'd slept right through Joanne getting up early and leaving to open up the Cauldron. She had slept on the couch through the night ... bummer ... and had left a note and a fresh pot of coffee she'd brewed for him before she left. The note read ...

"Had to leave early, as you might have noticed. I stayed awake as you drifted off (you snore quite loudly, by the way) and nothing out of the ordinary seemed to happen, thank God. I think we had enough crazy shit for one day. Don't forget to get the number from Wanda for her friend over at the U. I'll talk to you later on.   Jo."

After a couple cups of coffee, reading the morning news on-line, and jumping in the shower he got the number from Wanda and called her friend at the U. The secretary informed Henry the doctor wasn't in his office yet, and he could leave a message if he'd like. Henry declined and asked what time she thought he would be in. She told him he'd be there at any minute, or he may not show up at all.

"Pardon me?"

"Doctor Love marches to the beat of his own drummer, sir."

"Doctor Love? As in, *'they call me Doctor Love'* ... from the KISS song?" he asked.

"I'm not familiar with that particular song, sir. But he does have a poster on his wall of that band."

"I thought you were making a clever joke, you know, Doctor Love marches to the beat ... never mind. Should I just come over there and wait for him?"

"That's your choice, sir. Have a nice day."

Very helpful.

Henry grabbed his keys and headed over to the University.

After about thirty-five minutes of sitting out in the hall reading posts from Facebook and Twitter on his phone, a door at the other end of the hall opened up, and a man pulled out his cell phone as Doctor Love by KISS blared from it, echoing down the long hall. He looked at the phone, frowned, and killed the ringer.

He was an interesting-looking guy. About five-eleven, kinda chunky, and he wore the same fedora as Indiana Jones. His face was round and framed in a white, neatly trimmed beard, and white hair pulled back in a ponytail that trailed down his back to where his shoulder blades ended. He wore a tie-dyed green and red and blue Grateful Dead tee-shirt, faded blue jeans, and black Adidas shoes with white stripes. Not exactly what Henry was expecting. He looked at Henry for the first time through his round, wire-rimmed glasses. The intensity of the sharp blue eyes kind of took Henry by surprise. He looked a little like Santa Claus on an acid trip.

"Good morning, young man. And you are?"

"I'm Henry Trank. I'm a friend of Wanda's."

"Yes! She mentioned you! You're the guy with the funny name! Hank Trank! That's pretty cool, if I do say so myself. Your parents must have a great sense of humor!" he said as he wiggled his eyebrows.

"Yeah, they're a laugh a minute."

"Let's go in my office." He called back over his shoulder, "Annie, please hold all my calls and tell anyone that may come by I don't want to be disturbed."

"No problem, Archie."

"Archie?" Henry asked, amused.

"Archibald Love at your service, Mr. Trank. They call me Doctor Love, you know."

"Of course. And obviously you've got the cure I'm thinking of?"

"You're a quick study, Hank." Eyebrow wiggle again. He shut the frosted glass door behind him. The window rattled in its frame. Archie waved Henry over to the couch across from his desk.

The office was a study in organized chaos. The back wall behind his desk was a top-to-bottom book case filled with psychology books, volumes on the occult, witchcraft, a King James version of the Bible, and several other religious titles.

The bottom level held a section of at least two hundred vinyl albums from a wide variety of musical genres. The albums started with AC/DC's *Back In Black* and included titles from The Doors, The Rolling Stones, Foo Fighters, Led Zeppelin, Duran Duran, Roy Orbison, a bunch of classical titles from Bach, Mozart, Beethoven, and yet another section with stuff from Snoop Dogg, Run DMC, and Public Enemy. How he found all this stuff in vinyl was a wonder. And to top it all off at the end of the collection, of course, ZZ Top.

To the right of the bookcase, in the corner, was one of those antique globes set in a wooden stand. Reminiscent of, again, the Indiana Jones movies. He was sensing a theme here. In his mind he heard Joanne saying, *'No shit, Sherlock.'* To the left of the bookcase was the only window in the room. It was sectioned in small, rectangular panes, and in each pane were different symbols that appeared to be wiccan. Henry deduced this because in the top right pane was the exact same symbol Joanne had on her lovely thigh. The others he had no idea about but suspected, in time, he would know their meaning. It gave him an odd and unexpected sort of comfort.

The floor was wall-to-wall dark green carpet that gave the room a cozy feeling. The walls were an eclectic mix of rock-and-roll posters, occult artifacts on shelves, a large gold crucifix set right in the middle of the wall behind the black leather couch, and intermingled between all these various items were his degrees from the U. The arrangement of these items screamed out, *'I'm more than my degrees.'* Henry felt an immediate ease and comfort through this realization. Whether or not intended by the doc, he felt he could talk to this guy about anything.

"So, Henry. I've looked at the video Wanda sent to me. Several times. And I have to agree with her when she says she doesn't believe it's a ghost. It appears this entity is there to observe. What its purpose in observing you is," he shrugged, "we'll see. And it also appears, as she surely has told you, the bright flash toward the end of the video coincides with the dark entity shooting up through the ceiling—as she so eloquently put it—like shit through a goose. What I want to know is the *why* of it! Why are you, apparently, being observed? Why are you having these dreams? What do they mean? Who is this apparent Knight In Shining Armor protecting you? Why, indeed, do you need protecting at all? And I think I have an approach to all of this which may give us some answers. It's not guaranteed to work, but its effectiveness will depend on how much of an open mind you have. Do you consider yourself an open-minded person, Henry?"

"I'd like to think I am. What exactly are we talking about here, Doc?"

"One thing I specialize in is hypnotherapy. I will try to put you in a state that will allow me to lead your subconscious mind backward in time, to a point before all this started to happen to you. Before the dreams started. To rewind the tape, as it were. You'll never be in any danger. I wouldn't attempt it if I thought you would be. It may be emotionally uncomfortable to you but, no matter what, you will be in complete control, and you will have total say in whether or not we continue. There is no pressure here, Henry. My only aim is to help you get some answers and, hopefully, to the bottom of what's going on. Again, if you are at all uncomfortable about this, just say the word and we'll call it a day. The call is one hundred percent yours."

Henry gave it some thought. "Well, the way I look at it, if Joanne trusts Wanda and Wanda trusts you, I really don't have a problem with it. And I'd really like to find out what the hell is going on with these damned dreams. You know, last night was the first night since I've been here I actually got a good night's sleep?"

"Is that right?"

"Yes. In spite of some nut-job trying to grab Joanne out of the car last night, I slept like a baby for the first time in a few months."

"Someone tried to kidnap Joanne?" he asked.

"I don't know if he was trying to kidnap her, or rob us, or what. Thankfully, she had the presence of mind to headbutt the guy in the face to get him off of her. When she closed the door, I reached for a bat I keep in the back seat for baseball practice to go after the guy, but by the time I got around to the other side it was like the bastard vanished into thin air. The only living thing even in the area was a big Rotty ... and he was on the other side of the fence."

"What did this guy look like, Henry?"

"I couldn't really tell, it all happened so fast. He was dressed all in black and it was dark and raining out. The only thing I remember was he smelled terrible. Kinda like rotten eggs and burnt matches."

A look of concern mixed with anger and a touch of fear seemed to cross over the good doctor's face at that moment. Especially with the last comment about the aroma of the perpetrator in question. He was quiet for a few minutes, and it was making Henry nervous. He kept silent, however. He had the feeling he was about to learn something important.

Dr. Love rose from the couch and headed over to his bookcase. Donning his reading glasses, he scanned through the titles on the shelves and double tapped the spine on one of them. He removed it, and brought it over to the table. After a few silent moments scanning through the book he said, "Henry, I want you to look at some of these pictures. Tell me if any of those things look like the person you saw last night, okay?"

Henry took the book from him and looked over the two open pages. About midway down the second page was a figure loosely resembling what he'd seen. Although, he told him, he couldn't really be sure. It was dark and rainy, and to Henry it just looked like a guy in black.

"That might be it, doc, but given the circumstances …"

"Do you know anything about shape-shifters, Henry?"

"Um … I'm gonna go with no."

"Usually, it has to do with human beings believed to have the ability to metamorphose into an animal form, say a cat or a dog or some other animal. However … and this is gonna sound way out there … I believe what you came across last night was something a little more … sinister. That figure you pointed out to me on the page there, it's not dressed all in black. Although at night, in the rain, it may appear that way. It *is* the black. It's an entity devoid of color. It knows nothing of love or joy or happiness. Its purpose is to sow discord, to inflict pain, and above all else, do its master's bidding. Which, I believe, is what it was up to last night. Sent there by God knows who or what to gather information. It appears to be in human form when it needs to be. And it will transform into what it needs in order to hide in plain sight in the land of the living. I can't tell you for sure exactly what it is, but I know this … what you and Joanne were smelling was not body odor. Did you ever smell anyone with B.O. who smelled like *that*?"

"No."

"It was sulfur and rot and all things bad. It was something straight out of hell," Archie said. He continued, "Henry, there are many things that have gone on in this area for a long time. Hundreds of years. No one talks about them any more, though. Everyone is too busy in modern life to be bothered. We bury our faces in our cell phones. We're all too concerned about binge watching the next big thing on TV. We're told by people God and the devil and good and evil are old notions. That they're relegated to horror movies or scary books. And if you actually take any of that stuff seriously, you're an idiot or gullible or just some fucking whack-job. But regardless of what modern life has to say about it, those things don't go away. They're timeless. You see things everyday on the news. Shootings, rapes, murders, child abuse … cruelty in any number of forms. And, at the root of it, is our loss of *belief*! I frankly don't care what you *believe* in, Henry, but I do care that you believe in *something*! Whatever you choose it to be. All the world's great religions have, at their core, a belief in a power greater than ourselves. What they also have, unfortunately most of the time, is a bunch of people who think they know what that power wants everyone else to do and they are the chosen messengers to deliver instruction from on high! Fuck *that*! This is your journey, Henry! It's a spiritual journey, and it's also an inward one. I can help you, I think, find the answers you're looking for, but you have to be willing to give it a try. Will you let me help you, Henry?"

Henry considered what Archie was proposing. He wasn't the most religious or spiritual person to walk the earth—not by a long shot. But, given the events of the last forty-eight hours, his willingness to try anything, at this point, to get a handle on all the weird shit going on lately, was increasing ... and fast. So, after a few moments tossing it around in his head he said, "Let's do this, doc."

He reached over, tapped Henry on the knee twice, and said, "Let me get set up. Why don't you lie back on the couch, Henry, and close your eyes? I want you to breathe deeply, and try to relax all the muscles in your body from head to toe. Take your time."

He did as instructed. Henry could hear him puttering about, setting up whatever it is guys like him set up to do his thing. After a few moments, the room darkened and filled with the calming aroma of Dragon's Blood. Henry had really grown to love the smell of it lately. It reminded him of Joanne.

"Ok, Henry. Keep your eyes closed. Keep breathing and relaxing as you've been doing. I've set up a digital recorder so we can keep a record of this. When you are in the trance state, you will be fully aware of what is going on, but when I bring you out, you may not remember a lot of what's been said. We'll both listen to this together after the session. Here we go."

The following is a transcript of the session:

Dr. Love - *Okay, Henry. I want you to picture some place you love to be. A place that brings you peace and calm and happy thoughts. I want you to picture that place at the bottom of a stairway or a path, whichever you prefer. And to get there, we are going to count the steps backward from ten to one. When we get to one, you will be in this peaceful place. You will feel an utter and complete sense of well-being. You can do this silently or out loud. Let me know when you are there.*

Henry - *I'm there. I'm at the beach in Maine. It's sunny and warm. I'm having a vanilla and chocolate soft serve and it's awesome. It's running down my forearm and my mom is wiping it off with a napkin. She's smiling at me as she does it. She really loves me and I can really feel that. This is the best day ever!*

Dr. Love - *That's great, Henry. How old are you on this day? Do you know?*

Henry - *I'm nine. I know it because today is my birthday. Mom said I was good, and she was going to do something special for me on my birthday. I smell hot dogs. They smell goooooood!!*

Dr. Love - *Now Henry ... take the feeling from that beautiful memory with you, and we are going to go backward in time. We can do this because where you are, all things are possible. Do you understand that, Henry?*

Henry - *Yes sir. All things are possible.*

Dr. Love - *Okay, I want you to imagine you are flying backward in time, Henry. You can use whatever you need to do so. It's your choice. Let me know what you choose and when you are ready. Okay?*

Henry - *Okay. I'm gonna use the Millennium Falcon from Star Wars. It's really fast, and I can shoot down the bad guys. Well, Chewie will have to shoot them down cuz I'm driving. No one messes with the Millennium Falcon if they know what's good for them. And it's the fastest hunk of junk in the galaxy.*

Dr. Love - *That's perfect, Henry. Now I want you to take the Falcon, and point it backward in time. When you come out of hyperspace...*

Henry - *You know what hyperspace is?!?*

Dr. Love - *Of course I do! Fastest way around the galaxy, Henry!*

Henry - *You're pretty cool for a headshrinker.*

Dr. Love - *Thanks, Henry. Now, when you come out of hyperspace, I want you to land at docking bay four. That is also how old you are going to be when you exit the Falcon. Can you do that for me, Henry?*

Henry - *Piece of cake, doc. Okay, I'm coming down the ramp and I'm out on the tarmac at bay four. What's next?*

Dr. Love - *I want you to exit the station and head outside. When you go outside the Falcon, it will still be at the dock, but you'll be back in this world and you will be four years old. I want you to remember, as best you can, anything at all from when you were four. It can be any memory, good or bad, I just want you to pick one that stands out the most from that time. Can you do that for me, Henry?*

Henry - *Okay. I'm sitting in front of the tella-bizzun. I'm watching Bert and Ernie and they are mad at each other about something and it's funny cuz Bert thinks he's the smart one but Ernie is really smarter and they are waving their hands in the air and shaking their heads ... it's funny. Now the door is opening, and the sun is hurting my eyes cuz the sun is bright and my mommy is dressed all fancy and stuff ... only today ... she isn't my mommy. My today mommy is in the kitchen and her eyes are wet and she runs out of the kitchen and into the room where I am sitting on the floor and she gives me a really hard hug and she puts kisses all over my face and she tells me that I need to go with my other mommy, the one I told you about that was at the beach with me, and to be a good boy and that she will see me again someday, but to try really hard to pretend my beach mommy is now my real mommy and to practice forgetting what my today mommy with the wet face looks like. I'm scared and I tell her I don't want a new mommy, but she just has more water running out of her eyes and snots are coming out of her nose. I want her to stop leaking so much! I'm sad but I go with my new mommy, the beach mommy, who is asposed to be mommy now. She puts me in the small seat that's on top of the big seat in her big black car. I looked out the window of the big black car to see if my today mommy is waving goodbye, but the only thing I can see is the black and white birdie above our door. The door is closed. I hope she's not mad at me.*

There's a small lady with a hood over her head in the seat next to me. She says some weird things to me and then to my new mommy and daddy. They make us feel sleepy and far away ... and a few minutes later we are on the big road. I can read a little, but I don't know what some words mean. But I can say the letters. Can you tell me what they mean, mister doctor? The letters are N-O-R-T-H, then there's numbers 9 and 5 and then more letters underneath M-A-I-N-E and N-E-W-H-A-M-P-S-H-I-R-E.

Dr. Love - *That big road is called a highway, Henry. Those letters spell out North, the numbers are the name of the highway, and the rest of the letters spell out Maine and New Hampshire. Those are states that are north of Massachusetts. Which is where we are. And, apparently, where you once were.*

Henry - *Why does your voice sound all wet, mister doctor? You sound like my today mommy from the kitchen did.*

Dr. Love - *Not to worry Henry, it's probably just my allergies kicking up. It's that time of year where all this stuff gets in the air and it makes your eyes water and you sound all wet. I think we need to bring you back now, Henry. Let's get back in the Millennium Falcon and take off. I'll count forward from one to ten and when I reach ten, you will be back in the present and back in the room with me. Is that okay?*

Henry - *Okay, mister doctor.*

End Session.

CHAPTER FIFTEEN

HEADED NORTH

IT WAS THREE HOURS later. Henry was at home with Joanne, listening to the recording. His world had just turned inside out, and he was at a loss for words. But he wasn't about to let on to Joanne just how he felt at the moment. He didn't understand what he was feeling, and if he'd had a better grasp on it, he would have labeled himself as in denial. But he wasn't there yet. When the tape ended, he looked over at Joanne and was surprised to see tears in her eyes. "What's the matter?"

"The part about you being taken away from your mother. It sounds so sad. I wanted to reach out and hug the four-year-old you."

"Jo, don't feel too bad. The part about me being taken from my mother—it never happened. I've been with my mother all my life up in Maine. I'm not sure where the memory could have come from, but it sure as hell wasn't something that happened to me."

"Are you sure? It sounded so ... I don't know ... real. The emotions seemed so strong and the whole scenario was so detailed and ... "

"I'm sure. My mother is Jeanne Davis Trank and my father is Dominick Trank. And I've no memory of any sort like this. It's probably something I saw in a bad TV show once. Dr. Love may be good at what he does—I was sure as shit hypnotized—but I think whatever came out on that tape, at least the part about being taken away from whoever this lady is, it's pure fiction. That other part, with the ice cream. That was the real deal."

She didn't look convinced. "Henry, there is no way in the world I would want what I just heard to be true. I know we haven't been together long at all either, but I really care for you. So I'm gonna climb out on a limb here and suggest maybe, just maybe, it might be worth looking into." Her face said *please don't be mad at me*.

He stared at her a few moments before answering. "So, you want me to go to my mom and dad, who I worship the ground they walk on, and, I don't know, just casually ask them if I was, what? Adopted? Kidnapped? Taken out of the living room of some woman I've never met and wouldn't know who she was if she walked right up to me and said 'howdy-fuckin'-do Henry … oh by the way, I'm your long-lost mother?' Sorry, that ain't happening."

"I know, I know. I'm sorry. It's just … if it were me and I'd just gone through what you've gone through, I would, at the *very least*, want an answer. Think about it. You are probably ninety-nine point nine percent right, and it will be a wild goose chase, and you can come back here and point at me and say

I'm an idiot. But at least you can squash that tiny sliver of doubt that will, undoubtedly, creep into your mind and eat at it like a worm."

He had to admit it to himself, she had a point. They were new at being a couple, but they'd gotten to know each other pretty well before they started dating. She knew after all the bluster that, eventually, it would drive him crazy and he'd have to know.

"If you'd let me, I'd like to go with you. I'm gonna meet your parents sooner or later. Might as well be sooner."

He smiled at her. "Wouldn't have it any other way."

Twenty minutes later they were on I-95 North heading to Portland.

Chapter Sixteen
Wanda comes clean

"Wanda. It's Archie. We need to talk."

"What's up, Arch?"

"I just finished up with your friend, Henry. Some interesting things popped up in his session."

"What would those be, Archie?

"You're probably not gonna like this, but here it is. I brought him down into the trance state in the usual way, and he arrived at a comforting memory from the age of nine. He was with his mother, at the beach, having ice cream."

"That sounds nice," Wanda said.

"I then had him travel backwards in time, to the age of four."

"—okay. I think I know where this is going."

"You do?"

"Yes. Let me guess," Wanda said. "He had a memory of someone else being his mom. Or maybe a memory of being taken away from someplace?"

"That's exactly right. How did you know?"

"Because I'm the one who suggested we move him, back then. For his own safety and also the safety of his mother and the rest of us. I knew this day would come—have been dreading it for a long time now—but it was the only way I knew to keep his true identity a secret from them."

"Yes, but *I* didn't know this day was supposed to come. You said you wanted me to bring him back all the way to the lifetime he'd lived in the dream. Back to the witch trials. Back to when he was her! I had no idea this would come up. A heads up would have been nice. I was in tears listening to that!"

"Archie, you are one of my closest, best-est friends in the entire world. I would keep nothing from you unless I thought it was absolutely necessary. And it *was* absolutely necessary. He is the only one that can end all this. The only one who can travel the astral plane like he's lived there all his life. Like Madeleine used to do. I don't know why, it's just a natural thing within him. Well, within his soul.

"He was gonna find out eventually. And with the four hundred year period ending at the crack of dawn on Halloween, it's better off being sooner. He's the only one who knows the truth. We needed to protect him until now. His awareness is growing. I can feel it. He's not quick to dismiss what's going on. Actually, I'm a bit surprised at how readily he's accepting some of the things we've been revealing to him lately. It's not every day you get someone, in about two days, willing to accept something paranormal or supernatural may be happening to them. Especially in the age of science, above all else. But, in my opinion, it's the part of him we all know is so strong that's waking up. And at just the right time."

"He's gonna be pissed when he finds out the truth. I know I would."

"I know. I'm counting on him understanding why it had to be done. And he will. I've no doubt about it. He almost finished it last time, when he was her. He'll learn what went wrong, if we can convince him to go back, and finally take this bastard down!"

"What about his mom? His real mom? The one I've just recently been introduced to. Is she safe?"

"She's safe. And she's ready to do her part."

CHAPTER SEVENTEEN
HENRY AND DAD

THEY ARRIVED AT HENRY'S parents' house at about six in the evening. He'd called his mom on the way and told her about Joanne. His mother greeted them at the door wearing an apron and a little flour smeared on one cheek.

Jeannie was tall, just under Henry's six-foot frame. Her auburn colored hair was tied back in a bun. She towered over Jo. She was about two inches taller than her own husband.

Big warm hugs for both of them. The smell of garlic floated through the door with her like a silent companion—life as it had always been for him as far back as he could remember. How the hell was he gonna bring up what he'd learned from the session with Dr. Love? Shit, *he* didn't really believe it except, as Joanne had said, he had to know for sure. And she was right.

Henry settled down in the living room before dinner. The Red Sox were on the TV. His mom and Joanne were making small talk in the kitchen. It was just him and his dad sitting there watching the game. He had butterflies in his stomach the entire time thinking about how to bring up the subject that someone—a stranger no less—a few hours earlier had, for lack of a better term, told him he was adopted. And not in any normal sort of way, either. Life was so fucking strange sometimes. When it came right down to it he decided there was no easy way to bring it up, so he said, "Dad ... are you and mom my real parents?"

Dominick said nothing right away, but his body language said it all. He stiffened in his seat as if he'd just heard a cherry-bomb go off right outside the front door. He turned to look at his son then, and the look on his face was heartbreak, horror, and shame. His mouth formed a silent O, and his jaws were working like a fish that had jumped from its tank and landed on the carpet. And all at once he knew. All at once his world flipped on its axis, and it was all he could do to hold it together. They locked eyes for a few awkward moments and, while still looking at Henry, he said, "Jeannie, you need to come in here."

His mom came in with Joanne at her side. Jo took one look at Henry and the smile fell from her face. She knew he'd asked "the question." She made her way over to the couch and sat next to him. Jo took his hand into hers and just held it. He needed that. She said nothing. He knew right then, at the moment he was the most lost he'd ever been in his life—by the way she just knew the right thing to do at the right time—he loved her. And the weird thing was, though he didn't know why at the time, he'd felt he'd always loved her.

"Henry just asked me a question, Jeannie. He wants to know if we are his real parents. He wants to know the truth, Jeannie." His father clicked off the TV. The silence in the room was like a tomb. His mom looked down at the floor and said nothing for a few moments. And then ...

"Henry, you are my son. I've raised you since you were a little boy. I've loved you your entire life. Your dad and I brought you up to be a good man. I've watched you grow through grade school, nursed you when you were sick, cried with you when your first girlfriend broke up with you, watched you graduate high school and then nursing school, and we practically burst at the seams with pride. Nothing can change the fact that you are my son. And Dom is your dad. And through all this time, all the love and the tears, the happiness and the heartbreak, there has always been this little undercurrent of dread. Knowing this day would come. That it *had* to come. I've thought of a billion ways to say this to you and it never, ever seemed there would be a right way to say it. So I'll just rip the band-aid off and say it. I am your mother but, no, I did not give birth to you."

And there it was. It hung in the air like an emotional mushroom cloud, and now they all had to deal with the fallout. Henry didn't take a breath for at least a good minute. Without a word, he got out of his chair and headed straight for the front door. No one said a word (which he was grateful for) as he opened the door and headed outside. He needed some air. Needed to absorb it all. The emotions and feelings came fast and furious. He paced around his parents (could he still call them his parents?) front yard. It was cool outside as the sun sank low. Twilight had yielded ever so gently, allowing the first stars to pop through the veil dividing day into night. He'd always loved this time of day, and now it was a living metaphor for his life: things that seem so clear in the daytime appear totally different when darkness falls.

Time seemed unimportant as he stared into the night sky. The whoosh and gentle slam of the screen door behind him pulled his thoughts back to the new reality. Henry turned to see his dad walking toward him. The muted orange dot of his cigar gave his face a subtle orange glow as it hung askew out of the left side of his mouth. In each hand he carried a Miller Lite. He offered one to Henry, and he took it without a word. Two loud cracks as each of them opened a frosty brew. Dom offered his beer forward, and they tapped cans, as they'd always done.

Henry's dad was a stutterer. It wasn't terrible, and he had it mostly under control, but at times like this—emotional times, stressful times—it had a way of creeping back into his speech. He said, "I l-l-l-love you H-henry. I've always l-l-loved you like you were my own. And, as far as I'm concerned, you are. I-I-I don't know who your real dad is. And I don't really c-c-care. I just want you to know that. If you leave here tonight and you n-n-never want to talk to me again, I g-g-g-get it."

Henry turned to face him. Tears ran down Dom's cheeks and through the five o'clock shadow that encircled his now damp cigar. A single teardrop reflected the pale moonlight and stretched out, falling from the cigar to the grass below. Dominick Trank did not cry. In all the years growing up in this house he'd seen him mad, seen him happy, seen him proud, seen him scared, but never had Henry seen him cry. The truth about what he was feeling ran down his face. And the man who moments ago had become a stranger to him, in the house he grew up in, was just DAD again. His dad was hurting as much as he was, probably more, and Henry pulled him in and hugged him hard.

He let go of Dom and asked, "So what do I do now, dad?"

"I would g-g-go and talk to your mom when you're ready. But before you do, I just want you to realize one thing, Henry. The woman in that house *is* your mom. Make no mistake about it. I know you're mad and confused right now, but try to keep in mind there is a reason for all of this. I don't know what it is. All I can tell you is, for your own safety, I was left out of the loop. I love your mom so much. When she told me we were taking you in, I didn't question it. Jeannie does nothing without thinking it through, that's for damn sure."

Henry took a big swig from his beer and left it on the fence. He thought about what his dad said for a moment or two and made for the door. Time to talk to mom. God help me, he thought.

When he came through the screen door, Jo was still sitting on the couch. Staring at the blank TV screen. She looked up at him and put her arms out. Henry walked over to her, hugged her, and gave her a quick kiss on the lips and said, "Wish me luck."

He walked into the kitchen and saw his mom working on dinner. She went about her business, politely ignoring him and sniffling a bit as if she'd been crying. She had. Unsure how to bring the conversation they'd had earlier back up, he just dove in as he'd done earlier with dad. If there was one thing the Trank family all had in common, it was to get straight to the heart of the matter. No bullshit, thank you.

"Mom ... who is my biological mother?"

Chapter Eighteen

Henry and Mom

"HENRY..." SHE PAUSED, LOOKING very unsure how to proceed. "This is going to sound like the lamest thing in the world ... and it's probably not going to make you happy. But ... I have no idea. I don't even clearly recall the day we brought you here. I can't even explain to you why I can't remember." And then, frustrated, she threw the towel hanging over her shoulder down on the white-tiled kitchen floor.

"How is that even possible, Mom?"

"I wish I knew the answer to that, Henry. It's hard to explain but I know, in here," she tapped her chest, "that to follow that one down into the rabbit hole would mean danger to you and a bunch of other people ... who, by the way, I couldn't even tell you who they are, because I can't remember *that* either."

"Jesus Mom, how am I supposed to get to the bottom of all this?"

"Henry, I have one request. I would like us to have dinner together tonight, at least one last time, like the family we've always been." He started to talk, and she put up her palm like a traffic cop. "After dinner, I'm gonna go up to the safe in my room. I'm going to bring you something from the safe that, again, I don't know the reason, but I'm supposed to give it to you in case this day ever happened ... which ..." and she swept her hand out like a magician, asking him to observe.

"Okay, Mom. But let's stop with this talk about us not being a family after tonight, okay? You and dad *ARE* my family. Not maybe. And there is nothing in the world that could ever change that. Understand?"

She nodded, started crying, and ran over and hugged him. He held her as she sobbed and the lump in his throat threatened to strangle him.

Chapter Nineteen
Dinner and Discovery

Dinner was amazing. Being the spoiled only child they, of course, had lasagna with meatballs. Henry's fave. His mom and dad made small talk with Joanne, and he was jumping for joy inside they seemed to really like her. Which was good since, yes, after two days as a couple, he could safely say he was in love with her. It was unbelievable to him he could say this, but it was fact. Written on his heart like the name chiseled on a gravestone.

When dinner was finished, Joanne, Dom, and Henry were cleaning up. Jeannie made her way upstairs to the safe, and came down with a solid bronze box about six inches long, three inches tall, and about three inches across, front to back. The outside had different symbols etched into the front. Jo and Henry exchanged a knowing look as they both observed that one symbol was the exact same one she had tattooed on her thigh. Where the cover and the body of the box met, there was a row of four spinning dials with numbers on them. It had a combination lock.

"I don't know what the combo is, Henry," Jeannie said.

"Well, that's kind of a ball buster, now, isn't it?" he said.

"Maybe we can figure this out," Joanne chimed in.

"What?! I wouldn't even know where to start!" he shot back, frustrated.

"Why don't you try starting with your birthday, Henry?" Jeannie said.

He put in the digits for his birthday. If it *was* his actual birthday, he thought, and tried the lock—no dice. For the next half hour they tried his mom's birthday, dad's birthday, and several combinations of numbers from one end of the family to the other. After the futile attempts of the past thirty minutes, they all sat in silence, racking their brains for any combo of numbers that might spring the lock.

"Henry, just for shits and giggles, try my birthday," Joanne said.

She told Henry the digits for her birthday. It worked!

"I'll be dipped in shit," Henry whispered.

"That's f-f-fucked up. Why in the world would it work for Joanne's birthday?" Dom said.

"Dom, language!" Jeannie said, then smirked.

"Sorry. I got a little lost in the moment." His face turned a few shades of crimson.

Joanne laughed out loud and said, "I only even thought to try it because one of the symbols is something personal to me I recognized."

"Well, at least we can find out what the hell the big mystery is now," Henry said.

He opened the box. Inside were two items: a key and a note. He was careful unfolding the note. It had yellowed over the years, and it looked a tad fragile. It read ...

'Henry, if you are reading this note, that is a good sign. For the safety of all I haven't revealed who I am or why, as you undoubtedly know by now, you are the child of someone else. This will be revealed in good time, and at the right time. You need to now go to the Library of Salem. In the Vintage section, look up the book, "Malleus Maleficarum". Investigate the book from cover to cover. It will reveal to you the nature of what is happening to you in your life at this very moment. And trust me, you need to know! The sooner the better!'

'P.S. Don't forget the key! It opens up a lot more than one lock.'

"Great!" Henry said, throwing his hands in the air. "Now this has turned into a scavenger hunt!"

"I'm sorry, Henry," Jeannie said. "I thought the box might lead somewhere."

"It does," Joanne said. "So lets get going and find some damned answers!"

She was right. No sense in sitting around feeling sorry for himself, Henry thought. Time to rock-and-roll.

They all exchanged hugs and said their goodbyes. As they headed out to the car, Henry turned back to look at his mom and dad waving from the front steps. Maybe it was everything that had happened lately. Maybe it was stress. Maybe it was a doom and gloom streak buried inside him. He just felt something bad was coming their way.

Chapter Twenty

Jo's Ghosts

It was around nine-thirty at night when they made their way onto I-95 South, heading back to Salem. Henry fell asleep for about a half hour while Jo did the driving. They were already over the Massachusetts border when he woke up. It appeared the new woman in his life had a bit of a leadfoot. He looked down at the speedometer and saw it pegged at 90 mph.

"Are you late for a date?" he asked.

"Why do you ask?"

"Um, because you're doing ninety ... maybe."

She looked down and said, "Shit. Bad habits die hard."

"Have you always driven like a NASCAR driver, or are you new to the racing game?"

"Smart ass. No, it's kind of a thing with me from the past. I used to have to get out of some unpleasant situations quickly when I was younger."

"What situations would force you to drive like your hair is on fire?"

She considered this for a bit. The silence carried on until it became uncomfortable. Henry looked over in time to see her trying to wipe a tear from her eye before he could notice. She failed.

"Hey, Jo ... I'm sorry. You don't have to tell me anything you don't want to. I was just kidding around. I didn't mean to upset you."

"No, it's okay. I want to tell you about my past, Henry. I want you to know as much about me as possible. Before I do, though, I have a question for you. I think I know the answer, but I've been wrong in the past. We've known each other for a while now. These past two days, though ... they've been crazy. I don't know if you've felt it, but—"

"I love you, Jo. I'm pretty sure it happened the day I walked into your shop. I'm not one to buy into the 'love at first sight' thing ... but that's what it was. It sounds sappy, but there you have it."

His heart was pounding now, and he felt like a fool. It's a leap of faith when you really love someone. The fear of that love not being returned is terrifying, and rejection can be soul-crushing.

"I love you too, Henry," she said, and took her eyes off the road, putting them on him for an uncomfortably long time, given the ninety miles per hour thing. "I can't believe how fast it's all happened. Trust me when I tell you, I was not looking for a guy! But yeah, the day you walked into the shop ... I felt it too." She laughed. "It sounds like a corny movie!"

The relief Henry felt, when she told him she felt the same way, was overwhelming. They sat in comfortable silence for a bit. Then, just like Henry had done with his mom, back at his parents' house, Joanne dove right in about her own past.

"I love your parents, Henry. You're lucky to've grown up in a home like that. I, however, was not as lucky. My mother was a drunk, and my father walked away from both of us before I was old enough to remember his face. They found him about three or four years ago. He burned alive in a crack house down in New York somewhere. My mother is still alive and, thank God, finally got sober about a year ago. I don't really talk to her all that much. Wanda was the one who helped her out. Mom was court ordered to appear at the AA meeting Wanda is the treasurer of."

"How did you and Wanda meet?" he asked.

"Ironically, the same way as my mom. Only without the court order. I used to do a lot of drinking and drugs, Henry. I also drove getaway on some B and E'S for drug money, way back when, to answer your NASCAR question. I'm definitely no angel, but I was lucky. I had something happen to me that woke me up. After my father left, my mother did her best to hold it together. But eventually, like most alkies, she fucked up along the way. She got shit-faced on the way home from work one night. She'd picked me up from day care like normal. Apparently, that night, she felt the need to stop off at a bar on the way home. Just to keep the buzz going. Well, she definitely kept her buzz going. She kept it going *so* well she decided the cute guy chatting her up at the bar was gonna be the cute guy knocking her socks off later that night. Unfortunately, she forgot about me, about her car, and about pretty much everything else except booze and orgasms for the night.

"Thankfully, as the bar was closing, the bartender noticed the car in the lot. And looked inside and found lil' ole me sitting in the back, sleeping away, in the now freezing car.

"A lot of judges find that a bad thing. They took me from mom and dumped me into the foster care system. I bounced from family to family until I was almost eighteen. My last stop on the magical mystery tour of families ended when my new foster "dad" decided he wanted to be my new foster boyfriend. He climbed into bed with me and, within ... oh, about a minute ... left that bed with a black eye and a ruptured left testicle."

"You gotta be shittin' me." He was blown away.

"I shit you not."

"So, what woke you up?"

"I'm getting there. It's all about context, Henry. So, after *that* incident, I was done with foster care, but I had nowhere to go. I took a room at the Y, and a shitty job. I needed cash and a place to live. I ran into some shady people at the Y. They introduced me to the wonderful world of mind-altering substances and the various ways said substances get financed. I got hooked. The drugs took away all the fear, all the shame, all the terrible memories and feelings. I was trying to bury all those things deep down inside. Funny thing about those feelings though—when you bury them, you bury them alive. They all come back to the surface like fucking Jason or Michael Myers. So, when the drugs and the booze stopped working, I was in a world of hurt. I couldn't live with them … they were killing me. And I couldn't live without them. This, sadly, led my drug addled brain to the only conclusion it was capable of at the time. I couldn't live. I was actually thinking about doing myself in."

"Jesus, Jo."

"Ah, but that's where my lucky break comes in. I was sitting at a deli in town one day. Really feeling shitty about myself. Bad thoughts about doing bad things to myself were the *only* things on my mind. As I was sitting at the counter against the wall, all by myself waiting for my food, this guy comes out of nowhere and asks me would I mind reading a book he's writing. At first I was thinking, *'what the hell does this weirdo want?'* But the place was full, and it was the middle of the day, so I wasn't really too worried about him pulling some kind of crap on me. So, I asked him what the book was about. He tells me it's a book about quotes on happiness. At this point I was just thinking, *'let's get this over with'*, so I tell him, sure, I'll read his stupid book. Then something funny happened. Line after line, my mood changed. I couldn't stop reading it! It was like a fucking miracle, Henry! It took me out of the funk I was in and I realized for the first time in … I don't know how long ... I wasn't feeling sad, or mad, or suicidal. I handed the book back to him when my food order came up. I turned around to look for him and thank him, and he was gone. I asked the guy at the counter where the man at the table went that I'd just been talking to. He just looked at me like there was an arm growing out of my forehead."

"So, who do you think the guy was?"

"I don't know who he was. And I never found out. When I think back on that day though—you'll probably think I'm nuts, and I wouldn't blame you—I think he was a guardian angel. I think, sometimes, when we are at our lowest points in life, whoever or whatever runs things, on a spiritual level, will intervene. Whether we believe it, and whether we grab at the chance we've been given, is up to us. Even through the alcoholic and druggie haze I was in, I was, thankfully, at least able to see it that way. And that night I went to my first AA meeting and met the fabulous Wanda."

They were both quiet for a while. The steady rumble of the road, the constant rain, and the smooth hum of the Toyota's engine the only sounds. He was considering all she'd told him. Under normal circumstances, the story she'd just finished (especially the part about meeting a guardian angel) he would have dismissed out of hand. Now ... he wasn't so quick to do so. Not so quick to judge what another person believed, and not so quick to dismiss the shortcomings of another, and the choices (good or bad) they'd made under circumstances he'd no way to grasp. It reminded him of what his father had once said: *'We all have our own bag of rocks to carry in life, Henry. The only difference is how the bag got filled.'*

"So, now you know the real me. Still interested?" she asked.

"Are you kidding me? Bad girls are such a turn on!"

He looked over at her. Subtle green light from the dashboard painted her face. She smiled, never taking her eyes off the road, and punched him in the leg.

"Asshole," she said.

CHAPTER TWENTY-ONE

SOLOMON'S LAW

SOLOMON DOBSON WAS FEELING something he'd not felt in ages. Fear. This made him angry. For the first time in months, he could not account for Henry's whereabouts. And for Solomon, Henry's whereabouts were becoming a more urgent thing to account for. If he were not tailing him personally, he would have either Leonard or Delilah or one of the other "associates" keep tabs on him. If it weren't for the pint-sized witch across town protecting him, he could have taken Henry out as soon as he'd arrived in town. But somehow the little pain in the ass had known that particular soul had returned before Solomon himself had known. She could shield him until she knew he'd be safe. At least for now. Her and her goddamned protection spells!

She'd also figured out a way to hide him from the time he'd been born. When he found out who her co-conspirator was in *that* little venture, there would be, as he'd heard the kids in town say, a "fuck-ton" of pain involved for both.

He thought back through time. How he'd discovered, for the first time in his existence, someone had finally figured out his secret—what he'd discovered on the path to earthly immortality during the Crusades. How he could stay and rule here, on this plane. Forever, if he chose. How he'd learned to feed on the souls of others through their dreams. How you could siphon the life essence out of others and they were almost helpless to do anything about it.

The lucky ones—well, lucky for them, not Solomon—were the ones who suspected, correctly, there was something evil afoot. Invariably those few would seek spiritual protection. They would contact the local high priest or priestess, shaman, witch doctor, or whatever flavor of religious or spiritual practitioner dominated in their particular part of the world. The local authority would sometimes stumble upon something that could keep Solomon out of their dreams.

More often than not it didn't work, however, and he could steal their life force as he pleased. Often with devastating physical and psychological results. Faith was only as strong as belief, it turned out.

There was the occasional successful defense of a believer here and there. Though it at times proved frustrating, in the end it mattered little when you were dealing with eternity. And if the person you chose as *protector* was weak in their faith ... c'est la vie.

Not now, though. Somewhere along the way, he'd missed something. Most likely during the witch trials, when Henry had been an accused witch who had almost eluded him. He'd come within a whisper of recapturing that which could keep him protected forever. It would have ended his worries for eternity. He was so close! If only his followers could have controlled themselves. The insanity of the times back then (an insanity he'd helped provoke, he lamented) had proved overwhelming. The mania that was the Salem Witch Trials had taken Henry, who back then was known as Madeleine, and her secret knowledge of Solomon's condition, to the grave.

"I've called you all here tonight because Mr. Trank has taken a little trip. Normally this wouldn't bother me. Normally, we would have eyes on him around the clock. And the clock is ticking."

Solomon finished this by fixing his gaze on every one of his followers. The only sound was the hollow bang of the wooden shaft of his cane on the cement floor of the dank underground room in the mortuary (one of his many properties in Salem) as he paced back and forth. It's always in the eyes. Those gathered before him knew better than to look away. For *one* of his followers, it was going to be an awful night. Perhaps their last, depending upon what they had to say.

He stopped in front of a young man wearing a blue-on-white varsity letter jacket. Dean Samuels felt the blood in his body turn frigid as he looked into Solomon's ancient blue eyes. Dean felt a strange tickle in the middle of his head. A feeling akin to when you eat cake with frosting that is way too sweet. Dean would call it "brain puckers" when he got that sensation. Only, there was no cake here tonight. He could feel Solomon probing his mind, and he tried in vain to think of anything but how he'd lost Henry's whereabouts.

"Really, Mr. Samuels? Trying to keep me out by thinking about fucking your cheerleader girlfriend? I'd expected better. And so did she, apparently. My compliments on your selection, though. She looks like an absolutely fantastic fuck. Next time though, try to last a little longer than it would take to microwave a cup of coffee, my boy, or she'll be riding the baloney pony with the quarterback by next week."

Dean's face turned purple with shame, and tears formed in his eyes. He wouldn't let them fall down his cheeks, though. Weakness was not tolerated here. It could actually get you turned out from the group ... or worse. And once you started down the road laid out before you by Solomon, once you had stolen from others the very essence of their soul, there was no turning back. You were committed. It violated all things holy. It was the unforgivable sin. But when shown what you could have on this earth—the wealth, the power, the unlimited time to do whatever it was you wanted, forever—it seemed like the only choice. Solomon showed you the promise of that new life, and he made it seem so real! So close! All you could ever want! Just commit yourself to him, swear your loyalty, and it was yours. He would show you the way! And Dean had done just that! With enthusiasm! Dean wondered about that choice now.

"Please, Mr. Samuels, tell me how it happened."

"Mr. Dobson?"

"Are you really going to play dumb with me?"

Dean looked down at the floor. *He knows.* Better to come clean now and face the music than to fuck with a dude who's been around the block several thousand times.

"I followed him from the shrink's office, like Mr. Shrumm told me to do. I sat outside the house for a while and I saw him and his girlfriend get into their car and take off. I went to get into my car and follow them, and that's the last thing I remember. I woke up in my car about three hours later and on the other side of town. I didn't tell you right away because I couldn't. I was out like a light and I have no idea how it happened. I lied to Leonard and told him they were still in the apartment because I didn't want to fail you, sir. I booked ass all the way back over to their place, but the car was still gone. Then I was called here. I don't know where they went or who they talked to or anything after that. I still don't know where they are now."

It all happened fast. Dean shuddered violently in his seat. He grabbed at his head, screaming in pain. His legs shot out and hit the seat in front of him, pushing his own chair over backwards. The metal chair slammed to the floor with a loud bang and Dean writhed in pain, rolling left and right and kicking violently at something no one else could see.

"Stay away from me! Stay away from me! NO! Oh my God, what is that? Don't touch me with those! Please!"

His hands shot out as if to ward something off. Both hands forming the letter C as if they were grasping at the arms of an unseen attacker. For the briefest moment, everyone in the room glimpsed two arms covered in black hair. At the end of each arm were three razor-sharp black claws aimed right at Dean's eyes. They came within inches of ending Dean's window on the world forever.

And then as fast as it all started, it stopped. Dean was staring at the back of the guy in front of him. His head didn't hurt anymore. He was seated as he'd been before. He looked around. No one seemed to notice what had just happened. No chair was overturned. No one was even looking in his direction. It was as if he'd just had the worst daydream/nightmare of his life. Solomon was still up front, talking to everyone and inquiring as to the whereabouts of Henry Trank. When he looked in Dean's direction, the old man had the slightest grin on his face. Solomon winked.

)⊕(

Dean's attacker watched the front of Henry's house after walking back from where the car and Dean had been deposited. Just because one threat was neutralized didn't mean another couldn't be arriving soon after in its place. Henry's guardian settled down in the spot in front of the house again. It was going to be a long night.

Chapter Twenty-Two

Library Card

Joanne pulled the Camry off of Route 128 and down the ramp marked Salem/Beverly. It was just a few blocks back to Henry's apartment from there. They'd ridden most of the way back in silence. Henry had nodded off a few times during the trip. The events of the evening had left him feeling drained but oddly satisfied.

It wasn't every day that you'd just found out you were "adopted." But the satisfaction came from at least knowing part of the truth. The rest was yet to come. And as they got closer to Salem, the emotional and physical fatigue gave way to a spark of curious excitement about what was to be revealed next.

Questions swirled in his mind about the possibilities. What would they find at the library? What was the key for? Would he finally find the answers he sought about these insane dreams that, incredibly, ended with items from another world and another time in his bedroom? Most important of all: who was his mother? And was she still alive?

First things first. "What time is it, Jo?"

"It's eleven-thirty."

"Shit! The library's closed."

"Nothing is ever really closed, Henry."

"Huh?"

"I'm just saying, like the guy in that movie, "Taken" ... *I have a particular set of skills.*"

"Are you suggesting what I think you're suggesting, Jo?"

"Well, I don't know about you, Henry, but *my* gut tells me waiting until the morning to grab that book may be unwise."

"So is Breaking and Entering, Jo."

"Only if you get caught."

He couldn't believe his ears. Although, after all that had gone down, why the fuck should anything be a surprise right now? He tossed it around in his head, still unsure.

"How do you propose we do this, exactly?" he asked.

"Let's get to the library and see what I can come up with, okay?"

Again, he couldn't believe his ears. Or his mouth. "Okay."

The Salem Public Library is an older, three-story brick building on the corner of a major street and a quiet side street. There is literally no parking lot, save for a small space in front of the building large enough for one car. It's surrounded by residential homes with backyards Jo intended on using to sneak into the rear of the library and search for a place to gain entry.

Jo shut the headlights off about a block before they got to the library. She swung the Camry down one of the side streets and into a spot unlit by any street lamps.

"I need something to hide my face and my hair from the cameras inside," Jo said.

"Pop the latch on the trunk. I think I may have a hoodie from the gym back there. It may be a tad ripe, though."

"I'll manage."

They got out and rummaged through his disaster area of a trunk. Jo found the offensive smelling hoodie, a tire iron, and grabbed Henry's sunglasses from the top of his head. She got dressed for action.

"Well? What do you think?" she asked.

"I think you look like a mini version of the Unabomber."

"Thanks. Do I look enough like him to *not* pass for me?"

"Yep."

"Do you have any gum on you, Henry?"

"Fresh breath a priority for B and E?"

"Always. But what I need it for is the wrapper. If they have contacts on the windows I can bypass them, hopefully, and get inside without smashing any glass."

"Doesn't that kinda shit only work in the movies?"

"You'd be surprised," she said.

He didn't have any gum. But he had some foil, luckily. Ever since he'd seen a story on the news about how thieves could read the magnetic strip of a debit or credit card through a wallet, he'd taken to wrapping the bottom end of his debit card in aluminum foil. He pulled out the card, removed the foil, and handed it to Jo.

"I'm glad you had this, Henry. I'm sure there's a wonderful story behind it, too."

He started to tell her the news story when she put up a hand and stopped him.

"It can wait," she said. "Let me see the note one more time. I need to get the title of the book again. I'm gonna take the book from here and we can go over it back at your place. If you hear the alarm go off, don't come and help me. Take the car back to your apartment and wait for me there."

"You sure about that?"

"Yes. If the alarm goes off, I don't want to limit myself to one option or one route for escape. It's easier for both of us if you just trust me and let me act on instinct. Hopefully it won't come to that, but it's better we hash this out now than to make it up on the fly. Agreed?"

It was a good point, shitty as it made him feel about possibly leaving her on her own. Henry nodded in agreement.

She took the note, the tire iron, the foil, kissed him really hard on the lips, and slipped into the darkness.

)⚝(

Leonard had given the command, and Hercules was on the prowl. After the meeting with Solomon, everyone in the order was on high alert. The lovely couple must not be allowed to leave the city limits again. There were no more chances left to those who failed. This was a matter of life and death. And eternity. Solomon had made it clear to all who'd been in attendance just what the stakes were.

Sure, the newest of his followers would die a natural death after years of a "normal" life if they failed, but that would be the only thing it was. A death, nothing more. When you sold your soul for immortality, you turned your back on whatever the afterlife held for you. You turned your back on the cycle of life and death and rebirth. On the chance to grow as a soul over the ocean of time. To be cast into the void. But it was so worth it! You had FOREVER to do anything you wanted. You had forever to gain wealth, power, knowledge. To build empires if you so desired!

When midnight came on the 30th and the calendar flipped to Halloween, it would either be the end of Henry and Wanda and their kind. Or the end of Solomon and the *Order Immortalis*. And Leonard was playing hardball now. No more fucking around. He sent Hercules on a fact finding mission. They needed to know where Henry and Joanne had gone, who they'd been talking to, and what they'd found out about Solomon. By any means necessary.

))⬡((

Joanne made quick work of the library window. The contacts were old and worn and easily bypassed. Truth be told, few people even went to the library anymore. The internet had taken care of that. So it wasn't much of a surprise the security wasn't exactly akin to Fort Knox.

Cameras—those could be a problem. It was actually a stroke of good luck they hadn't been able to park close to the library. The darkened yards of the houses surrounding it provided the perfect cover. All Jo had to do was take out the camera hanging over the rear entrance with the tire iron. She did that by sticking to the side of the building after breaking cover from the shrubs. If she were on camera at all, it was only for one or two seconds.

Once inside, she removed the sunglasses and gave her eyes a second to readjust. She consulted the note again for the name of the book. "Malleus Maleficarum," she whispered to herself. She needed to find the vintage book section.

She made her way to the middle of the room and came to a bookstand that was a series of hexagonal shelves. The largest of the shelves were on its bottom and then two more rows of shelves decreased in size the higher the stand went. It was covered with books, but mostly newer titles. Not the spot she was looking for. Behind the stand was a staircase leading up to the second floor. Thankfully, the floor and the stairs were covered by indoor/outdoor carpeting. In a building that looked this old from the outside, she'd assumed dealing with any stairs would be a creak-fest. It wasn't.

When she got to the second floor, it didn't take long to find the vintage book section. It was tucked away in the back. Vintage Books was a smallish room containing about seven or eight sections of shelving, and had a green, formica-topped table at its center surrounded by four wooden chairs.

Jo took out her cell phone, activated the flashlight app, and set about finding the *Malleus Maleficarum*. It didn't take long. She tucked the book under her arm and readied herself to leave and meet Henry back at the car. And that's when she smelled it. The same smell from last night when she'd been attacked—sulfur and rotten eggs. She heard the soft panting of a dog. It sounded like a big dog. So, now the bastard had found her again. How? She couldn't possibly imagine. And now he had a dog with him. Must be the same one Henry saw last night, she thought.

She tossed those thoughts aside and locked in on survival mode. One big problem. She was on the second floor and the open window she'd come through was on the first. She crept to the edge of the railing, quiet as a mouse, and risked a peek over the edge. All she could see was the massive Rotty as he passed by the window at the front of the library. Its long shadow cast from the street lamp stretched across the floor. It mingled with the shadows of the raindrops, which made it appear as if it were melting in little rivers of black. No sign of her attacker from last night, though. They must have split up to make the search for her a quicker task. It's what she would have done.

She backed away from the railing and tiptoed toward the back of the building. She made her way down a narrow row of bookshelves that ended with a window overlooking the backyard she'd just sneaked through twenty minutes earlier. At least, she thought, it puts a little distance between me and them. She looked through the window. Though she couldn't see him, she could roughly pinpoint Henry's location. She had to call him. Had to risk it. There was no other way. Or was there? As she was thinking this, she turned around to check the end of the aisle she'd been hiding in. The silhouette of the Rotty came into view. She now had only one option. She silently texted Henry. The light from her phone caught the big dog's eye, and he slowly turned down the aisle. She was trapped.

Henry looked down at his phone. There was a one word text message from Jo.

RUN.

And then he heard the alarm from the library go off.

Seconds after Jo sent the text message, the dog turned down the aisle. Her understanding of reality immediately came into question. The Rotty seemed to get taller. Impossible! But, nevertheless, happening right in front of her eyes. All four legs of the massive canine seemed to fold in on each other. As the legs in front receded, the ones in back grew. Joanne heard an audible snapping that reminded her of the sound Mr. Stinky's nose made when she broke it with the back of her head. Then, a different sound. It reminded her of what you'd hear when you pull a strip of duct tape from its roll, only wetter. She watched as the head changed shape—the ears and nose shrank and folded in on each other. *I'm trapped in the Salem library with Freddy Fucking Krueger* was the only thing that came to mind. And then, almost before she could take another breath, the animal had rapidly transformed into a man. And the recognition, for her, was instant. And terrifying.

Henry saw a quick burst of movement at the window on the second floor. The library grounds were instantly bathed in brilliant white light. Adrenaline poured into his system, and everything seemed from that moment on as if it were in slow motion.

He saw Jo's silhouette. Her arm shot through the window a split second after the lights came on. The glass from the second-floor window shattered. Jo, in what looked like controlled panic, jumped through the now empty window frame, clutching the book. He saw her, without hesitation, jump from the second floor fire escape and into the bushes below. And then he saw the man in the window. The man in black from the night before—an impossibly deep-black, featureless mass—silhouetted against the glare of the bright lights. He thought of the picture he'd seen in the book Dr. Love had shown him.

Henry threw Jo's plan out the window. He jumped in the Camry and floored it. He drove straight over the lawn of the house across the street, through the yard, through a wood fence that splintered into a million toothpicks, and right up to the shrubs Jo had just landed in. In one fluid motion he stomped on the brakes—tearing the grass of the library lawn up in bunches under the car—grabbed the baseball bat from the back, flung open the driver's side door, picked up the now dazed Joanne from the top of the bushes, ripped open the back door and laid Jo, book still clutched to her chest with both arms, down in the back seat as gently and quickly as he could. He slammed the back door, jumped in the driver's seat, and with his left hand slammed the door shut as his right hand ripped the gear shift into drive. He stomped the accelerator, and the car fishtailed forward across the lawn that ran along the side of the library. Still trying to regain control, he plowed through a ring of bushes surrounding a circular fountain in the middle of the lawn. The metal of the fender on the passenger side squealed in protest as he scraped by it, narrowly avoiding a head on collision with the fountain, which would have put a sudden end to their getaway. He got the car straight just as it hit the asphalt of the main road, and they went screaming away into the night.

Chesrule, the actual name of the demon that could shape-shift back and forth from a dog to a passable human form, watched as his prey leapt from the second floor library window. He watched as her mate scooped her away in the red car. He was, however, not at all concerned about their escape. True, he would like to have caught her up here, maybe played around with her a bit before killing her, but that could come later. He had achieved his primary objective. He had obtained some blood from a cut she had sustained when leaping from the window. He touched the blood and closed his eyes. In his mind's eye he could trace back in time—rewinding as if on an old VCR—the events from the present, back to what she'd seen and said and done over the past few days.

The trail only led back so far when he used this method—not as reliable or enjoyable as torture—three days at the very furthest, but it was more than enough time to learn what he needed to know. He would bring this information back to Leonard and Solomon and receive his next orders. In his dark, soulless heart, he imagined all the things he wanted to do to the dark-haired woman after all of this was over. He leapt through the library window and headed for the mortuary and his masters.

Chapter Twenty-Three

About That Dog...

Are you okay, Jo?"

"Yeah. I'm sore, cut, and bruising as we speak, but I'll live."

"What the hell do we do next?"

"I don't think going back to your apartment is a good move at all. This changes things. We need to go somewhere we'll be safe and protected. We need a little time to figure this all out. And, I hate to say it, but we both need to sleep."

"Sleep? I don't think I could fall asleep anytime soon, Jo. And how the hell are we supposed to protect ourselves from these psycho assholes if they can invade our dreams?" he asked.

Jo fished her cell phone (with new and improved cracked screen from the fall) out of her pocket and tapped the contact for Wanda. She waited a bit and got no answer. She left her a message.

"Wanda isn't answering. Let's head over there, anyway. I've got a key. It's the one place I know of for sure we'll be safe."

"How do you know that? It seems like these nut jobs are one step ahead of us at all times. What makes you think they won't be waiting for us at Wanda's shop?"

"Because it's protected. They wouldn't dare go near there with the spells she's laid down around the property. And if they did, it would be *beyond* painful. Wanda may not look like much, Henry, but she's a powerful witch. She's like Yoda on steroids."

"I hope whatever she's done to protect the building can keep that dark dude out, too."

"About that "dark dude," Henry. He's not what he appears to be. When I first noticed there was someone else in the library, I smelled the rotten egg smell and knew right away it was the asshole from last night. And then, up front where the big windows facing the street are, I saw the silhouette of a dog passing by them. I just assumed he'd brought a dog with him and they'd split up to find me. When I sent you the text, I'd just watched that fucking dog change from a Rotty into a man. I flipped my shit and smashed the window to get the hell outta there as fast as I could."

Henry's conversation from the session with Dr. Love flooded back into his memory. At the time, he'd been almost humoring the old guy. He never really considered what the doc was trying to tell him about the incident with Joanne and some bullshit about shape-shifting beings could actually be true! Now his mind had, again, taken a hard left turn, and Henry was face to face with another reality-altering fact. This was not coincidence. He'd seen the same guy last night seemingly disappear in the span of about ten seconds. And behind him was a Rottweiler, just staring at him from behind the cemetery fence. Tonight, same guy and a Rotty. And Joanne had just filled in the blanks for him on how the motherfucker could have disappeared. It was time to fill *her* in on the missing piece of the story.

"Jo ... last night, after we got attacked by that guy, I kinda forgot to tell you something. Well, two somethings. First, there was a Rottweiler staring at me from the other side of the fence after the smelly guy disappeared, or seemed to disappear. So now we both know neither one of us is nuts. Second, before I had the session with Dr. Love, I told him about what happened to us the night before. He showed me a book that had some images of different dark figures. Had me point to which one the guy reminded me of the most. After I pointed out the one that resembled Mr. Stinky, the good doctor sermonized to me about evil entities and shape-shifters. I kinda blew him off because, in spite of all that's happened in the last couple days, it still sounded kinda nuts to me." He looked at her and swallowed hard. "I have since reconsidered that position."

"Timing is definitely not your strong suit, Henry. But at least we have a better grip on the situation. All the more reason we need to get our asses over to Wanda's shop. We need to be protected tonight. And I need to get a hold of that woman. It's kinda strange she's not there."

Well, he thought, *she took that better than I thought she would.*

CHAPTER TWENTY-FOUR

WANDA'S SURPRISE

WANDA HAD BEEN BUSY. She'd driven over to the University to pick up Archie and bring him back to the shop. It was an unusually late night for the good doctor at the U. He'd been held behind for a faculty meeting and, as per usual, it had devolved into a shouting match about funding for different departments. Whose work should take priority? Why should his department even be considered for any increase? After all, some of the other professors proclaimed, his was "junk" science. That got his blood boiling. So he reminded them that, after fifty years plus, they still couldn't accurately figure out what the fuck gravity even was! Or whether matter was better explained through string theory or loop quantum gravity! That always shut them up.

He stormed into his dimly lit office and plopped down in the soft leather chair. He removed his glasses and rubbed his eyes. When he took his hand from over his eyes he cried out, "Jarsus Murphy!" Wanda was sitting across from him in the dark, leafing through the book he'd shown Henry several hours earlier.

"I know it's presumptuous of me to ask you this, Wanda, being that this is my office and all. But do you think, maybe, I don't know, you could let me know ahead of time you are coming? Maybe a heads up you're here? Maybe turn the lights up a bit so I don't think I'm seeing a ghost sitting in front of me? You know, so I don't actually *become* a ghost that recently died of fright? Just a thought."

"It's nice to see you too, dear. Now, why would you have this particular book out on your table, opened to this particular page? With this particular ghoulish figure circled in red?"

"That, my dear, is a recent development in the story with our young friend, Henry. It seems that particular shitbag paid a visit to Henry and Joanne last night. As Henry put it, this fine gentleman smelled like rotten eggs and burnt matches and tried to rip Joanne right out of the car. Henry chased him off ... or so he thought. Turns out this lovely individual is a shape-shifter. It puzzled Henry that the guy seemed to slip away so quickly. Then he informed me that when he turned around, he noticed a large Rottweiler staring at him through the cemetery fence. Henry, being ill-informed on exactly the type of danger he faces, didn't—nay, couldn't—put those two things together. I informed him of the possibility the dog and the man in black may, in fact, be the same being. He didn't really seem to warm to the idea. Your thoughts?"

Wanda stared at her friend for a few seconds. He returned the favor. She said, "Archie … why didn't you tell me this yesterday when we were talking about Henry's session?"

Now it was Archie's turn to stare. Wanda waited. "I guess it slipped my mind. I was so startled about the revelations of Henry's past it never occurred to me to mention it to you."

"That's kind of a big thing to forget, Arch."

"So is not telling me about Henry's mother!" he shot back.

In all the years Wanda and Archie had been friends, there had been hardly, if any, harsh words between them. Wanda was not about to let it happen now. She got up off the couch and made her way over to her friend's desk. She took his hands in both of hers and kissed them.

"I'm sorry, Archie. I've not been totally honest with you about all of this. Not because I don't want to. Not because I don't trust you. I'd trust you with my life. And, in a way, that's what I'm doing at this very moment. I haven't been straight with you because my hands are tied. I've had no choice. Tonight, all that ends. Everything is going to come out in the wash, Archie. It has to. I've asked you to do a lot by accepting it as necessary. Some things you've done, in the past, were to help me out … help this cause out, and they were set up by me, without your knowledge sometimes. Before this all ends, you will know everything. I promise. All I'm asking is for you to trust me. I don't blame you if you have your doubts, but I think we know each other pretty well. I'm asking you to hang in there just a little longer. Just follow my lead a little longer, okay?"

He couldn't stay mad at her. He wasn't even really *that* mad at her now. Just a little frustrated. But Archibald Love was also a pragmatist. He needed something concrete. A morsel of truth. A good will offering, as a sign of trust from Wanda.

He asked, "Wanda, now that I know about Henry's parental situation, I have to ask. Who is Henry's mother? His *real* mother?"

Wanda closed her eyes and let out a long sigh. And she told him.

CHAPTER TWENTY-FIVE

OBEDIENCE

CHESRULE ENTERED THE BASEMENT of the mortuary. Solomon and
Leonard sat in silence at opposite ends of a large, dark mahogany table ringed
with over-sized, over-stuffed, over-priced black leather chairs. Both men were
smoking cigars, and each had a glass of JW in front of them. The demon,
and his aromatic trail, took a seat in the middle, equally distant from both of
them. Solomon got up from his seat and walked over to where Chesrule sat.
He placed his hands on top of the demon's head. It felt like ice. "Show me,"
Solomon commanded.

Solomon closed his eyes. Images from the girl's point of view flooded
his head. He heard the conversation, somewhat muted, of the revelation of
Henry's parentage. He watched with great interest as Henry and the girl tried
to open a familiar box laden with symbols he recognized; they succeeded. It
stunned him to find out the coffee girl's birthday was the combination that
finally opened the box. It was not the combination he'd set for it when he'd
possessed it. She would definitely have to be further investigated. He would

use Delilah for this. She was so good with historical facts and figures. What she was doing with a dolt like Leonard was beyond his own imagination. *The guy probably had a foot-long dick, he thought.* He felt a ripple of fear as they read the note about the book. A title he knew well.

The key. That was new. And he knew instantly this was the item they'd not been able to recover from Madeleine. His thoughts turned to the key he kept with him at all times. It opened the box containing the item he, as well as the *Foedere In Luna*, so desperately sought. Could there be another? And if there was, how was that possible?

He needed more information about the key. He listened in on their conversation as they rode home from Maine. He became annoyed with the girl and her story. Self-pity, as the famous quote went, was such bad box office. He had no patience for what he perceived as weakness. The rest of the conversation on the ride home yielded no fresh revelations about this key.

The scenes from inside Joanne's head came to an abrupt end. The last scene from the movie inside the polluted mind of the demon was of the girl staring up at him through bushes she'd landed in after the jump from the fire escape. Her last thought: the dawning recognition of what Chesrule actually was. The words in her mind; *'That thing is a fucking shape-shifter, oh my God! Gotta tell Henry...'* And then—black. After that, the running dialog of whatever passed for the mind of the demon resumed. Solomon quickly removed his hands, but not before he glimpsed the dark one's thoughts about the black-haired girl, and all the ways he planned on violating her. Even for Solomon, it was disturbing.

It was time to lay out an alternative course of action. Solomon told Leonard what he needed Delilah to do. Leonard didn't say a word, he nodded and left. Solomon had a mission for the demon. It would require some travel, but that was of no concern for Chesrule. Being from another dimension, the dark entity was accustomed to certain shortcuts others of this world were not. Time and space could be altered under the right circumstances. And this close to Halloween, with the veil between the living and the dead being much thinner, it would make what Solomon had requested easier. Chesrule morphed back into Hercules and padded out of the room and into the rainy night ... toward Maine.

CHAPTER TWENTY-SIX

SANCTUARY AND SUBTERFUGE

JOANNE LET BOTH OF them inside the shop. They headed straight for the back room because, as Joanne had explained to Henry on the way over, Wanda had set up the room as a sanctuary. And not just for Wanda. It was a place for all who were part of Wanda's coven. It was time, Jo had decided, to open up some more to Henry about the coven to which she belonged. She dragged two of the black beanbag chairs that ringed the room over to where Wanda's chair sat, dead-center, of a large golden pentacle emblazoned on the shiny black floor. She beckoned Henry to sit.

"Henry, you remember the symbol you saw on my thigh the other night?"

"Um, yeah. That's not something you forget. Unless I'd seen it on some hairy guy's ass—which would make me want to gouge my eyes out. But since it was on your thigh ..."

"Thanks for that wonderful image. Aaaanywayyyy, I told you I would explain what it meant. I intend to do so now. You need to know about it, given all that's happened in the last couple days."

"I'm all ears."

"Okay, since I already explained the symbolic meaning of it the other night, there's no need to go into that again. I am not, however, the only one who wears this symbol. All the members of my coven wear it and ..."

"Coven? As in a bunch of witches?"

She reached over and placed another imaginary gold star on his forehead and continued.

"Yes ... a bunch of witches. Ever since I got sober and met Wanda at the AA meetings, I'd heard the speakers up front mentioning about trusting and relying on a power greater than yourself. I was never much of a believer in religion of any kind, not that I have anything against that, it just never seemed to work for me. What I noticed, at least about some people at the meetings with some sober time, was they had a peace about them. None of them pushed me about going to church or anything, they just kept bringing up this "power greater than themselves" stuff. And said I didn't have to choose anything they were into. I had to find out what worked for me. I talked to Wanda about it, and she invited me to this very room one night. And I don't know how to explain it, but the moment I stepped into this room a few years ago, I instantly felt at home. Like I'd always belonged here. And from that night to this very moment I've been a member of *Foedere In Luna*."

"League of the Moon?"

"Henry ... how the hell do you know what that means?"

"Jo, I'm a nurse, remember? I can read prescriptions written in Latin."

She slapped her forehead and let out a very Homer Simpson-like, "Doh!"

Henry went to do the gold star thing to Jo, and she stared daggers at him. They both laughed.

"So, what exactly does the *Foedere In Luna* do?"

"We are a coven sworn to protect the people of Salem, and other places, from swine like Solomon Dobson, honey!"

Both Joanne and Henry almost fell backward off the beanbag chairs as Wanda said this from behind them. She seemed to appear out of thin air, with Dr. Love at her side.

"Holy shit! You scared the hell out of both of us!" Joanne said.

"I'm sorry, my dears," she said. "But it appears I've arrived here at just the right time in Jo's explanation. And I'm sure whatever Joanne was about to tell you was going to be a very thorough explanation of what the *Foedere In Luna* does, but I think I can give you a more in-depth explanation of the movement if Jo is okay with that. Jo?"

Jo extended her hand, palm-up, "By all means."

)✷(

At the same time Wanda was beginning her explanation of the *Foedere In Luna* to Henry (and, for that matter, Joanne), a dimensional portal ripped opened in Maine. Chesrule, in the form of Hercules, strode through it. The demon barely acknowledged the group of six disciples of Solomon, clad in black cloaks and sitting around a fire. And they were okay with that. The smell was awful.

He slunk through the alleyways and backyards of Portland until he arrived at the gate to the Trank residence. He sniffed the air and caught the faint scent of Henry's mate. The house was dark. The gate was open. The yard was lit by the full moon and made the grass into a dark silver carpet. The demon crept around the perimeter until he reached the backyard. He noticed the bulkhead to the basement had been left open. Fools! He strode with confidence toward the opening and caught the faintest whiff of a cigar. In the visions he'd obtained from the woman's blood, he'd seen Trank's father smoking a cigar in the living room. He followed the scent toward the bulkhead and made his way into the cellar.

Chapter Twenty-Seven
The Foedere In Luna

"The *Foedere In Luna* has been around for a very long time, Henry," Wanda said. "When I say a long time, I don't mean thirty or forty years. I'm talking centuries. It was started in Europe—though no one knows for sure in exactly which country—around the time between the end of the Crusades and the beginning of the witch trials that occurred throughout Europe. Roughly 1486, if memory serves me. The year of the publishing of the book you acquired tonight. Solomon had been practicing his "trade" for almost four hundred years by then. But our particular chapter, here in Salem, has been around since the sixteen hundreds. And all of us in this room, including you, Henry, have been a part of it at one time or another over that period."

Henry and Jo looked at Wanda like one might look at someone who had walked into a room naked, carrying a torch, and singing The Star-Spangled Banner.

"Um, what the hell are you talking about, Wanda?" Henry asked.

Wanda took her time before answering. So much to tell this poor soul, and so little time to get him to understand the magnitude of who he was back then. Who he still is *now*. Time was short, but not so short she couldn't help him wrap his head around it. But where to start?

"Wanda? Earth to Wanda! Are you still with us?" Joanne asked.

Wanda began, "The last time you were a part of this coven, Henry, you were a woman named Madeleine. You were a witch in the *Foedere In Luna*."

Henry sat and listened. When he didn't offer any comment on this revelation, Wanda continued.

"I have a small confession to make. When you and Jo brought the tape to me the other night, though I hadn't seen it yet, I knew what to expect even before you downloaded it to my laptop. You see, all this has happened before. It seems to happen roughly about every four hundred years. Why roughly every four hundred years? I can't say for sure. I have a hunch it takes a soul grouping roughly that amount of time to align properly in order to carry out whatever purpose they are intended to achieve.

"The souls involved get close to finding the secret that will take Solomon, or whatever name he's going by at the time, down. But the one soul who's gotten closest—you, Henry—met an untimely end. And that end is always engineered, in one fashion or another, by Solomon.

"The last time, when you were Madeleine, the *Order Immortalis*—Solomon's group of immortal ass-hats—used the superstitions of the time to whip the people up into a frenzy. Much as he'd done in Germany in the 1560s and 1570s. He just imported it to America. That is the crowd you see in your dreams, Henry. You have been dreaming about the night you died at the hands of Solomon's angry mob."

Henry sat staring at Wanda, expressionless. Trying to sort through his emotions. There were so many questions. Where to begin?

He said, "First, this sounds completely fucking nuts. But let's just say, for shits and giggles, I believe this. I have to admit, I've seen some really strange things these last few days, so I'm inclined to give you the benefit of the doubt. But what I don't understand is why, when you've known all along what's going on, did you not just come out and tell me not only I, but Joanne, my parents, and whoever else may be involved in this, is in some kind of danger? If you knew Solomon and his buddies could invade our dreams, why wouldn't you tell us up front? And that's just for starters. I got a lot more I wanna know." His voice was much louder at the end than the beginning.

"I know you're upset with me. You have every right in the world to feel that way, too. If I were in your shoes, I would be feeling the exact same way. The only defense I have for myself is I've seen all this happen before. After I got sober and got back in touch with the spiritual side of my life, as I walked my path, I started to have my own dreams. At first I chalked it up to my mind clearing up. That maybe it was just the physical effects of sobering up affecting my dreams. But, much like your dreams, mine wouldn't stop. That was, until I left the city limits for the first time. I noticed when I got away from Salem, the dreams stopped. Not slowly. Not a few here and there. They stopped. The first night back in town, they started right back up again. This made me more than curious about what was going on. You remember me telling you the other night about Big Jim?"

Henry nodded.

"I told Jim about the dreams. He just nodded and said, 'Yep, you're the one'. I looked at him much like you're looking at me now. He'd told me, right before he died, he was part of the *Foedere In Luna*. He said the League had almost disbanded because, for years, they had awaited the organizer. The one who, back during the witch trials, had been in charge of the League back then. They couldn't, for the life of them, figure out why I hadn't appeared yet. And if I hadn't had that accident out in front of my old apartment, none of it would have happened. How does the saying go? We make plans and God laughs! Ha! But when my mind cleared up from the years of boozing, and all the synapses in my head reconnected, sure as shit, the dream factory started working overtime. Almost like it was trying to catch up on lost time. So after Jim enlightened me on what the hell I was supposed to be, he introduced me to this handsome young guy." She pointed at Dr. Love. "Archie was just starting the parapsychology curriculum at the University. I told him what I'd been dreaming about, and he brought me back to those times through regression therapy. And I have to say, much like you Henry, even after all I had seen and all Archie had revealed to me, I still had a hard time believing any of it was true."

"So what changed your mind?" Henry asked.

"One day, back in ... ohhhhhh, I'd say around 1986, or '87, I was out for a walk on the Salem Common. It was twilight. Sun just going down, leaves blowing around on the ground. A little October chill in the air. I was in my own blissful little world. Happy to be sober. Trying to think of things to be grateful for and succeeding. I was in such a wonderful space that day. I'm not sure what made me look up at the gazebo in the middle of the Common. The only way I can describe it is that feeling you get when you've eaten a piece of cake and it's too sweet. You know how you get that irritating tickle in the middle of your head?"

Henry, Jo, and Dr. Love all nodded.

"Well, I got that feeling, and for some strange reason it made me want to look up and in the direction of the gazebo. Smack dab in the middle of it, standing all by himself, is a man in a black, three-piece suit. This guy was dressed to the nines! He didn't say a word. Didn't lift a finger. All the same, I found myself walking over to the gazebo. I climbed the steps and stood in front of him. It was cool that day, but it was freezing up on the gazebo. I could see my breath. I stared up at that man's eyes. The feeling I got looking into those ice-blue eyes was something I never want to feel again. All at the same time I felt his anger, his cruelty, his hatred ... and his *timelessness*. I can't tell you how I knew he was something almost ancient, but I could see it in those eyes. Then it dawned on me, right there in the middle of the park. This was the man who'd invaded my dreams. He didn't look the same, physically, but the eyes did. They were the same eyes I saw in the dreams, and in the visions Archie led me back to through regression. They were the eyes at my execution back in sixteen ninety-two. The only reason I couldn't recognize them right away was, in my dreams, I was looking through fire. The normal mode of execution, back then, was hanging. Solomon decided that, for me, they were gonna have a little get together in the woods. He'd summoned me to the gazebo to warn me off. He never said a word, but I got the message. And then I promptly spat in his face. I never said a word back, but *he* got *my* message."

"If this guy is so "all powerful", then why hasn't he just tried to take me out? It's not like I've been in hiding since I got here."

"Well, there are two reasons I know of for sure. The first is he needs to know what *you* know from the last lifetime. And it is surely within his power to do so, you know, with the cakey-brainy thing. The second reason is me. I've been protecting you since you were a boy. It was me, with the permission of your birth mother, who arranged for you to live with the Tranks up in Maine. So, in a nutshell, he needs to keep you and all of us alive so he can get his hands on whatever it was Madeleine had found out about him—or took from him—so he can get a hold of it, more than likely kill all of us, and destroy it. Otherwise it will be a continual threat to him century after century."

"So you know who my birth mother is?" Henry asked, almost falling backwards off the beanbag chair as he tried to stand up.

"I do," Wanda said. Her tone matter-of-fact.

"Who is she? Is she still alive? What's her name?"

"Yes, she is still alive. And no, for the time being, I cannot tell you who she is."

Henry opened his mouth to protest and Wanda put up a hand to stop him.

"I want to tell you who she is, right this very minute if I could. If I did that now, she would be dead within the hour. I cannot speak her name out loud to you. That's part of the spell since the day we moved you. To do so would reverse the protection surrounding her. You would never get to meet her and, even more tragically, all of this would be for naught. All the years she's sacrificed being without her son—knowing you are out there—it would become wasted time and wasted lives. There could be no more gut-wrenching burden carried by a mother than to see her child die before she does. And it's also the precise reason we are at the point we're all at today. She did it, and I agreed to it, to keep you protected for all these years."

Henry went silent then. It was a lot to absorb. He seemed to cycle through different emotions minute by minute. He was mad at Wanda for hiding all this from him and pretending to know nothing. Could he really even trust this woman? He'd known her for all of two days. She'd pretended to be fascinated by the video he and Joanne had shown her, yet she was forthcoming with what she thought was on it. She put on a good show when they'd arrived here, pretending not to know the peculiar rhyming scheme of his name, Hank Trank. But the humor had seemed so genuine. Almost as if she was caught off-guard by it. More questions than answers! This train of thought led him to his next question.

"I'm curious about something, Wanda. When we brought the video from my apartment here the other night ... did you know what you were about to see on it? Was that all an act?"

"I had no idea what you were going to show me. If you recall, it was your idea to set up the camera and record yourself sleeping. I had a feeling about it, based on the history of this entire situation. But no, I didn't know what I would see. I only commented on what I saw. On what you captured," she said.

"But you knew immediately what you were looking at, and you still held back all this information about my past. Why wouldn't you just come out and tell me?"

"Henry, even though that video is not yet forty-eight hours old, you are thinking about it in terms of everything that's happened *since* you showed me the video. Not where you were at *mentally* when you showed it to me. If I had laid all the new information you've learned in the last couple days on you right after we'd watched it the other night, you would have thought I was a crackpot. But think about all that's happened since we watched the video. All the things you and Joanne have been through in that short amount of time! I'm just asking you to consider how differently you view the video now versus the night you first saw it. Can't you see why I would play it that way? Imagine what may have happened had I just blurted out everything right then?"

"She's right, Henry." Joanne said.

Henry turned to look at Jo. He thought about all they'd been through together in such a short amount of time. How she had literally laid her life on the line for him back at the library. How she'd been there for him at his parents' house. How she'd known exactly what he'd needed in those trying moments when his entire world had turned upside down. And, most of all, how he'd fallen so hard for her, and she for him, in such a short amount of time. Like it was all meant to be ...

He turned back to Wanda. They stared at each other for a few moments. Henry nodded slowly, and said, "You were the one outside the coffee shop that day, weren't you? Yes! You were the one who asked me for ice! You didn't need ice. You needed me to go into the coffee shop. You needed for me to meet Joanne, didn't you?"

Wanda nodded. Her eyes teared up thinking about the day she'd reunited these two soulmates. Her friends! Two lovers who'd been together in the last life. And now in this one. She stared at Henry, chin up, defiant ... even though her jaw was quivering. She knew she'd done the right thing. She'd felt terrible about all those she'd had to deceive, but she loved all of them so much she would do whatever she had to do to keep them safe, and to see this all the way through—Henry's feelings be damned. He would just have to accept it. They all had no choice.

Henry looked from Wanda, to Jo, to Dr. Love, and back to Wanda. In that moment it all clicked together, like the feeling you get when the last few pieces of a puzzle are sitting there, and before you even go to put them in, you see exactly where each one will fit. He walked over to her and put his arms around her. She ground her face into his chest and sobbed. He held her until she was all cried out. Wanda looked up at him and said, "I'm so sorry you've had to go through all this, Henry. I never wanted it to go this way."

The rain pounded down on the skylight above. For a few moments, it was the only sound in the room. Everything hinged on Henry's reaction at this moment—the night before Halloween.

He took her face in his hands and tilted her head up. They were eye to eye. He thought about all that had happened in the last forty-eight hours. How he felt about Jo. About all the things he'd learned about his mom and dad. About the revelation his birth mother existed, and she was a part of this—was probably, no, definitely laying her life on the line for him, for all of them, right this very minute. He heard himself say the words, "I believe you," to Wanda. And he meant it.

Relief washed over Wanda. A huge weight, gone! Years of careful planning. Years of reluctant deceit. Years of guilt. Years of doubt. All gone. It was late, and the night was just past young. They had a lot to do in a short amount of time. No one was going to sleep, or dream, tonight.

)☾☆☽(

Solomon was alone in the darkened maternity ward of the hospital. He'd come here after he'd dispatched Chesrule and Leonard on their errands. No one at the hospital questioned his presence there. He was on the board of advisors, after all. Several newborns slept in their incubators, dreaming the dreams of the innocent. The purest form of the energy he needed for the battle that lay ahead. It was late, but things were just starting. Solomon fed.

Chapter Twenty-Eight

One Door Closes...

CHESRULE MADE HIS WAY to the center of the almost pitch-black basement and took in his surroundings. He could see perfectly well in the darkness—he was born of it. He saw the stairs before him leading up to the first floor. He could smell the man's cigar. He made his way over to the stairs and saw the glow of the television illuminating the smoke. The flashes from the TV made the smoke appear like wispy cobras writhing in mid-air. This pleased him.

As he put his front paw on the first step, there was a loud crash from behind him. The other end of the room instantly filled with pure white light. He growled and sprinted toward the bulkhead and had to pull up short. Painted on the doors of the bulkhead was a crucifix. Through his demon eyes, the crucifix lit up the bulkhead. It burned! He fled for the stairs leading up to the first floor in a total panic. As he reached the stairs, the doorway that had hypnotized him with visions of dancing cobras just a few short moments ago, slammed shut in front of him. An identical crucifix painted on it. He fled back to the middle of the cellar. All arrogance driven out of him, he looked for somewhere ... anywhere, in the cellar to hide from the light. He was trapped. They'd known he was coming.

Leonard arrived home to deliver Solomon's instructions to Delilah. He called out her name after he found she was not in her favorite nighttime spot—by the fire, reading a book, and enjoying a glass of wine. He went upstairs to check if maybe she'd gone to bed early. The king-sized bed was still made. He was getting a little agitated with her. He pulled out his cell phone and called the real estate office to see if maybe she was working late. The real estate number would automatically forward itself to her cell phone. It did, and the cell went straight to voice-mail. He wasn't sure what to think of this. On one hand, he was annoyed with her, on the other, he was worried about her. He grabbed his keys and headed back out. No fucking way was he going to tell Solomon about this until he found her.

)✪(

All four souls in Wanda's shop sat in a circle in the center of the room. A beanbag chair supported each. Henry was still somewhat in shock from these newest revelations. He still had questions he needed answered. But the atmosphere in the room had definitely changed. Joanne had lit some Dragon's Blood and left it burning on the counter, turned down the lights, and sat down next to Henry. She took his hand in hers and gave him a reassuring squeeze. Then she turned to Wanda and asked, "So, what's with the book, the key, and how the hell did my birthday open that box?"

Wanda laughed. "Not one to beat around the bush. That's what I love about you, sweetie. First, the book. It was published in the year 1486, and the title, Malleus Maleficarum, means *Hammer of Witches*. It was basically the handbook a discredited Catholic clergyman wrote to prosecute witches. What's not in any of the history books is the real inspiration for the book is the very soul we are fighting here in Salem to this day. Solomon, as he is named now, has been behind movements like these for centuries. He uses the turmoil surrounding these hideous atrocities as cover for what he really wants—to steal life force from others so he can survive and grow his empire. With all that's been going on lately, I wouldn't be surprised if the bastard isn't fueling up for the fight as we speak."

"How would he "fuel up" as you put it?" Jo asked.

"He would probably try to find the purest form of dream energy he could surround himself with. Dreams of the young are the purest, most innocent, and mainly uncomplicated for him to invade. Fortunately for them, he'll just steal their dream energy. They have nothing he could actually want to use against them. It's like stealing paper from a mill so he can use that paper to write his own despicable story. Mainly one which has us dead at the end.

"But that's not what we need to be focusing on right now. It would not surprise me if the book was placed there as a way of drawing Solomon and his buddies out of hiding. He knows what that book represents, and how it ties a lot of things to him. Still, I don't really understand the point of hiding it in the library, other than there must be something else about what's in it I'm not aware of."

As Wanda continued to talk, Henry opened the book. The only thing remarkable about it, at least to him, was a black swan stamped on the inside cover. The ink from the stamp looked fairly recent compared to the overall condition of the rest of the book. He filed it away for later and focused on what Wanda was telling them.

"Solomon's been at this immortality thing for quite a long time now. How far before that book?" She shrugged. "I guess I can't say exactly. But he is tied to the ones who wrote it by the same warped ideas that gave us the trials here, in Salem."

"Now, the key. That key was found, a little less than four hundred years ago, on the body of Madeleine. On you, Henry, when you were her. She saw it in Solomon's thoughts when he foolishly tried to invade her mind the day they encountered each other in the town square. She was able to recreate it exactly from memory. Although, knowing Madeleine, it more than likely does much more than the one Solomon still possesses. Through some miracle, it evaded Solomon and his followers. Madeleine's husband hid the key. Buried it in an old box with a combination lock. Ironically, the same box the original key used to be in. The key Solomon keeps on him at all times, now. It was unearthed the year after you were born, Henry. By your mother. Your biological mother. She wrote the note contained within. She is the one who reset the combination to that date, the same date as Joanne's birthday."

"But how could she know Jo's birthday? I'm three years older than Jo, for starters. And there is no way in the world she could ever have foreseen what day Jo would be born. Or that we would even meet and fall for each other."

"That's correct, Henry. And, as wonderful a coincidence as it is, the combination on the lock is not actually, well originally, intended to represent Joanne's birthday."

Henry and Joanne both looked at her then. Kind of like a dog that's already outside, and then you ask the dog if he wants to go outside. The poor pooch will tilt its head and look at you like, "What the fuck are you talking about?"

Wanda looked at them with kindness. Then she stared straight at Henry. "That is the date of your mother's birthday. 0626."

Henry, Jo, and Dr. Love's jaws all dropped open simultaneously.

"That's seems like the most unlikely coincidence I think I've ever heard," Dr. Love said.

"Yes, Archie," Wanda said. "But in my experience, I prefer to call things like that miracles. True blue miracles. It's God's little way of telling you he's got your back."

"So, as unlikely as all this sounds to, well, all of us, there remains the key," Wanda said. "We have an explanation for the book, in my opinion not a good one at the moment. We have an explanation for the birthday ... divine intervention, but I do not know what the key is for, exactly. I do know it represents the one thing in the world Solomon wants to get his hands on. Even more than any of us. Though I doubt he knows a key is the thing he's been chasing for all these years, since he couldn't find it to begin with. If he could get the key and whatever it leads to, he could end all of this. He would win and be free to roam the earth forever, doing as he pleased. We need to take that key and acquire whatever it's intended to open. At least that's what it feels like to me."

"But you've no idea what it opens. Or if it even opens anything," said Archie.

"This is true, Archie. But what I know for certain ... we have all we need right here in this room to find out the mystery of the key. And without ever leaving this room. Well, at least physically," Wanda said.

"Okay, Mrs. Houdini. How, exactly, is *that* supposed to happen?" Jo asked.

Wanda turned her gaze on Henry. "Do you remember the other day, Henry, when we were all talking about the things happening in your apartment? How, after you woke up, you were finding pine needles, puddles of water, dirt, et cetera?"

Henry nodded.

Wanda continued, "You asked me how that was possible and I filled you in on apports, and how they worked. I have a theory they work the other way, too. That if you can bring something back from the dream realm into this world, then it should be possible to do the same thing in reverse."

"You may be right, Wanda. But you are talking about using a key that was buried back in 1692, unearthed in the current century, and present with us right here, right now. And to open whatever is still locked, one would presume, to this very day. Then, once we've unlocked said item, bringing it back from not only a place existing in a dream, but that existed four hundred years ago. I'm an optimist, Wanda, but that sounds like the longest of long-shots I think I've ever heard." Dr. Love sat back down with a thud in his beanbag chair and rubbed his palm along the length of his face.

Wanda looked at Archie. Her face was a mix of amusement and slight disappointment. She said, "Archie, given your line of work, I would think this challenge would be right up your alley. And since there is no time to lose, I suggest you get your ass up off that beanbag chair, get your mind in the proper frame, and get Henry back to where he needs to be."

She turned to Henry. "I need you to lie over here, Henry." She said this as she pulled a black-clad massage table used for Reiki treatments into the center of the room, kicking aside the beanbag chairs along the way. "When you lie down, I want you to do your best to get into a state of relaxation. Then, Archie will bring you back to the time when you were Madeleine."

Henry was past the point of questioning any of this. He did as he was told, with neither hesitation nor fear. He intuitively knew the time was now. It seemed like he was watching himself from outside of his own body. Like it was a waking dream.

"Joanne," Wanda said. "We need the key. Please put it in Henry's hand, and then come join me in the outer circle. Take the chair on the other side of Henry, directly opposite from me."

"What good is the key going to do for Henry if it's in his hand on this side?" Jo asked.

"I have a theory on that Jo. As long as it's on his person in this realm, it will prove useful in the other realm. It's really the only thing that seems to make sense. I can't think of another reason we'd have the key, and the letter doesn't exactly clarify why we have it. So I'm going with my gut on this one."

Joanne came to the center of the room. She leaned over Henry, put her right hand gently on the left side of his face, and kissed him on the lips like she meant it. "Get back here safe, handsome."

She took Henry's left hand (the magic hand, she thought), put the key in it, and folded his hand around it with hers. She kissed his closed fist. Jo then strode to the beanbag chair opposite Wanda's, and to Henry's right, dropped into it, and assumed the lotus position.

Dr. Love, now all business, shuffled over to the bar. He turned the lights down as low as the dimmer would allow without plunging the room into blackness. He refreshed the Dragon's Blood incense in the tray on the bar. He grabbed a barstool and placed it next to the massage table to Henry's left. He pulled out his amethyst pendulum and prepared to bring Henry down to a state where he could regress him back to the year 1692. Before he started, he looked at Wanda and said, "What are you going to do while I bring Henry back?"

The grandfather clock next to the bar chimed. The rain pelting the skylight grew more intense. The first seconds of Halloween ticked away.

"I am going to open the door, Archie."

CHAPTER TWENTY-NINE

CELLAR DWELLER

CHESRULE HAD MORPHED BACK into his "human" form and cowered in the basement's corner, beyond the reaching fingers of holy light. He wasn't used to being prey. He was trapped and desperate. In what passed for his fevered mind, he wondered how this could have happened—and what the penalty for being captured meant. Either the old hag from the store would banish him from the earth for good, or Solomon would snuff him out forever. He tried to put it out of his mind now. Escape was all that mattered. He shifted into survival mode, desperate for a way out. The demon took in his surroundings. The bulkhead, ceiling, and cellar door were bathed in holy light. Out of the question

He quieted himself and ran the memories of the girl back through his mind, paying particular attention to the layout of the Trank's house through her eyes. He saw the cellar door pass by on her left as she entered the living room. Saw her looking at the father and then turning to her left as she went to sit down on the sofa. And there, in the corner, out of her eyes, he found what he was looking for. A heating grate. On the floor, to the left of the couch.

Above his head and to the right of where he stood was the aluminum piping that led to the grate. The piping was half-in, half-out of the holy light. It would have to do. It would be painful, but it was his only option.

He laced both hands together at the fingers and formed a hammerhead with them, and swung with all his might. He dented the pipe, and it tore slightly from the metal ring holding it in place where the ceiling met the bottom of the grate. Dust plumes flew across the beams of light and disappeared into the darkness. His hands (they were hands in his current form) were scorched raw, even though they had only passed through the light for the briefest moment. He heard footsteps pounding down the stairs from the second floor in response to the loud crash. They were coming! He needed to get the pipe loose from its frame before they could think to put something over it, trapping him for good. Ignoring the pain in his hands, the demon swung a second time as hard as he could. The pipe moved again, but not enough. His hands were now covered in blistering, steaming sores. Footsteps above raced across the living room. This was it! The pipe had to come down now or he would face the most severe of consequences.

He heard something heavy scraping across the living room floor. Chesrule brought his tattered hands together, raised both of them above his head, and swung them into the hollow aluminum piping. It came crashing to the cement floor with a deafening, hollow boom. In that instant he looked up through the grate and saw the woman's leg. She was working with her husband to drag a large mahogany chest over the opening. He leapt from his spot, right arm extended, smashing his ruined hand through the grate. The steel cover flew up from the living room floor with such force the corner of it impaled the ceiling above. It hung there like the strangest mistletoe ever. Only, it wasn't kissing about to happen under it. As gravity pulled the demon back to the cellar floor, he reached out and grabbed hold of Jeannie Trank's left leg, and pulled for all he was worth.

Chapter Thirty
That's Gotta Hurt!

Delilah had avoided Leonard for most of the night. It wasn't too hard. Her fiancé was not the brightest bulb on the Christmas tree. She knew what Solomon wanted without Leonard having to tell her. And also, thanks to the Ring doorbell app on her phone, that Leonard had come by the house looking for her. Probably to tell her about a change in plans or some other dictate from Solomon. Fuck him. She was tiring of taking orders from that wrinkly old prune ... and from Leonard, for that matter. She knew exactly what she needed to do. Delilah exited the car a block from Wanda's Wicca'd Emporium and walked through the pounding rain to the dark alley behind the shop. She pulled the hood up on her coat and waited in a shrub-covered corner of the lot. The plan was in motion whether Leonard realized it or not. If he and Solomon didn't like it, too fucking bad. She always knew at least one of them wouldn't like this part, anyway.

Leonard was frantic. He had to find Delilah and get to the bottom of the coffee shop girl's connection to all of this. It made no sense that her birthday would open the combination box buried so long ago. Solomon needed to know all he could about that bitch so they could figure out what to do next. If that meant roughing miss coffee shop up, so be it. But it would be so much easier to just have Delilah sneak around in her past and dig up the information.

"Think, Leonard!" he said to himself as he drove around Salem. It had been at least two hours since he'd talked to Solomon. He was desperate and hoping to spot her car somewhere around town. At least with the current monsoon that was making its way through Salem, he didn't have to deal with the huge Haunted Happenings crowds that always walked the streets, night after night, leading up to Halloween. The place was as deserted on the night before the big day as he'd ever seen it.

He drove past the Salem Common and down Congress Street. Essex Street was to his left. And as he passed by Essex on his way toward Derby Street, he noticed Delilah's white Lexus parked on Congress, halfway between Essex and Derby. He made the left at Derby and parked.

What the hell would she be doing in this part of town? At this time of night? He made his way, on foot, back up Congress, took a right onto Essex, and about halfway down he had his answer. The sign for Wanda's Wicca'd Emporium, though not lit at this time of night, nevertheless glowed bright gold in the dark. As if lit by some internal flame. He knew better than to approach the building from the front. He made his way toward the back alley Delilah had just traveled only thirty brief minutes before.

As he entered the lot behind the shop, he made for the far side and walked along the perimeter. He didn't want to be seen by the owner, for obvious reasons. As he got to the back corner of the lot, Leonard was yanked violently into the bushes that concealed the immediate area. He felt a hand clamp over his mouth. When he looked up, he was only mildly surprised to see it was his fiancée's face glaring back at him. And she was not thrilled to see him.

"What the hell are you doing here, Delilah?" he shout-whispered.

"I was about to ask you the same question, dear!" she spat back.

"I was sent to look for you by Solomon. He needs information on the coffee girl. Something unexpected has come up regarding her, and he needs you to do a deep dig on her background. And he needs it now!"

"Why couldn't you just do it, Leonard? It's not like it's top-fucking secret information! There's this thing called the internet, now. It's loaded with all kinds of information. You could probably find everything you need to know about her in about ten minutes, tops!"

"Not *that* kind of information. I *have* looked up all I can about her on the web. But there are other things, such as sealed records, I can't get to. But *I* know, and *Solomon* knows, you can get that info. Such as her actual birthday, for instance. It says on her driver's license her birthday is April nineteenth. However, dear, Chesrule was able to see through her eyes after he attacked her earlier tonight. Solomon read its mind—in that creepy Solomon way he has of doing it—and in the visions from Chesrule, he saw the real numbers for her birthday. And they were not April nineteenth."

This was quite a surprise to Delilah. It was information she knew, of course. It was *not* information, however, she wanted Leonard or Solomon to *know* she knew. At least, not yet. She had plans of her own for the *Foedere In Luna*.

She could take care of Leonard right now. Solomon … she could figure *that* out when the time came. Before she did anything, though, she had to be sure. "What were the numbers?"

"0626," said Leonard.

Delilah's mouth formed a surprised O. When her mouth closed and the shock had worn off, she knelt down and picked up her satchel. She rummaged around inside it and brought out a square black box with a curved U-shape on its top. She pressed a button and held the taser to Leonard's neck. He dropped to the ground with a satisfying thud.

CHAPTER THIRTY-ONE
HENRY TAKES A TRIP

"ALRIGHT HENRY, I WANT you to count backwards from one hundred to one. With each number counted off, I want you to make your body calm and relaxed. Breathe in deep, and relax more and more with each exhalation. As you do this, I want you to picture yourself descending a flight of stairs toward the place you feel most comfortable and safe. It can be any place in the world or any place you can imagine. What matters is you feel safe, protected, and at peace. Let's begin."

At Dr. Love's request, Henry started. In his mind he saw an opening in the ground in the middle of a brilliant green field of grass. The color of the grass reminded Henry of Fenway Park on opening day in 1997—the first baseball game he'd ever attended with his dad. Even though the Sox lost to Seattle and Randy "The Big Unit" Johnson, it was a happy memory. It comforted him as he descended through the opening and took his first steps downward.

It was much cooler the further down he went. Even though it was in his imagination, he could actually feel the temperature dropping. In his mind's eye he ran his hands across the cool, dark-grey stones. He could feel the bumpy texture of the rocks and the thin, green film of moss covering them. As he looked down, toward the bottom of the staircase, he could see bright white sand. He could smell the ocean brine. He'd always loved the smell. It was rejuvenating. With only ten steps left to reach the beach, he saw little tongues of ocean lapping up the shore. The smell of hot dogs and his mother's perfume mixed with the salty air. He was back to the time of the first session he'd had with Dr. Love. He told Archie this, and it came out to the others in the room as a barely understandable mumble.

"That's great, Henry. Now I want you to go back even further than the last time. I want you to reach back to the very earliest memory you can recall. When you get to it, I want you to tell me what you can see. Take your time."

Henry relaxed and let his mind take him where it needed to go. A small light appeared in his mind's eye. He focused on that, and the surrounding darkness faded back as the scene enlarged before his eyes. There was a large circle floating above his head. It spun slowly around and had several odd shaped figures attached by strings hanging beneath it. What his infant mind in the vision could not comprehend, his adult mind in the here and now announced out loud to the room he was looking at a mobile.

"That's great, Henry. You're doing really well. Now I want you to take a deep breath, and relax a little more."

Henry did as requested. He felt like he was floating in space—weightless, free, and with an uncanny sense of well-being. "Where am I now?"

"You are in the in-between, Henry. The place where we are before being born into the next life. The place where we take stock of the lessons learned from past lives. It's a safe place. You've nothing to fear here. Consider it the most wonderful classroom you've ever been in. Enjoy it for a few moments. Look around. You can talk to the others ... share your thoughts and feelings. They are there to seek knowledge and share it with you. Time there is not as it is here, Henry. Here, all things take place in sequence. In the in-between, you can move back and forth through time. You can review past experiences from any of the lives you've lived. They understand why you are there, and they are more than willing to help."

Henry felt himself being gently stood up. A room took shape around him. On the floor was a plush white carpet his bare feet sank into. It felt wonderful, and he groaned with pleasure. The walls were a cool blue reminding Henry of the shade he'd seen in swimming pool liners. The room had only two walls, and those walls stretched out as far as the mind could see. Both walls were lined with huge wooden doors. Each door had golden hinges and silver doorknobs. Every door was labeled with gold script, but the lettering was only readable when you stood directly in front of it. And even then, some were unreadable. It allowed you to only focus your thoughts on one door at a time.

At that moment, Henry sensed the presence of someone else in the room. He turned around, and before him stood a man. He was taller than Henry by about four or five inches. He was wearing a black cloak that stretched all the way to the floor. At his waist was a golden-roped belt, tied in the middle. The hood rested on his shoulders. He had a heart-shaped face framed by a wiry goatee, and tufts of white hair that looked like they were about to take flight from his head in a thousand different directions. He had brilliant green eyes that reminded him of Joanne's. The shape of the eyes reminded him of Wanda. The hair was remarkably similar to Dr. Love's. When the man spoke, his lips remained still.

"What do you need to know, Henry?"

"Um. Let's start with who you are," Henry said.

"I am one of the guides here. I'm here to help you find the answers."

"The answers to what, exactly?"

"All you are experiencing now, in your current incarnation, has led you to this point. All you've lived through in all of your lifetimes, has led to this point. You are not here by accident. You are here because, despite your own doubts, your intuition spoke louder. I ask you now ... why do *you* think you are here, Henry?"

Henry thought back on the events leading up to now. He thought about Jeannie and Dominick Trank. He thought about Joanne. He thought about Wanda and Archie. He wondered about his mother. He thought about Solomon and Leonard and Delilah. He thought about moving to Salem from Portland. He thought about all the crazy conversations only a few short days ago he would have considered ludicrous. He thought about the key in his hand. He looked down at it now. It glowed silver in his astral hand. He never noticed before, but there was an etching at the top of the key. It was a picture of a swan with a capital letter I next to it. I-swan. It kept ringing a faint bell in his mind, but he couldn't quite grasp what it meant to him, even though the symbol had again popped up. Just as he'd done with the stamp in the book, he filed it away for later.

Suddenly, the answer to the guide's question came to him. "I'm not here to question, I'm here to act. I'm here to follow where my intuition has led me in spite of my questioning."

The guide smiled at Henry and said, "Now, you understand. Follow the small, still voice inside you. It will take you to the door you next need to pass through. Don't question. Act."

And with that, the guide was gone.

Henry turned to the doors on his left. He walked along that side of the room, turning his head toward one door after another as he passed them. Each door's etching had a unique feeling for Henry but, for a while, none of them would come into focus. When he reached the twelfth door, he felt the slightest magnetic pull. The key in his hand vibrated. He turned toward the door, and the gold etching upon it immediately came into focus. On the door was one simple word. 'Madeleine'.

CHAPTER THIRTY-TWO

TUG OF WAR

DOMINICK TRANK WATCHED IN horror as his wife did the most amazing split right in front of him. In his stunned mind it looked to him like some bizarre imitation of the Rockettes from Radio City Music Hall in New York. He barked a maniacal laugh. He couldn't help himself. Jeannie, through gritted teeth, said, "What the fuck are you laughing at?"

Hearing his wife swear, which happened as rarely as the passage of Halley's Comet, snapped him out of it. He rushed over to her and grabbed her outstretched hand. He pulled and brought her up about two inches from her current position, and she was yanked back down with a thud. She screamed in pain. Chesrule hissed with laughter from below. "Open the bulkhead or she loses a toe."

"Go f-f-fuck yourself. You demonic piece of shit."

Chesrule didn't hesitate. He took Jeannie's big toe in his mouth and clamped down hard. Fangs digging in. Jeannie screamed in pain. Chesrule released the bloody toe. "The next bite takes it off, husband."

Jeannie glared at her husband. The look said it all. *'Don't you dare open that bulkhead.'* It tore at Dominick. He couldn't stand to see the woman he loved being tortured. But he feared more the consequences of giving in to the demon.

Just as Henry went to reach for the knob of the door labeled 'Madeliene' , he felt a searing pain in his foot. At the same time, one door to his left slammed open. A scream flew through its open space. It sounded like his mom. And she sounded like she was in pain. Acting on instinct, he bolted for the newly opened door and ran through.

Back in Wanda's shop, Henry's corporeal body jounced around.

"Henry, what's the matter?" Dr. Love asked.

"It's Mom. She's in trouble. I have to go to her."

Archie looked over to Wanda as if to say, *'Can he do that?'*

"He seems to think so, Archie. He's the true leader of all of us. Let's trust him and help him as much as we can. Keep him calm, though. If he gets panicked, he may drop out of the plane he's in. And that would be a disaster for all of us."

"Henry," Archie said. "Do what you have to do. We are here for you."

Henry tumbled through the door. There was a moment of complete darkness and then a blinding flash of light. He was in his parents' living room. He went over to where his mom was and immediately tried to help her up from the floor. He reached between Dominick and Jeannie and tried to help by pulling on her arm. His hands passed right through her, and he stumbled backward toward the china cabinet. As he fell backwards he tried to brace himself for the crash. Instead, he kept falling backward through the cabinet, through the wall, and into the middle of the kitchen. And he would have continued falling had his mind not registered the absurdity of the situation. He willed himself to stop.

If anyone had actually observed him, they would have been reminded of the old Road Runner cartoons Henry used to watch on Saturday mornings. Wile E. Coyote would chase the Road Runner toward a cliff and invariably Wile E. would go over the edge of the cliff and, floating to a stop in mid-air, look at the camera, gulp, and fall to one of his numerous Saturday morning deaths.

This was Henry's introduction into the power of his mind in the astral realm. If he could think it, he could do it. The power of thought in the astral realm was his currency now. He needed to learn how to spend it.

"Henry?" Dr. Love asked. "Where are you now?"

"I'm in my mom's kitchen. I just fell through the china cabinet, the wall, and halfway through the kitchen before I realized I could stop myself. She's in pain. Her leg is through the floor and my dad is trying to help her get unstuck, but he's not having any luck. It's as if she's being held down. But I can't see anything *holding* her down."

"Archie, tell him to go into the cellar. He'll find what he's looking for," Wanda said.

Archie was a little surprised at this, and it showed on his face.

"I thought they might try something like this. Going after Henry's parents makes sense. The black figure you spoke of the other night ... he's there now. I'm sure of it. I had Jeannie set up the trap years ago, though I doubt she is aware of it now. There are crucifixes painted in glow-in-the-dark paint on the inside of the bulkhead and the cellar door. To the dark one, they will appear as blinding white light because I had the paint blessed before I sent it to the Trank's. Now, tell Henry to go through the floor and into the cellar, please."

A little bit in awe of Wanda's foresight, Archie did as he was told.

Henry imagined himself in the cellar, and there he was. It was almost completely dark to him. No blinding white light, just the light from the hole in the ceiling leaking in from around his mother's leg. Under that sparse amount of light he could see the silhouette of the man/dog in black thing that had attacked Joanne twice, and now his mother. He could feel the anger within swelling. He was gonna take this motherfucker out once and for all. But how?

CHAPTER THIRTY-THREE

HIDDEN REGRETS

DELILAH LOOKED DOWN AT Leonard's prone form and stepped over him. She made her way to the back of Wanda's Wicca'd Emporium and climbed the rust-flaked fire escape to the roof of the store. She would have to travel lightly. Gravel covered the roof, and she didn't want the crunch under her feet to alert those inside to her presence. After what seemed like forever, she came to a stop at the edge of the skylight that served as Wanda's window to the stars. Under the opening, she could see all four of them. Henry was on a table. The doctor guy by his side (he looked familiar to her) whispering in his ear. The coffee girl was to the left of the table and the witch was to the right of the same table. The two women seemed to be in prayer or chanting. She just had to bide her time until Solomon made the next move.

Solomon Dobson arrived back at the mortuary. He was refreshed and revitalized from his feeding at the hospital. He also appeared to look like a man in his mid-forties now. He took in his reflection in the mirror. His hair had regained its dark-brown luster, with just a touch of grey at the sideburns. His posture had assumed its previous upright rigidity.

He hated having to stoop to the pains of old age and sciatica. But one needed to keep up appearances, if only for a couple of decades. After all of this was over he would burn down the mortuary, (preferably with the members of the *Foedere In Luna* in it), make it appear as if he'd died in the fire, and start anew right back here in Salem. Maybe he'd acquire the coffee shop from the soon to be dead owner. It was good to have options.

The last time he'd laid eyes on Henry was at *Rockafellas*. He took the risk of being in proximity to Henry one more time. He had to be sure he was the one. When Henry reacted to the spot Solomon had vacated across from the restaurant, he knew Henry was who he sought. He knew it was Madeleine.

He allowed himself a moment of self-pity. He thought back to the night the crowd had killed Madeleine. They had beaten her to death out of fear. And stupidity. But he had only himself to blame. He'd been the one who had pushed them too far. A mistake he would never allow again. Still, he'd never found out what happened to the item lost in the beating. Try as he might, in the short few months Henry had been in Salem, Solomon could not force the dream past the point where Madeleine's loss of consciousness and death had finally occurred. Thus the need to keep Henry alive. To keep all of them alive. Only together would they be able return to that time. He needed to capture what was lost, what was taken from him and remained safe, if unaccounted for, now. Tonight was the last chance, and he knew it. They were going after whatever Madeleine had taken and hidden. He had to let them get it. There was really no choice in the matter, as he saw it. What it all came down to was one simple thing. Allow them to find whatever it was they thought they were going to kill him with, kill them, and take possession of it again.

Done with his pity-party (and a little disgusted with himself), Solomon turned out the lights in the mortuary and headed out of the funeral home, one way or the other, for the last time.

Chapter Thirty-Four
Lost and Found

HENRY TOOK IN THE scene before him. The entity had a hold of his mother's toe in its mouth. Blood dripped down the man in black's chin and pattered in little droplets onto the floor, kicking up tiny plumes of dust as each landed. He released the toe from his mouth and stuck a talon into the open wound. Henry's mother writhed in pain. Anger swelled up in Henry now—red and raw. He didn't need any further instruction from Wanda on what to do. It came to him without thought, without hesitation, and without remorse.

Henry hurled himself forward at the demon and slammed into him full force. Though he could travel through walls and floors and ceilings with no effort at all, he collided with this entity almost as if it were a solid being. The part he'd hit, however, was the pure and evil spirit inhabiting the shapeshifter's body. He'd knocked that spirit energy out and into the holy light that flooded the cellar. The body of the entity crumpled to the ground in a heap. The spirit of the demon, now exposed fully to the light, recoiled in torment on the floor. Its black form twisted and contorted as patches of white light formed on its obsidian skin. It reached up to Henry, all confidence and arrogance driven out of it, and pleaded with an outstretched claw for Henry to help it out of the light. To show it mercy.

Henry knelt down in front of the demon. He didn't need to speak to it directly, he simply showed the entity an image from his mind. The image was from a bumper sticker he'd seen on the very day his mother had taken him to the beach for his birthday. It was a blue bumper sticker with white lettering. It read, *'Jesus loves you! Everyone else thinks you're an asshole.'* Chesrule got the message.

"I will tell you anything you want to know about my masters, Warlock! Anything!!"

Henry thought about it for a second and said, "What are they trying to prevent us from getting? And where is it?"

"First, you take me out of the light. Then I tell you what you desire!" Chesrule screamed.

Henry laughed in its face. "You aren't exactly in a position to bargain right now, shitbag. Answer my question ... or I'll find it out eventually, anyway. Your choice. But by the looks of you, you better make it quick."

Holy fire had consumed much of Chesrule's body. He was in danger of slipping into the void of nothingness, forever. He would become part of the ether. Dissolved into the fabric of the universe—without thought, without consciousness, without a spirit—good or evil. He panicked and spilled his guts to Henry. In Henry's mind, he saw the place and time he needed to go to. He sent an image from his mind back to Chesrule. It was an image of Henry spitting on the demon. And the last thing Chesrule would ever see was from one of Henry's Saturday morning cartoons. It was a giant blue lollipop with the word "SUCKER" written in large black letters across its face. Henry rose slowly up and out of the room, looking down at Chesrule as he did so. The evil entity let out a scream filled with agony, rage, hatred, and above all else, outright terror. The scream shot through Henry's mind like the pain from a thousand ice cream headaches. Then, silence. Chesrule knew no more.

)⊕(

"Sir, are you okay?" Solomon's driver asked him.

His driver was reacting to what he'd heard and then seen in the rear-view mirror. Solomon had barked out in pain and had stiffened up as if his entire body were in spasm. He knew instantly the dark entity he'd commanded for centuries had been erased. It felt as if a piece of his own body had been torn off. Except it was much worse. Chesrule was his eyes and ears in places he could not go. Though Solomon may be immortal, he was very much bound forever to the physical plane. He could travel the astral plane as he saw fit, but he could never, ever fully leave the physical realm. That ship had sailed a long time ago.

Much like his former master, he decided it better to rule in his own kingdom than serve in another's. Thus he needed Chesrule as a go-between—his bridge between the living and the dead—to ferret out the groups of souls who, in their next incarnations, would regroup and try to put an end to Solomon's reign on earth. The demon could sniff them out. This particular group had eluded him twice now. And they'd managed something none of the others had—they'd blinded him. Taken away his advantage. Things were getting desperate now.

"I'm fine! Just get me over to the witch's store. Park in the back!"

)☾(

Henry's body still lay safe on the massage table in Wanda's Wicca'd Emporium.

"I know *where* it is. And I know *when* it is. But I still don't know *what* it is," he said to the others. His voice sounded groggy and far away, but they received the message clearly enough. "I have to go back to the room with the doors. I have to go back to my other lifetime and get it. But how do I know what to bring back if I don't know what I'm looking for?"

Archie looked over to Wanda for guidance.

"Archie, ask him if he still has the key."

"Henry, Wanda wants to know if you still have the key. Do you?"

A brief wave of panic passed through Henry. He shot both hands into his pockets and his left one produced the astral plane equivalent of the key. He hadn't lost it. It occurred to him it was an odd question—considering the key sat in his hand back at Wanda's place. Then he remembered the lessons learned from his mother's house a few short moments ago. Thought was everything over here. Out of mind, out of site. He flipped the old saying in his mind to fit the moment.

"Yes. I have the key. Thank her for reminding me."

Henry thought about where he needed to go next, and after a brief moment and a quick flash of light, found himself back in the room with the doors. The one he'd just returned from shut silently behind him and the sign on it instantly blurred, becoming unreadable again.

"Why are some labels on the doors unreadable?" he asked out loud to himself. Not really expecting an answer.

"They are parts of your current life that either you haven't experienced yet, Henry, or they are events from a past life which have already happened. The ones that have already happened in a previous life are blurred until such time arises it's necessary for you to alter them." The guide had appeared out of thin air at Henry's side.

"How is it determined what's necessary? And by whom?" Henry asked.

"I'm afraid the answer is above my pay-grade. But, as in the case with this door," the guide pointed to the original door Henry'd been at when he'd arrived, "I believe said powers have deemed it necessary. One thing I do know, call it intuition, is that you are only allowed through certain doors to alter history if that history has been altered in a way deemed unnatural."

Henry was a bit surprised to find himself directly in front of the door marked "Madeleine." He didn't remember walking over to it. And then he realized he'd been thinking about it. The power of thought over here was still new to him. It continued to surprise and amaze him.

"Do you know what I'm supposed to find on the other side when I go through this door?" Henry asked the guide.

"I do not," was the guide's simple reply. And he was gone again.

Henry turned to face the door. He removed the key from his pocket. It vibrated as it had before. He put the key into the lock on the door, turned it, and walked into 1692.

Chapter Thirty-Five

...Another Opens

WANDA FELT IT FIRST. She looked across the room at Joanne to see if it had registered with her yet. Joanne was sitting in the lotus position directly across the room from Wanda. A much prettier mirror image of herself, Wanda thought. Jo's eyes were closed. She was deep in meditation. She slowly opened her green eyes and her gaze locked with Wanda's. Jo gave the slightest nod in the affirmative to Wanda that she was feeling it too. The portal was opening. The connection between the two witches was complete.

Archie was the last to notice. The hair on his arms rose. Thin little grey soldiers standing at attention, each on its own mound of gooseflesh. The wiry white hair on the top of his head rose slightly and the loose strands in his ponytail stuck out like porcupine quills. He looked at Wanda and opened his mouth to ask her what was going on, and she gave him a look he'd seen many times before. He deduced its meaning instantly. *'Not Now.'*

The room buzzed with a low electricity. Directly over Henry and Archie was a faint, blue-tinted arc of light. At the top of the arc, a razor thin tendril reached down and connected directly to Henry's chest. The rest of it stretched across the room and terminated at each end where there was a witch attached.

Wanda had to concentrate a little harder than usual. She had to keep from looking at Archie and bursting out laughing. Under the glow of the blue light Archie looked like a cross between Jerry Garcia of the Grateful Dead and Papa Smurf. But she was a pro and just turned the humor into more positive energy. Still, she thought, it was fucking funny.

The interior of the room changed. They all sensed this at the same time. The first thing they noticed was the temperature drop in the room. It was at least ten degrees cooler than it had been only moments before. The smell of pine filled the room immediately after. A faint, icy breeze swirled about them. The candles blew out, plunging the room into almost total darkness, save for the blue light emanating from the arc. The first faint snowflakes fell in the room. Wanda and Joanne had opened the doorway.

)⊛(

The driver pulled the limousine, headlights extinguished, into the darkest corner of the lot behind Wanda's store. He killed the engine and, per

Solomon's instructions, left the keys on the dashboard, got out, and left the area.

Solomon sat alone in the back seat. His only companions were his thoughts and the ticking of the cooling engine. He ran several scenarios through his mind about how to breach the witch's store. Walking through the front door was possible, but not worth the trouble or the pain it would cause him. She'd protected it too well with white magic. He hated her with a passion, but he respected and feared what she could come up with. And today being Halloween, where the veil between the living and the dead was at its thinnest, he was not about to commit to a full frontal assault. It would be akin to walking into the room with a marching band and announcing his arrival. No ... she and her coven hadn't survived several centuries by being stupid or unprepared. He needed the element of surprise, but it had to be at just the right time. To kill them all right away would just set the whole thing back in motion again. Another one hundred to two hundred years of plotting and planning and waiting. Unacceptable. It had to be done tonight, and it had to be done right. It could only be at the moment Henry arrived with whatever he was astral traveling to retrieve. Solomon knew he had to get a hold of it, kill them all, and figure out what to do with it after his business with them was finished.

Delilah looked down from the skylight in awe. She'd always known Wanda was powerful, but she'd imagined nothing like what she saw before her now. What she had *no clue* about was how powerful the coffee shop girl had become. No wonder Solomon was so worried about her. Together, Henry and Joanne had become a formidable team. And knowing what she knew about Henry, she realized he had chosen his mate wisely. Part of her actually felt a tug of jealousy. She pushed the feeling away. Why should she feel jealous of Joanne? It made no sense.

She was so wrapped up in her own thoughts and the spectacle taking place beneath her, she hadn't noticed the wired glass of the skylight in front of her fading out of reality bit by bit. She watched as the top of the pyramid-shaped skylight disappeared completely. Inch by inch it faded from the top down. It reached the metal base holding it in place on the roof and then, much slower but just as steady, the metal base began to dematerialize in front of her. She realized she needed to move or she would tumble to the floor beneath and land directly on Henry. That would put an end to the entire plan right then and there.

As quiet as a mouse, she backed up to the far corner of the roof closest to the fire escape. Judging by the rate of the disappearing roof, she figured this probably bought her about a half hour. If whatever Henry'd gone to retrieve hadn't been found in that time, she would have to vacate the roof and alter the plan.

She heard a sound from the parking lot below. It came from the place where she had dropped Leonard with the taser. She could barely make out Leonard's tall, lean frame as it emerged from the bushes. He brushed himself off, and she heard him say, "That fucking bitch!"

"Leonard?" It was another man's voice. She didn't recognize it right away, but there was something familiar about it. She watched as Leonard made his way over to a large, black SUV. She hadn't noticed it in the lot when she'd gotten here earlier. It looked a lot like Solomon's limo. Leonard made his way over to the black Caddy. The man in the back seat beckoned Leonard into the vehicle's driver seat. When the dome light came on, she recognized Solomon. Only, he looked like he'd just returned from a dip in the Fountain Of Youth. She couldn't believe her eyes. Leonard shut the door and the two men engaged in muffled conversation. She couldn't decipher a word of it. Delilah ducked below the level of the roof, out of sight from both of them, and waited.

Chapter Thirty-Six

Madeleine

Henry found himself in a cabin in the middle of the woods in 1692 Salem. Although physically not there, for some strange reason he could smell the pleasant aroma of the pine logs comprising the cabin's walls, and the cozy smell of the fire that heated the place on this cold Halloween night.

It was a simple cabin. A plain wooden table sat in the middle of the room, bookended by two plain wooden stools. In front of the fire was a rod stretching the length of the hearth. It held a kettle on a hook at one end, and various items of clothing were draped over the rod's length. Small puffs of steam rose from the drying clothes. Other than dishes and tools hung on hooks planted in the log walls, the only other things of note in the sparsely furnished cabin were the carved symbols in the slats holding the roof up. He recognized many of them as the exact same ones that adorned the walls leading to the back room of Wanda's shop in 2018, Salem. He speculated, correctly, they were a form of protection.

The door to the cabin opened. Snow blew in with a tall, thin woman in a black hooded cloak. She turned her back to Henry and leaned on the door to force it shut against the angry Halloween wind. The latch caught with a loud metal snap and silence dropped back down on the cabin like a warm, soft blanket. The woman whirled around, exhaled in relief from the struggle with the door, and using both hands reached up and removed the hood surrounding her head.

Although he'd only seen her in his dreams, Henry couldn't fight off the odd sensation he was looking in a mirror.

It made no sense to him at first. They looked nothing alike. She was tall and thin. Her hair was wavy, long, and dirty blond, surrounding a heart-shaped face. She had full lips. Her nose was thin and slightly upturned. It somehow complimented her lips. When Henry got to the eyes, he realized why he'd felt the effect of looking into a mirror. They were identical to his eyes. Not in color. Hers were brown and his were blue. They were identical in spirit. Again he was amazed by the perception he possessed here—a knowing without the need to learn. He realized he was looking back through time at the mirrors to his own soul. It left him feeling both awestruck and dumbfounded.

Henry snapped back to reality. Well, this reality, in a hurry. He watched as the woman he used to be walked toward him. Her head was tilted slightly to the left, and she reached out with her hand as if sensing his presence. She closed her eyes and said aloud, "I knowest thou art there. Thy presence is plain. I knowest thou meanest no harm. Wouldst thou show thyself to me? Makest thine intention plain, kind spirit."

Henry wasn't quite sure what to do. He'd just assumed he was here to simply follow her through the events of that night. And through following her, he could figure out what he was supposed to bring back to the present. It never occurred to him this might be, for lack of a better term, an interactive experience. The world's weirdest Disney ride.

He looked around the cabin, seeking some sort of inspiration, and failing. He almost gave up and surrendered to the idea of just letting events play out. And then something occurred to him. It was so simple he felt stupid for not thinking of it right away. He would wait until she fell asleep. He would talk to her in a dream.

CHAPTER THIRTY-SEVEN

DECISIONS, DECISIONS...

LEONARD WAS SQUIRMING A bit in his seat. He knew he'd fucked up. Big time. And having Solomon sitting behind him, in the state of mind Leonard could only assume he was in, did nothing to alleviate his unease.

"So, Leonard, where is your beloved on this fine evening?"

"I don't know, sir. I wasn't able to find her," Leonard lied.

"Why were you in the bushes, Leonard?" Solomon asked.

Leonard hesitated before answering. "I came here, after failing to locate my betrothed, to monitor the store. I thought maybe I could try to figure out what Henry is up to. Get the jump on them."

"I see. Did part of your surveillance include rolling around in the dirt in your five thousand dollar suit? Did it include rubbing dirt on your face, maybe as camouflage?"

Leonard looked down at his clothes. He had given little thought to how he'd appeared as he left the bushes. He was too bewildered when he'd awoken on the ground, and then pissed beyond belief when the memory of what

Delilah had done to him with the taser had come back. He barely had a full minute to gather his thoughts when Solomon had called him over to the limo. He realized the more he spoke, the deeper the hole was he'd been digging.

"You know what I think, Leonard?"

"What, sir?"

"I think when you got here, Delilah was waiting for you. I think she somehow got the better of you. I think you interrupted her as she was carrying out her own agenda."

"Her own agenda, sir?"

"Oh yes. Did you ever notice how whenever I ask you to have her do something she is *never* around. Any time there is an urgent need for *The Order*, she can never be counted on?"

"She's a very busy person, sir. Between what she does for our real estate business and the things she does for *The Order* ..."

"Oh, for fuck's sake Leonard, just stop."

Leonard shut up. He looked in the rear-view mirror and met Solomon's gaze. He didn't like what he saw there. He wondered if these were the last moments of his existence.

"What to do with you, Leonard?" Solomon looked out the window to his left. He brought up the gold-plated lion's head cane and tapped it lightly against the window well for several minutes as he contemplated Leonard's fate.

The room inside Wanda's shop was turning into winter 1692. Snakes of blueish-white flakes covered the gloss black floor as the centuries old air blew through the electric-blue portal created by Wanda and Joanne. In the dead of night in 1692, Salem, Henry would have no trouble finding his way here when he'd found what he'd been looking for. He probably wouldn't have much trouble finding it, regardless of the blue-tinged portal. There was a reason Wanda had picked this particular spot to open her shop. This was the site of Madeleine's last breath.

Chapter Thirty-Eight

Hidden Agendas

Madeleine had given up trying to contact the spirit she'd sensed in her cabin. It had been a long day, and it was time to rest. She'd sneaked into town earlier that day, against David's wishes, to buy some supplies. And the stares and whispers of the townsfolk had ground her usually upbeat spirit into a budding despair. She knew they thought of her as a witch (well, their version of a witch) and she knew what happened to witches in Salem. Today, however, it was as if she could reach out and touch the hate in the air. It was all driven by one man. Dobson Molonos. He was a recent arrival in Salem. Word was he'd arrived on the supply boat from England within the last year. And he'd wasted no time spreading his doctrine of fear.

The first time she'd laid eyes on him, she could sense the evil that poured forth from him. When their eyes had locked in the town square, she felt a peculiar feeling in the middle of her head. It seemed to her as if a spider had begun crawling around in there, searching, looking for something to feed on. When she concentrated with all of her soul, she was able to stop it. She violently cast the feeling out of her head, but right before she cast him out, she caught sight of an item Molonos believed to be a secret. She watched, surprised, as Dobson Molonos fell to one knee, letting out a sharp cry at just the moment she'd cast the spider out. She watched his fawning followers help him to his feet. And then she met his gaze. She saw the briefest glimmer of fear in his eyes, and felt it in her mind as if it were her own. It was in that moment Madeleine realized this was a soul she'd dealt with before. He knew her, and she him, but she didn't understand how. She decided, right then and there, she would need to deal with him again. She would have to be clever and careful. Allies were few and far between for anyone accused or even thought to be a witch in Salem.

That same night, she came home from town and, having dwelt on it for days, told her husband about Dobson Molonos. When she finished, David Tranch sat back and considered what his wife had told him. He'd heard rumors about the newcomer. None of them good. He knew what this meant for his wife and, ultimately, for him. David was not one to shy away from a fight, but he was also not fool enough to confront a formidable foe without a carefully considered plan.

Madeleine watched David in silence. He had the same pattern of behaviors and physical tics whenever he considered something of importance. He would absentmindedly stroke his beard with his left hand, then run both hands through the thick bird's nest of red hair atop his head. He would repeat this several times. As if trying to summon the answer by coaxing it through his scalp and into existence.

He was a practical man. Not a skeptic, exactly, but not as reliant on nature and craft as she was. She knew he respected the power she could wield. It was one of the many things she loved about her husband—that, and the sincerity and heart which seemed to radiate from his brilliant green eyes.

They'd met in the very square in which Madeleine had encountered Dobson Molonos. They'd been introduced to each other by a mutual friend neither of them realized the other knew. A man named Henry Wandell. After they'd been introduced, they watched as Mr. Wandell walked away. A little bounce in his step. Almost as if he'd planned it all along. They turned to each other and laughed. David and Madeleine stood together that day in the square and talked for hours. It was as if they'd known each other for years. Two months later they were happily married. And now they sat in their little cabin in the woods, finished with their cooked rabbit and carrots, and contemplated their next move and how to stay alive in a town gone mad.

David finally came out of his reverie and laid out a plan. He would get to know this Dobson character. Try to find out what he could about him from others he worked for in town. David was a master hunter, and he would leverage his skills against the dependence others in town had on his expertise. Everyone needed to eat. And winter was coming.

He knew better than to trust the others in town by solely using idle gossip to gather information. People talked, but hungry ones would be far less likely to betray those who put food on their tables. The one stipulation he had was Madeleine, for the time being, needed to stay out of town as much as possible while he did this. It would do no good for either of them to be seen together by Molonos until David could gather the information he needed. She agreed.

Over the next month, David put his plan into action. He bartered game he'd killed for morsels of information about Molonos. He was very careful about it. Making the conversations he'd had with his customers seem, to them, as if they were imparting a confidence to him, instead of the other way around. Even going so far as to give them a wink and a nod.

David had the gift of gab and the power of persuasion. And, to be honest, the ladies were quite taken with him. Another reason, though Madeleine didn't know it, he wanted to keep her from town as much as possible. Most women in town were jealous of her, and occasionally outright hostile toward Madeleine because of her marriage to David. Things would go much easier if the illusion of availability existed, though it never did. He was madly in love with Madeleine.

At the end of the hunt on All Hallows' Eve, several hours before the storm that blew Madeleine into the cabin where she was with Henry now, David was bringing three fresh-killed rabbits to the home of a widower on the outskirts of Salem. She was one of the women Dobson Molonos paid a pittance to clean his home. David had been "wooing" her for the past few weeks. It was a one-sided affair, of course, but she didn't know. David felt a pang of guilt about it on two levels. Even though he had no ill intentions, he still felt, in some way, he was betraying Madeleine. And he felt awful about leading on this woman who had not a chance of truly gaining his affections. But, what must be done, must be done.

Katherine Andersen invited him into her home to lay the rabbits down to be salted and preserved for later use. She asked him to stay for tea and he agreed. They talked for several minutes. Eventually the conversation wound around to her employer. She complained about how hard Molonos had worked her that day. How he had repeatedly admonished her for not cleaning the floorboards in his chambers properly. He'd made her clean them three times this very day! David nodded and sympathized with her in all the right places. When she asked him to rub the pain out of her shoulders, he obliged.

After several moments of uncomfortable silence (at least for David it was uncomfortable), she talked about her master's chambers. How he was meticulous about his cleanliness—to the point of insanity, it seemed. David kept rubbing and kept quiet. She continued on about her master. He needed his coat folded a certain way. He needed his clothes for the next morning stacked just so. His books had to be aligned perfectly. His dresser was to be dusted daily, and any items removed for the dusting were to be returned in precisely the same spot. All furniture was to be dusted and cleaned and set back exactly as before. And the trunk at the foot of his bed was to be dusted and cleaned but never, under any circumstances, was it to be asked about, or even spoken of. When she asked Dobson why, she told David she wished she hadn't.

"He set his eyes upon me. He spoketh not once. But I understood there wouldst be no debate of the matter."

"What dost thou thinkest he hides, dearest Katherine?" David asked.

"I knoweth not, David. But it is of utmost importance to him. On occasion, I've heard him speaketh four numbers in whisper ... 0622. I knoweth not why, but he sayest these at the trunk in his quarters."

David, to keep up appearances, changed the subject to make it seem the information she had given him about Molonos were just another tidbit of a larger conversation. He kept rubbing her shoulders and making small talk for several minutes more. He released her shoulders after a time, put on his coat and said his goodbyes. As he opened the door Katherine reached around him and slammed it shut.

Outside, a raven cawed.

"Why not stayeth with me tonight, David?"

She pressed up against him, pinning David against the door. It was not at all an unpleasant experience, David thought. His next thought was of Madeleine, and guilt flooded through his being. But not enough guilt to keep his, as Madeleine called it, "Hunter's Compass", from pointing north.

A fact not lost on Katherine. She kissed his neck and ground her hips into his. He hadn't noticed she'd undone the laces of her corset as his back had been to her while he put on his coat. He looked down at her as she kissed his neck. Her wavy black hair smelled fresh and clean, despite a hard day's work. She'd let it loose. It ran long down the front of her corset, over her shoulders, and disappeared down her back. Her ample cleavage threatened to send the laces to points east and west. He felt the want rise within him. David reached for her shoulders and slid the sleeves of her corset down to her elbows and the laces in the middle parted without fuss. He tilted her head up toward his with a finger under her chin. She stood on her toes and met his lips with hers, driving her body harder against his. Her tongue dashing and retreating, as if testing for a response. David responded in-kind, driving them both deeper into the moment. David slid his arms down her back and in one swift motion lifted her by the bottom and brought her over to the table where only moments earlier they'd been discussing the business of the day. He madly swiped the tea set from the table to the floor, the cups and saucers smashing and the metal pot clanging out loud in protest. David looked down at her. She was beautiful, and he wanted her. He pulled her forward to the edge of the table by the hips and slid her dress up to mid-thigh. She moaned. He ran his hands along the front of her thighs, his thumbs along her inner thighs, and gently parted her legs. She was ready for him.

"David ... David? Hast thou not heard a single word I've said?"

David hadn't realized how much he had slid down the path toward infidelity until this very moment. And not a moment too soon. He'd been absentmindedly fantasizing about having his way with Katherine on the very table they'd been discussing, at least from David's point of view, life and death matters! It was best to take what he'd learned and move on. Before fantasy became reality.

"I beg thy forgiveness, Katherine. Lost in thought was I on the foulest treatment exacted upon thee by Molonos."

Katherine looked genuinely touched by David's concern. She reached out to take his hand. David, considering his most recent thoughts about Katherine, was not about to push his luck. And it wouldn't have taken much in his current state. He gave her hand a gentle squeeze and release. He kept his eyes on Katherine as he gathered his coat and opened the door. He bid her goodnight, closed the door, and waited a beat or two before re-entering her cabin. He had one last question.

"Dearest Katherine, I wish to speaketh to master Molonos about his treatment of you. Where wouldst I findeth him on this foul October night?"

Katherine looked terrified at David's suggestion of confronting Dobson Molonos.

"Thou shalt do no such thing, David Tranch! I wouldst be without employ! And one doth not traverse the foul side of Molonos!"

"Nonsense!" said David. "I shall head to his quarters at once!"

"Molonos is with the town fathers. They preparest for winter this very evening. I implore you, thou shan't speak of this on my behalf! I beg of you, David. Please!"

David relented. He comforted Katherine and assured her he would not confront Dobson Molonos. When he had sufficiently calmed her down, he took his leave. If Katherine had had her wits about her, she would have realized David was heading in the wrong direction. With the final tidbit of information of Dobson's whereabouts, he headed toward the estate of Katherine's employer, the direction exactly opposite David and Madeleine's home. The first flakes of snow landed on David as he headed west.

Chapter Thirty-Nine

Almost There...

Wanda's Wicca'd Emporium's roof space had dwindled down to almost nothing. Delilah kept her distance from the middle as the portal dissolved it. She needed to make a decision, and she was running out of time. She made her way around the edge of the roof, keeping low to avoid detection by Solomon and Leonard. She stopped at the end opposite the parked SUV. Luckily for Delilah, the building was only one floor high. Still, with the three-foot rise of the wall around the perimeter of the building, it was somewhat of a fall to the ground. She slung the strap of her satchel over her neck and under her right arm, sat atop the wall, and twisted her body into position in order to slide, as much as she could, down the wall before letting go. She landed successfully on both feet, but her momentum carried her backward, her hands pinwheeling in the air as she tried to gain her balance. She came to an abrupt stop as her back slammed into Henry's red Toyota Camry. She righted herself and scurried to the other side of the car to hide. She looked up at the edge of the roof to Wanda's shop just in time to see the upper part of the wall begin to dissolve. "It's all about the timing," she muttered.

Leonard saw it first. The top of the wall to Wanda's Wicca'd Emporium had disappeared. A thin strand of brilliant blue light seemed to eat away at the very fabric of the brick that comprised the wall.

"Um. Mr. Dobson. There's something happening to the store I think you need to see."

Solomon had been tapping away with his cane on the window well, contemplating Leonard's fate. The tapping stopped and Solomon leaned forward in his seat. "Leonard, you know better than to interrupt me when I'm thinking ... "

And then he saw what Leonard saw.

"Consider yourself lucky, Leonard. I may yet have a use for you tonight."

Both men watched and waited as it consumed the wall, inch by inch.

)✪(

Twilight had descended on All Hallows' Eve in 1692, Salem. David Tranch had made his way to the estate of Dobson Molonos. The freshly fallen snow cast a luminous silver carpet over the property. He made a cautious approach to the house from the woods, staying off the well-worn paths leading up to the property. He remained concealed in a stand of bushes just outside the wooden fence ringing the backyard pen where Molonos housed his livestock. He only stayed there long enough to determine there was not a soul present who would thwart his plans to enter the home undetected. There wasn't.

He made his way to the wooden fence with as little sound as possible. He hopped over the fence to the mild clucks of startled chickens. He tiptoed his way to the back door. The lock was child's play to a master hunter. He'd set more secure traps to catch rabbits!

Once inside the building, he waited for his eyes to adjust to the gloom. He was in the kitchen area. It was immaculate, and he thought of poor Katherine and the others forced to work here for whatever slim earnings Molonos would pay them. This only made him more angry and determined.

He made his way silently through the kitchen and into the main room. With the sparse light that filtered in through the windows, he could map out his route to the bedroom containing the chest. He made his way around the large (and no doubt expensive) mahogany dining table. The table was ringed with chairs the likes of which he'd not seen in Salem. All eight chairs were upholstered on the seat and arms in what appeared to be black velvet. The chair at the head of the table was identical to the others, except the back of the chair rose much higher and had a headrest for the master of the house. Just another sign of this man's arrogance, David thought. The table itself was set for dinner. Expensive plates and silverware sat at the ready in front of each chair. Monogrammed linen napkins lay neatly atop each plate. The walls were adorned with framed paintings. Most were of famous landmarks from European cities around the world. An obvious boast to anyone being entertained by Molonos.

David reached the other side of the room, opposite the high-backed chair, to a closed door. This would be the master's chambers. He opened the door and stepped inside. The light was fading fast now. He would have to hurry. Again he had to wait for his eyes to adjust to the ever darkening interior. Disturbing a single thing in this room would tip off Molonos there had been an unwanted guest. A few moments passed, and he could ascertain the layout of the room. It was just as large as the dining quarters and exactly as neat and orderly as Katherine had described it to him. David heard the wind whistle through the windows. The storm outside was strengthening. He made his way over to the trunk at the foot of the bed.

Chapter Forty

Madeleine's Dream

ON THE OTHER SIDE of 1692, Salem, on All Hallows' Eve, Madeleine had fallen asleep and begun to dream. In the dream, the townsfolk had their backs to her. They lined both sides of the path leading through the town common. As she walked the path, both sides were closing the distance, narrowing the path. In front of her, their backs toward her, they moved together in unison to cut off the path. She turned around in time to see the others behind her doing the same. They encircled her. The air became still. The crowd hushed, and no one moved. She tried to push her way through them. They shoved her back onto the path so hard she fell backwards onto her behind. Startled and angry, she got up and tried to push her way through the crowd again. Again they resisted. She got back on her feet to make another attempt. As she approached the crowd for the third time, one woman turned on her. The woman's face was old and wrinkled. Her eyes were completely black. Wiry grey hair jutted from the tip of her nose and under her chin. She got up close to Madeleine and pointed a long, gnarled finger in her face and screamed, "Wiiiiiittttccchhhh!" The *others in the crowd turned around, one by one. Accusatory black eyes bored into Madeleine. The weight of their accusations became heavier by the moment. It felt to Madeleine as if it were a physical force, reaching out to smother her.*

They closed the circle. The women in the crowd chanting, "Witch! Witch! Witch!" The men chanting, "Burn her! Burn her! Burn her!" The men in the crowd grabbed her and hoisted her above themselves. It would have looked like crowd surfing to someone in modern day America.

As one, the crowd moved down the path toward an unlit bonfire that seemed to appear out of nowhere in the middle of the town common. They lowered her to the ground and poked her with sharpened branches toward the waiting bonfire. She tried to ward off the crowd as best she could. She frantically swiped at the branches in a futile attempt to keep the rabid mob at bay. Her hands were bleeding and raw from the sharpened points. Madeleine, left with no choice, climbed the waiting bonfire to escape the mob and their weapons. She cried out to God for help and this only further enraged the mob.

The old hag, who'd instigated the mob from the start, stepped forward through the crowd toward the edge of the dormant bonfire and looked Madeleine in the eye, flashing a wicked, toothless grin. She silenced her followers with the wave of a hand. The hag reached up to her own face with both hands. She began to peel the wrinkled flesh from her skull. It came off in ragged, blood-covered strips which she flung at Madeleine's feet. They landed with a sickening splat. With each strip she peeled off, the old woman's laughter became more intense. Madeleine looked down at the pile of ragged flesh at her feet, too scared to take her eyes from it and face what would surely be the nightmare to end all nightmares. When she finally drew the courage to look up, she was dumbfounded. There was no blood, no mess, no hideous exposed skull with black eyes. She was looking into the ice-blue eyes of Dobson Molonos. And he had a torch in his hands.

"Madeleine Tranch! Thou hath been accused of witchcraft and sentenced to death. Dost thou havest any last words?"

Madeleine said nothing. She would not give him or his mindless followers the satisfaction of grovelling for her life.

Molonos lowered the torch to the bonfire and then paused. He raised his head, nose in the air, looking left and right. A look of confusion crossed his face. The crowd surrounding Molonos and the bonfire muttered amongst themselves. A slight wind swirled around the bonfire. The torch flickered as the wind picked up in intensity. The wind became a gust, and the crowd had gone from a low mutter to a budding panic. The gust became a gale, and the torch was extinguished. The wind caught tiny embers from the torch and cast them back toward the crowd. The embers landed on the crowd, and men and women screamed in pain as their garments caught fire. Panic consumed the mob, and they ran from the bonfire and out of the town square. Madeleine could smell the burning hair and flesh as it swirled in the wind that ringed the bonfire in a wicked vortex. Only Dobson Molonos remained in place, facing Madeleine.

The look of terror and bewilderment on his face in that moment was the first time she'd felt genuine joy in ages.

The wind stopped then. The only ones left in the town square were Madeleine and Molonos. They stared at each other for what seemed forever. Madeleine could only take her eyes from those of Molonos when, on the outskirts of the town square, she saw a man making his way toward the area of the bonfire. Molonos had not taken notice of him yet. He was too shocked and angry by his failure to execute Madeleine.

The man was dressed in a way she'd not seen before. He had pants of what appeared to be a rough blue fabric, and a red shirt with no collar and shortened sleeves. On his shirt was the most peculiar profile of a man with a blue hat, sporting a star, and what appeared to be two red pieces of cloth trailing out behind it. The stranger wore the oddest looking footwear she'd ever encountered! His shoes were white, and they had three dark-blue stripes on each side. And they had the laces of a corset where there should be buckles! She wondered if this were what God looked like, as she had cried out to Him only moments earlier. And he strode with such authority! She sensed no fear in him of Molonos … but rather contempt.

After a time, Molonos came to his senses and realized Madeleine was no longer looking at him. He turned his body to follow her gaze. Unlike Madeleine, he was not surprised by the way the man was dressed. It was the furthest thing from his mind. Also, unlike Madeleine, he recognized the soul who now approached him. What she could feel was the fear that poured forth from Molonos in waves. He exited her dream without so much as a word. Gone in an instant.

Madeleine made her way down from the unlit bonfire and approached the strangely dressed man. It was the same presence she'd felt in the cabin earlier. She had no doubt.

Henry, still physically on the table at Wanda's fast disappearing shop, with Doctor Love still faithfully (if not fearfully) by his side, asked for the Doctor's help. He needed to explain to Madeleine how it was possible he could have, at one time, been her.

"I'll walk you through the basics, Henry. Speak out loud what she asks. Be brief and concise with her. Time is short. And be careful not to let your emotions about her fate get the best of you."

"Why hast thou entered my dreams, spirit?"

"I am not a spirit, Madeleine. I am a traveler from another time. My name is Henry. You and I share the same soul."

"How is this possible, Henry?"

"I'm not entirely sure, but apparently the souls of men and women travel through many lifetimes. And often, groups of souls travel together."

"And why hast thou come to me?"

"The man you dreamed of tonight, in my time, is named Solomon Dobson. I'm not sure what you call him in this time, but ... "

"He is Dobson Molonos, Henry."

"An anagram of the name. Figures ... pompous prick that he is."

"How does pricking thyself makest one pompous, Henry?"

"Never mind. Not important. This Dobson Molonos, as you call him, avoids death. He was, at one time, born just the same as we were. Though I don't know that for sure. Somehow along the way he figured out how to become immortal, or to at least appear as immortal to his followers. He's done this to avoid the cycle of birth and death. To bypass learning the lessons from one life to the next needed to perfect one's soul, and to grow in love and understanding and service. What he's done is unnatural. When a soul avoids those lessons, it craves power, it craves wealth, it craves to dominate and destroy others to keep what it has. It learns to subvert the will of God, or the Universe, or whatever higher power someone may believe in. It also learns how to spot those that, over time, are tasked with restoring the natural and spiritual order. We think there is a way to kill him, which is why I've come back to talk to you."

"I sensed something unnatural of him on the common the very day I layeth eyes upon him. I'd no idea of the depth of his depravity. My husband, at this very moment, seeketh to expose him to the townsfolk. We must stop him."

Henry grew uncomfortable. He knew how all this ended for Madeleine. It was tearing him up inside.

"Madeleine, where is your husband now?"

"He seeketh to gain an advantage over Molonos. I knowest not where he is at this moment."

"I need to know what he looks like, Madeleine. I can find him. Think of him now and focus your thoughts on me."

She did so. An image of a stout, red-haired man came into Henry's mind. All Henry could think of was the cartoon character in those old Rusty Jones commercials he used to see on TV when he was a kid. The jingle played in his mind, *"Hello Rusty Jones, goodbye rusty cars."* And then Henry focused more closely on the face. The eyes! He'd recognize those eyes anywhere! They were Joanne's eyes!

The last layer of denial about his current situation fell away. In that instant, all doubt Henry had about what Wanda or Doctor Love or Joanne had been telling him over the last few days vanished. It was like his own personal road to Damascus. He'd been transformed now. Much as Saul of Tarsus had become the disciple Paul—the scales fell from his eyes. He believed! And from that belief, the power and abilities he'd possessed as Madeleine flooded back into *him. He was a Warlock! He'd been confused when the man/dog thing in his mother's basement had called him that. Now it was all making sense.*

At that moment, the dream dissolved. Madeleine had been awakened by a pounding at her door. Henry found himself back in the cabin and slightly disoriented from the dream's abrupt ending. The pounding at the door became more persistent and forceful. A voice boomed from the other side.

"Madeleine Tranch, in the name of the Governor of Salem, thou art accused of witchcraft! Submit immediately!"

Henry sent one thought to Madeleine, *"Run."*

Madeleine wasted no time. She threw off her blanket, slammed both feet into her cracked and worn leather boots, grabbed a key sitting on the nightstand next to her bed, shoved it into the pocket of her nightie, and bolted through the back door of the cabin and into the unforgiving snow storm.

Chapter Forty-One

The Road to Nowhere

DELILAH WAS STILL HIDDEN on the far side of Henry's car. Time was growing short, and soon she would be forced into full view of everyone. Even the car would fade into the portal opened up inside Wanda's shop. 1692, Salem, would expand outward until this business was finished. She began her preparations. She needed to remove the spells protecting the interior of the shop and the land surrounding it. She was a powerful witch in her own right. A fact Leonard was not, surprise surprise, aware of. Delilah proceeded to undo the protections Wanda had set up.

The wall to Wanda's Wicca'd Emporium was three-quarters dissolved now. Snow flew over the shortened wall and out into the parking lot, mixing with the pouring rain. Leonard turned on the wipers of the Caddy so he and Solomon could see better what was going on, and be ready to breach the perimeter the moment it was safe.

"When do you think we should approach, sir?" Leonard asked.

"I'll tell you when. Your fiancée seems to have a different agenda than us tonight, Leonard. I'm not entirely sure of what she's up to, but it works to my advantage, nevertheless. She assumes I don't understand the talents she possesses fully. She is, at this very moment, lowering the defenses protecting the grounds. When I can feel the shift in energy, we will proceed. And they will, finally, pay the price for their transgressions."

"What talents are those, sir?"

"Come now, Leonard! You don't actually think she is a simple accountant, do you?"

"I'm not sure I understand, sir. As long as I've known her, I've never seen her doing anything out of the ordinary. I mean, she's exceptionally talented with numbers. And she has a genuine gift for research..."

Solomon threw his head back and laughed. "Leonard, let me ask you something. When you and your beloved are fucking, have you ever noticed any odd marks on her body? Perhaps on her thigh? Or maybe on her back?"

Leonard was quite offended by the way Solomon casually talked about private matters between himself and Delilah. But he still didn't have the sack to confront him about it. He swallowed whatever pride he had left and answered the question

"Come to think of it sir, there is a darker patch of skin on her thigh. She told me it was a botched tattoo she'd had removed years ago. Why do you ask?"

Solomon laughed even harder this time. Leonard, in spite of the fear he had of this man, was getting pissed. He didn't like that this arrogant prick seemed to know more about his fiancée than he did.

"What the fuck is so funny, Mr. Dobson?"

Solomon stopped laughing.

"Watch your tone, Leonard. If you're not careful, I might begin to suspect you are in possession of a spine." Solomon leaned forward, all mirth absent from his face. Leonard felt the old, familiar ass-puckers coming on. "It's amazing to me, Leonard, I've allowed you to live this long—given the amount of times you've completely fucked up even the most simple assignments. Let me enlighten you about your fiancée. I've known her a lot longer than you have."

Leonard's eyes widened with surprise.

"That's right, old boy. She came to me after she had a falling out with the old hose-bag who runs this little shop disappearing in front of our eyes. It was well before you brought her to the mortuary ... matter of fact. When she came by with you that day, we'd already agreed to discuss our mutual problem—Wanda Heinze. I told her I would be more than happy to have her. And oh, Leonard, my good man ... I've had her. In the bedroom, on the living room floor, in the garage. Good times.

"As a condition of joining *The Order*, she would have to renounce her vows to Wanda's little group and swear allegiance to us. She did. She took the vows, drank the dreams of others, and removed all trace of the *Foedere In Luna* from both body and soul. Once she drank of the essence of others, she became one of us. The little ceremony we all had the night you brought her by was only for your benefit.

"But I had a problem, Leonard. One downside to being immortal is I have to keep feeding on the dreams of others in order to sustain myself. However, I can't *overdo* it. I can't one day look like I'm in my late sixties, early seventies, and then the next day appear as I do now—a man in his mid-forties to early fifties. You see ... there are limitations, even for me. I have to at least *look* like I'm aging normally. At least within the span of the lifetimes of the mortal associates I surround myself with in daily life. One has to keep up appearances in order to stay, for lack of a better term, undetected. But, fortunately, that all ends tonight."

These revelations rocked Leonard. He stared at Solomon with impotent rage. He realized he'd made a deal with the devil. His *own* immortality depended on whether this man decided he should live or die. It hardly seemed fair.

Solomon continued, "I was the one who set up your meeting with Delilah. I needed to keep her around for her many talents, especially, but not limited to, what she is using them for tonight. It wasn't like we could actually be seen around town together. The associates in my *other* businesses would talk. A man almost in his eighties with a woman who looks like *Delilah* does? She's close to fifty, but she looks like she could be thirty-five! No no no. People today *say* the difference in age is no big deal. But what they *think*? That's another story. And I need them to think a certain way to protect my business gains. So I tell them I'm a widower. The sympathy is such a powerful selling point!"

"I don't understand. Why even have her pretend she wants to marry someone like me? If, as you say, I'm this incompetent buffoon you can't rely on?"

"It's simple to understand, Leonard. When you get right down to it, you can't trust anyone. There was a time, several decades ago, when you were reliable. That time has *long* since passed. But while Madeleine and the others were in-between lives, your incompetence wasn't really a threat. I kept you around because I thought you still might prove useful someday. And you did. You see, as much as I enjoy nailing your fiancée, I don't really trust her. So I needed you to keep tabs on her. I don't mind that you get to play with her now and then. But, at the end of the day, she's mine.

"Lately though, I can't seem to find her when I need her. It was making me nervous on two fronts. The first; I needed her for tonight to take down Wanda's protections. She is doing that as we speak, so no problem there. The second; I needed her to prove to me she'd not switched allegiance from me to you. And she proved that tonight by incapacitating you earlier this evening. So I'm good there too."

"So where does that leave me, sir?"

Solomon had been slowly twisting the gold-plated, lions-head handle from the top of his cane the entire time he'd been conversing with Leonard. He raised the handle of the cane, pressed it to Leonard's forehead, and pulled the trigger.

"Nowhere, I'm afraid."

Chapter Forty-Two

Nobody Home

DAVID SMASHED THE LOCK and opened the trunk at the foot of Molonos' bed. It had grown so dark in the room, however, he could not make out the contents within. He would have to use his hands and sort through the innards of the trunk to find whatever it was Molonos deemed such a danger.

David was pleasantly surprised when there were only two items stored in the trunk. One small box felt as if it had a combination lock, while the other slid through his fingers, as if it were wrapped in silk. As dark as the room was, there was no telling what they could be. He removed the items from the trunk, threw the broken lock and its pieces back into it, and shut the lid. He tiptoed his way back through the dining room, then into the kitchen, and reached for the door that led out through the back and toward the livestock pens.

Henry stood outside of the house, not in the least affected by the cold. He watched as David slid the door closed behind him, exiting the large cabin. David made his way to the woods in seconds and the forest swallowed him up. Henry followed close behind. He needed to know what David would do next with the packages he'd secured from Molonos' trunk.

)✪(

Madeleine ran for her life. She gulped in cold air with each stride, and her nose and throat were going numb. The crunch of snow under her feet was, for the moment, the loudest sound in the world. She knew she wouldn't last long out here, but the alternative ... well, there really was no alternative. She chanced a look behind her. In the distance she saw the faintest hint of a reddish-orange flicker. It looked to her like a sunrise in the middle of the forest—only she knew this was not the welcoming light of a new day. She ran harder, but her strength was flagging. She looked back again and saw the forest now painted in the bright-orange flicker of torchlight. The voices echoed from tree to tree, rock to boulder, and they carried waves of fear and anger and ignorance with them. Then she felt the familiar crawl of the spider behind her eyes. Molonos was trying to read her again. She could feel his fear and desperation as if it were her own. Molonos had worked his way into the corner of her mind that held the plan she'd hatched with her husband. She felt him going there, and she slammed her mind shut.

Madeleine risked another look back, and this would prove to be her last mistake. A broken tree branch, weighed down by the heavy, wet October snow, had fallen in her path. She tripped and went sprawling into a bed of bark, snow, and pine needles that had shaken loose from one of the trees. She scurried to her feet, only to collapse in agony. Madeleine looked down in disbelief at her left foot. She hadn't realized, until tonight, it was possible for a human foot to still be attached to one's leg at such a severe angle. Madeleine knew then she would die here, tonight, in the middle of the forest. Never would she see David again. Crying, exhausted, and terrified, she lay her head down in the pile of needles and branches and snow. It was the last bit of comfort she would ever feel.

)✪(

David made his way to the cabin to tell Madeleine the good news. And to open the boxes with her and decide on their next move. As he crested the hill, all thoughts of victory, discovery, and celebration were driven from his mind. The home in which he'd shared so many happy moments with Madeleine was now a raging inferno. Snowflakes poured onto the burning cabin only to die a hot orange death. He tucked the package into his backpack and bolted for his home. There was no entering. The fire was all-consuming. David rushed around to the back of the cabin, hoping to find Madeleine safe and out of the fire. She was nowhere to be found. Panic threatened to swallow his mind. He began calling out to her, desperate to hear her voice. It was full dark now. A late autumn blizzard raged. Where could she be?

It was then his hunting instincts kicked in. He'd been in situations like this before—in fact, a lot worse. He willed himself to be calm. To think. David approached, as close as he dared, to the back of the cabin. He took in the scene with hunter's eyes. There! Madeleine's footprints! He followed their path as they led to the woods. Looking up from the trail of prints, he could clearly see where they were leading. The footprints disappeared between two distinctly shaped bushes and into the forest. The bush on the left he'd trimmed, so it was high on its left side and sloping downward to the right. The bush on the right was trimmed to its mirror opposite. They formed an arrow that pointed to a trail leading deep into the woods ... to Madeleine's shrine. David wasted no time. He burst full bore through the bushes and after his wife ... and the several sets of footprints surrounding hers. Henry followed.

Chapter Forty-Three

A Falling Out

THE WALLS TO WANDA'S shop were gone now. The passenger side of Henry's Toyota faded as the portal edged further into 2018. Delilah had finished the countermeasures to Wanda's spells. It would soon be safe for her to enter the grounds where the shop had stood.

She risked a peek over the top of what remained of the Camry. Wanda and Joanne still sat in their lotus positions, partially covered by snow and buffeted by the winds. The rain that had been falling outside the portal was quickly incorporated into the snowstorm within. Archie still stood sentry over Henry, bracing himself against the wind by holding on to the side of the table on which Henry still lay. Henry himself hadn't moved the whole time. Delilah found this amazing and was seized by an irrational sense of pride in Henry. The last time she'd met him, she sensed the decency within him. Regardless of which side you were on, it was hard not to like Henry Trank.

She caught motion beyond the four companions. Solomon opened the door to the Caddy. When the dome light came on, she could see Leonard slumped over the steering wheel. A crimson splatter to Leonard's right told her all she needed to know about her former fiancé. She felt a twinge of regret, but not much more. Leonard had been a means to an end. And the end was coming fast. *Leonard's* end had been a forgone conclusion almost from the start.

She thought about the day they'd met. She had dropped by his real estate office several weeks after the court case against Wanda. There had been a time when Delilah and Wanda were close. But, as happens so often with business partners, they didn't see eye to eye on how the shop should be run. Delilah was insistent on charging more money for things such as psychic readings, tarot card readings, the prices on various types of merchandise, and classes on witchcraft—pretty much anything to do with profit. Wanda saw the business as much more of a service. She was completely happy to survive on thin profit margins. To Wanda, their customers' happiness was her primary motivation. Delilah agreed on that point, but she argued most of the other shops in the city were charging almost double what the Emporium charged. And what they were taking in was barely enough for one, never mind both of them.

One day, Delilah decided she'd had enough. She lawyered up and presented Wanda with papers. When they ended up in court, the judge had decided almost every point in Wanda's favor. Delilah suspected Wanda may have cast a spell on the judge. Of course, in a court of law, there would be zero chance of proving it. So, Delilah took her lumps, and the settlement money deemed "fair" by the court, and left.

She'd come in, several weeks removed from court, to Leonard's real estate office. She was determined to move on from her business divorce with Wanda. She arrived there with what, to Leonard, appeared to be a singular intent on finding prime commercial real estate to compete against Wanda. Maybe even drive the Emporium out of business. Her second agenda item, for the time being, would remain between her and one other.

Leonard was taken with her right away. She was a tall, gorgeous blonde. She had an easy way about her, and she reminded Leonard of a cross between Kim Basinger and Michelle Pfeiffer. Then, when they got down to business, everything changed. The "easy" way was gone. Leonard would show her an image of a site, and she would ask him question after question about the various properties. He was as impressed by her business acumen as she was by his wealth. After a couple of hours of back and forth (and with nothing agreed upon), Leonard mustered up the courage to ask her out for dinner. She agreed. They dated for several months.

One day, deep into their relationship, Leonard decided he trusted her enough to introduce Delilah to a man in town he had done several real estate deals for—Solomon Dobson. They met Dobson at the mortuary he owned on the other side of town. The three of them shared lunch in the mortuary's office. The conversation eventually swung around to Delilah's falling out with Wanda. Before the conversation had gotten fully underway, Leonard's phone chirped. Leonard excused himself. He needed to head across town to close a deal. He asked Delilah if she minded keeping Solomon company until he returned. He wouldn't be long.

"No problem, sweetie," Delilah assured him.

Leonard left the two of them alone.

"Ah, Ms. Heinze. A thorn in my side for a long time now," said Solomon.

"Wanda? Still haven't been able to scratch that itch I see."

Solomon considered what she said, "Delilah ... what are your feelings toward Wanda these days?"

"Cold would be an understatement. Not my favorite person in the world right now."

"What would you be willing to do to get even with her? Maybe drive her out of business? Maybe something else?"

"Something else?"

"I have a proposal for you, Delilah. It may sound crazy at first, but hear me out."

Delilah leaned forward, elbows on the table, arms up, fingers interlaced under her chin. "I'm all ears."

"Do you believe in reincarnation, Delilah?"

"I've never really given it much thought, actually."

"What if I were to tell you it is real? And when I say real, I mean provably real."

Delilah raised an eyebrow. "Prove it."

They stared at each other. The challenge in Delilah's eyes meeting the intense gaze of Solomon. Delilah felt a peculiar buzzing in the middle of her forehead. She was scared at first, but fear receded as she grew intrigued by a scene unfolding before her eyes.

The room seemed to dissolve in front of her, and she felt as if she were at the world's strangest drive-in movie. On the "screen" in front of her, she saw a man riding a horse through a battlefield. He was covered in blood, but it appeared not to be his own. The man on the horse wore chain mail armor. He lifted the helmet from his head. It was a much younger Solomon Dobson. He barked out orders, directing other soldiers on the battlefield this way and that, and then, without warning, the scene shifted. She now saw a man in a Capotain—the traditional hat worn back in the 1600s. To Delilah, he looked like a Pilgrim. Again, a much younger Solomon. He was in a courtroom. He was holding a book under his arm. The only visible word on the book's spine she could make out was Malleus. A man was standing next to him, his back toward Delilah. The man turned around to talk to Solomon. It was Leonard! She could hear them in a serious discussion about the rampant problem of witchcraft in Salem.

All in the room agreed it was a curse upon the town. And then, just as suddenly as it appeared, the scene before her vanished.

"Okay, what in the hell was that?, Delilah asked.

"That, miss Davis, was myself over the centuries. I've been alive now for over nine hundred years. I told you I would prove to you reincarnation was real. I've not sufficiently done so, yet. But I showed you that, to show you this ..."

Delilah felt the crawling sensation behind her eyes again. The room opened up once more, and she was returned to 1600s Salem. There was a light rain falling, and the sky was covered in grey, puffy clouds. The wind blew the rain sideways. Solomon stood in the middle of the town square. He was in conversation with a short, stout little man. They seemed to be arguing about something, but Delilah couldn't make out the words. The conversation between the two was, however, not the point. The scene shifted. It concentrated the focus on the shorter man's face. Delilah studied it for a few moments and sucked in a quick, shocked breath. Even though it was a man that stood before her, there was no mistaking the eyes of Wanda Heinze. The scene before her faded out.

"Now you know, Delilah. That man's name, back in 1692, was Henry Wandell, aka Wanda Heinze. I offer you a chance to even the score with her ... and much more. My proposal is simple. I can offer you immortality. Forever to build the wealth, the power, the prestige you deserve. And not only that!

But also the chance to permanently remove the problem of Ms. Heinze from your life.

"You see how Leonard lives. He isn't as wealthy as he is from real estate alone. Leonard is worth well over a billion dollars. He lives well, don't get me wrong. But he only shows those in Salem what he wants them to see. Mr. Shrumm has properties all over the world. I only ask he keeps it low-key. To protect the *Order Immortalis* from unwanted scrutiny. I can make you one of us, Delilah. What say you?"

Delilah was shocked. She didn't speak for several moments. Solomon patiently waited. It wasn't like he was short on time or anything. And the arrangement they'd discussed outside the courtroom the day she'd lost her court case to Wanda now came much more into focus. It was way more than just a business deal (as she'd assumed at the time), and it was also more than the sexual encounters the two had engaged in since that day. She didn't really want to dwell on sex with Solomon for any length of time, but business was business. She had her own agenda items.

In the end, greed and revenge got the better of her. She decided she wanted in. Solomon explained the stakes to her. What she would be giving up. She weighed the pros and cons and declared to him she thought it better not to have to start all over again. And again, and again. Why bother if you could circumvent the whole process and never have to give up the things you'd gained? She swore allegiance to the *Order* that very night, with Leonard by her side and the other members in attendance. There was no going back. She didn't care. She was too excited by the prospects the future held ...

And now she watched as the man she swore her allegiance to stood outside the SUV and across the grounds from her, calmly screwing the gun he'd killed her fiancé with back into the top of his cane. A cane he no longer needed to lean on. He looked young and vibrant now. It was the image of the man she'd chosen to spend the rest of time with. And they were about to end the singular threat to that future.

Chapter Forty-Four

Burials

DAVID REACHED THE BODY of his wife. She was barely recognizable, save for her bedtime clothing. He pulled her up from the ground, cradled her in his lap, and wailed.

Henry stood behind him. The agony coming from David hit him in almost unbearable waves. He wanted to do anything he could to alleviate the pain the man was in. After all, it was the pain from the same soul of the woman he'd fallen in love with on the other side of the portal. He couldn't wait to get back to her. Just to be with her. Through this man's agony, he understood the depth of feeling she'd shown him (and that he felt for her) in such a short amount of time.

He thought back to the first day he'd met Jo. It was like a bolt out of the blue. Of course, there was the physical. Jo was a knockout. But he'd seen plenty of knockouts in his time. Dated his fair share, too. None of them had the instant connection he'd experienced that first day in the Cracked

Cauldron when, even though intimidated by her beauty, he found the courage to start up a conversation.

She was sarcastic, but not in a mean way. She did this thing where she would cock her head to one side when she was truly curious about what you had to say. It made you feel important to her.

She would wink at him when one of the other patrons in the shop would hit on her. As if to say "watch this." And then the guy would leave with a smile on his face, never knowing he had zero chance with her. Henry didn't see it as cruelty. She could have just blown guys off—been mean to them. It wasn't her way. She was kind. There was a time Henry wasn't sure if she was doing the same thing to him—being nice and then adios amigo. It was a major reason it took him two months to work up the courage to finally ask her out on a date. Well, she'd asked him. But still! It seemed like ancient history now. Had it really only been three days ago since all this began? It didn't seem possible. But it was. And now here he stood, in the middle of 1692, Salem, at the height of the trials, trying like hell to save the lives of the woman he loved and their friends.

David lay Madeleine back down in the blanket of branches, needles, and snow, and slowly rose. He wiped his eyes with the back of his sleeve, reached around behind him, and took the sack from his shoulders. He emptied the sack he carried and pulled out a spade he used to dig traps. He began digging his wife's grave. Henry understood the reasoning behind it. They would never allow her to be buried with dignity in the town cemetery. To them, witchcraft was an abomination. They were too blinded by piety, too afraid of what they didn't understand, and too consumed by the mania stoked by Molonos and his ilk to succumb to reason. Henry felt a touch of shame. Not so long ago, he'd scoffed at the same things. This was David's way to honor his wife. She believed in the magic contained by the natural world, and she would want to be given back to it.

When done, he laid his wife in the hole he'd dug. He picked up the boxes and turned them over a few times in his hands. Then he searched the body of Madeleine. He held something up in front of his face and examined it. Henry couldn't make out what it was, but he suspected it was the very same key he held in his hand back on the table in Wanda's shop. David took the smaller of the two boxes and put the item into it, then placed both items in the grave with his beloved. He mumbled something Henry couldn't quite make out. It sounded like a prayer or chant. David said aloud to the world, "Now, it matters not." He covered the hole back up, disguising it to blend in with the landscape, and whispered, "Our time cometh, in the next life, dearest."

Henry watched in disbelief as David filled in the last of the dirt of his wife's grave—powerless to stop it. He'd not seen this coming. None of them could have. He thought for sure David would have opened the boxes and revealed their contents. They would at least know what they were up against.

David picked up the spade and pulled a large hunting knife from his bag. Henry watched as the bluish-green aura of sorrow surrounding David shifted to an angry dark-red. He headed off in the direction of the footprints leading away from his wife with revenge as his shadow.

Henry was torn. Part of him wanted to follow David and help him in any way he could. But he fought back the urge he shared with David to seek revenge. He now knew where the items were buried, and he had to tell the others.

Chapter Forty-Five

Green Eyes and the Raven

The Camry was completely swallowed by the ever-expanding portal. The ground under her feet was the snow covered terrain of 1692, Salem. There was nowhere for Delilah to hide now, nor was there any need. She'd finished removing the spells Wanda had surrounded the property with that kept her and Solomon and the others from the *Order Immortalis* out. All that was left was to finish what she'd started with Solomon back on that fateful day she'd committed herself to him.

It seemed so surreal to her. We all make plans. We dwell on those plans and labor hour upon hour and day after day to make them into reality. And then, when those plans actually turn into reality, it's still, unbelievably, a surprise it all worked out. But here were the fruits of her labor laid out in front of her. And like anyone who invests their time in something so important, she had insurance. She pulled the nine-millimeter Glock from her bag and moved toward the center of the portal.

Solomon took in the sight before him. The spells Wanda had cast around the property went out like the lights at the beginning of a concert. The excitement and anticipation, for him, were the same.

He was impressed by the power of the two witches and how they'd brought 1692 into the present. He'd always suspected Joanne of being a witch, especially since she was the one Henry finally settled on as his mate. Chesrule had confirmed it for him later, through the viewing at the mortuary. And he'd seen her eyes. It was all the confirmation he needed.

As he made his way toward the center of the grounds, he thought about those green eyes. The way those eyes came at him, barreling out of the woods on that night back in 1692, when the eyes had been David's. Knife in one hand, spade in the other. He felt no pity for David. He was amused by him. David and his wife *actually thought* they could get away with plotting against him. The day he'd seen Madeleine in the town common he knew he'd have to watch her. She'd cast him out of her mind like no one had ever done before. But they never knew about the raven.

Solomon laughed out loud at the memory of the bird as he strolled toward the portal. All the while David had been snooping around the village a large, black raven had tailed him. The bird followed his every move, sat witness to his every conversation as David tried to pry information from the villagers (albeit with admirable cunning, Solomon had to admit).

Molonos' feathered informant didn't stay to watch the direction David took when he left Katherine's home, however. For its own entertainment, it tried to instigate a sexual encounter between Katherine and David. The reason? Who knew? More than likely boredom or depraved curiosity. Chesrule was extremely useful, but he'd had his faults. One of them being a streak of rampant perversion. He'd almost succeeded, too. Had the bird stayed long enough, it may have happened. Instead, it took for granted human weakness in matters of the flesh. It knew nothing of the power of love and was incapable of grasping the concept of fidelity. Confident in the direction the bird had pointed David and Katherine, it had left its post too soon. A mistake that had almost cost the demon its existence back then.

The dark messenger came to him the night of the meeting of the town fathers. They'd been preparing for the winter ahead when the bird rapped three times on the window. Molonos excused himself and met it outside. The bird had morphed back into its human form (the one it used to invade Madeleine's dream—the old hag) and informed Molonos about David's movements. She told him David was on his way back to Madeleine to plot their next move against Molonos, and that he should assemble the villagers and arrest them. Charge the wife with witchcraft and the husband as an enabler. Molonos placed his full trust in Chesrule and acted upon that advice. It was the only mistake he'd made in entrapping the members of the *Foedere In Luna*.

Because of the bird's mistake, they had assumed David and Madeleine were together. And they *never* figured she would defy their orders and run. None of the other accused witches, to that point, had defied the authority of the town fathers. None had even dared. Madeleine, however (and he cursed himself for not seeing it then) was different. And he should have been prepared, given her display of defiance against him in the town common.

Now it had come to this. Madeleine had been beaten to death, and her husband was charging at him for revenge. David bludgeoned and stabbed his way past six of Molonos followers. Molonos watched in quiet admiration at the skill and ferocity with which David dispatched the other six. Such a pity a man as powerful as this wasn't on his side, he thought to himself. When David came flying at the target of his rage, Molonos let David stab him. David plunged the knife into Molonos abdomen with such force it knocked both men to the ground. David rolled from atop Molonos' body and lay beside him, panting from exhaustion and staring up into the raging blizzard. He watched his own heated breath ascend into the fat flakes and trail into the night. No revenge could bring his love back from the grave, but this would have to do. At least in this lifetime, he lamented.

The powerful redhead groaned as he lifted himself from the ground. He had not home nor wife to return to. He planned to make his way to the home of Katherine Andersen. It was the only thing his tattered mind could latch itself to.

He bent to pick up the spade and begin his journey to Katherine's, when he heard movement from behind him. David turned toward the sound. It was Molonos, and he was standing up with the knife still sticking out of his belly. Not one drop of blood darkened the man's overcoat.

David questioned his own sanity. Perhaps, he thought, his grief had been too much to bear. He watched in silence as Molonos strode toward him and pulled the knife from his own belly as casually as pulling it from a sheath. He stopped in front of David and smiled. Every tooth in the wicked man's mouth glowed a malignant yellow. His frosty blue eyes seemed lit from within and ringed with red. It was the last thing David Tranch would see in this lifetime.

Solomon smiled with the memory. And he continued his leisurely stroll toward the four souls in the center of the storm.

Chapter Forty-Six

1692 Meet 2018

Henry popped back into his body. He opened his eyes as he lay face up on the massage table. It seemed strange to him, at first, because he expected to be back under the skylight in Wanda's shop. Instead, he saw much the same scene as only moments before when he'd witnessed the ending to his previous life. It's not every day you get to see that, he thought.

He looked to his left and saw Jo. In the distance, about fifty yards behind Jo, he saw a tall blonde making her way toward the others. She looked vaguely familiar. To his right, slightly over fifty yards away, he saw a tall man in a dark, three-piece suit. On his head sat a fedora with a feather sticking up from the left side. To Henry, he looked like a walking cliché. He twirled a cane in his right hand, leisurely making his way toward the center of the grounds. He'd never seen this man before, but he knew it was Solomon/Molonos.

Henry looked down to his left and would have laughed had the moment been less threatening. Down on one knee and holding on to the table for dear life was Archie. He tapped the doctor on the shoulder and made a shooing gesture with both hands. At first the Doctor was confused by what he meant, and Henry had no time to explain. He pushed his friend backwards and Archie went ass over ponytail and flopped in the snow. Henry seized the bottom of the massage table and flipped it on its side. He had no other choice but to dig with his hands to unearth the box that lay in the grave containing his former body.

Solomon took in the scene in from afar. He threw his head back and laughed loud enough to be heard through the blizzard by everyone at its center. Henry paid him no mind. He dug at the cold, hard dirt like a man whose life depended on it. It did. He made little headway at first—just scraping the top layer of grass and dirt away. The nail on his left middle finger caught on a rock and tore halfway off. He ignored the pain and kept flailing away, finally able to dislodge larger and larger chunks of dirt. He flung them to and fro. He snuck furtive looks to check on the progress Solomon was making toward the middle, but never stopped his frantic digging.

"Oh, Henry. Henry, my boy. You may as well save your strength. It's not there," Solomon said.

Henry ignored the taunt and kept digging.

Wanda and Joanne never flinched at his voice. Not one iota. They continued their lotus-bound vigilance and kept the portal open.

Doctor Love heard Solomon, and it jarred him from a state of confusion. He pushed himself up off the ground, ponytail flapping in the wind, and ran over to the spot across from Henry. He also started ripping up big handfuls of earth.

Another bout of grating laughter from Solomon.

Delilah, gun in hand and satchel at her side, mirrored the pace of her master.

Henry and Archie both dug.

It was Archie who hit the box first. "Henry, here! Help me!"

Both men flung dirt until the box was unearthed. Archie pulled the box out of the ground, cradling it in both arms as if it were a newborn, and stood behind Henry.

Henry stopped digging and just stared into the hole. He saw the stark-white skeletal hand of Madeleine jutting from the dark-brown earth. It looked to Henry as if she were begging him to help her out of the grave. Sadness crawled over him. He felt like crying. He'd only met her for the briefest of moments, and he knew she was the embodiment of both of them, but all the same he felt as if he'd lost a beautiful friend. Literally, he felt as if he'd lost a part of his soul. And weirdly, he realized he had. It was all because of this arrogant, selfish, evil prick. The anger swelled in him now.

Henry stood and faced Solomon, never taking his eyes from the target of his rage. He motioned with his left hand for Archie to hand him the box, and the doctor obliged. The box felt oddly light to Henry. Not good. Nevertheless, he peeled away the black silk wrapping surrounding the box, releasing it to flap wildly like a black, silk raven into the whipping wind of the blizzard.

The box was constructed of dark, cherry wood. It had two gold hinges on its left side and a silver lock halfway down the right front side. It looked exactly the same as the doors in the room from the in-between. The keyhole looked to be the same shape as the ones that adorned the doors in the room with the plush white carpet and the guide who talked in riddles. At the top of the door, covering the front of the box, there were letters matching the words etched into the key in his pocket. ISWAN. The etching on the key looked fairly new. Again, Henry got the feeling those letters meant something to him, and it was something recent, but he still couldn't put his finger on it. The strange thing was, these letters didn't look like they belonged on the box, either. They were puffy, silver-glitter letters—like those adhesive ones you would buy at a Michael's craft store. As confused as he was by this, he never let it show on his face. He gave nothing away. To do so would probably mean disaster.

Henry, keeping his eyes on Solomon, reached into his pocket, and brought out the key. He held it up so his adversary could get a good look at it. Solomon broke stride for the briefest moment. Henry saw it. The fear Solomon felt was plain to see as he observed the key he could never recover. Henry had the feeling the cocky fuck wasn't exactly telling the truth after all. Now it was Henry's turn to smile.

Solomon was close enough now to be within the walls of where the shop still existed three hundred twenty-six years in the future and on the other side of the portal. The blonde lady was, Henry knew, most likely in the mirror position behind him. He didn't chance taking his eyes from Solomon.

"Archie, who's the blonde standing behind me?"

"It appears to be the fiancée of that real estate guy ... Shrumm, I think his name is."

"Was," Delilah said. "I'm afraid the wedding has been recently canceled."

"That's too bad. Who's gonna take care of your big scary dog now? Oh wait, never mind. I took care of him for you, sweet cheeks," Henry taunted her.

Delilah fumed.

"Yes, Chesrule is no more, my dear," Solomon yelled to Delilah. "I'm afraid our old friend Henry here has had the last laugh when it comes to our dearly departed friend. That one hurt Henry, I have to admit. Oh, not nearly as much as it must have hurt both David and Madeleine, well," Solomon looked toward the sky, "today, as it turns out. But it did hurt, nevertheless. He was a good and faithful servant. And a valuable asset. One you took from me. Just another reason it's going to be so satisfying to put an end to all of your lives tonight."

"So sure of yourself, Solomon. Yet here I stand with the very box you tried to keep from David and Madeleine. You think of yourself as this omnipotent being. Some immortal King Shit. But you couldn't keep the box away from a simple hunter and a witch! And you think I'm afraid of you? You think any of us are actually AFRAID of you? Get fucked, pal."

Despite the seriousness of the moment, Jo covered her smile with a hand. She'd never heard Henry this mad before. And his colorful New England temper shone through in his language.

Any trace of the mirth and cockiness of a few moments ago had left Solomon's face. He stared at Henry with the unvarnished hatred he really had for him. For all of them. "Open the box, Henry. Let's see who's got reason to be afraid."

Wanda and Joanne were still in position on the floor and holding the portal open.

Henry put the key into the silver lock and turned.

Solomon, unsmiling, watched.

Delilah held the gun aimed down at her right side.

Archie held his breath, scared shitless.

When Henry opened the box, he was confused for the briefest second. Inside the box were three branches. The branches seemed glued to the back of the box and they formed an upside-down U. It looked to Henry like a makeshift doorway. In the middle of this doorway was a small bag that appeared to contain either sugar or salt—Henry couldn't tell. Above the topmost branch was a sign on a post-it note that said, "READ THIS OUT LOUD: I ORDER THIS PORTAL CLOSED!"

Henry, well past the point of questioning things, did as the note instructed.

"I ORDER THIS PORTAL CLOSED!"

The snow fell harder. The wind whipped faster and blew sheets of snow sideways, forming a vortex encircling all five souls and Solomon. The six of them had all they could do to remain upright. And then, as if God himself had snapped his fingers, the snow and wind stopped. All was black for a few seconds. The lights of the shop flickered and came to life. Candles previously lit in the four compass points of the room sparked back to life. The Dragon's Blood incense, earlier lit on the bar top, glowed anew. Whatever snow remained caught in midair floated without a sound onto the gleaming obsidian floor of Wanda's shop, turning into shining black puddles. And Henry stood dead-center in the middle of the pentacle which held the body of Madeleine just six feet below.

Wanda stood up slowly. She'd been in the lotus position for what, to her, seemed like ages. She was having trouble getting up. Archie moved out from behind Henry and helped her to her feet—his eyes on Solomon as he did so. He guided her over to Henry's left and stood slightly in front and to the left of her in a protective position. Joanne moved to Henry's right and then turned to keep an eye on Delilah.

Delilah moved around the circle of friends in the middle of the room, gun drawn, and made her way over to Solomon's left side.

Solomon had expected a look of total defeat when Henry had opened the box. He expected Henry and Wanda and all the others to be begging for mercy. He'd savored the image for years. He would be in control—maybe play with their emotions a bit—slowly torturing them with hope before he snuffed out their lives. What he didn't expect—not in a million years—was to be in the position he was now. Three hundred twenty-six years he'd waited for this day. He looked around at the walls of the shop with eyes that saw what most others couldn't. All the protections Wanda had set up to keep him out of this shop, to keep him away from her and the other members of the *Foedere In Luna*, were all exactly where they had been before. And he was on the wrong side of them now.

He still knew the box was empty, Delilah had made sure of that. What he hadn't counted on was being trapped in Wanda's Wicca'd Emporium. And he never suspected Henry to possess the power to shred the countermeasures Delilah had used to bring them down. Either he'd underestimated Henry, or he'd put too much faith in Delilah. It had been a long time since Solomon had felt this unsure of his next move. Henry, suddenly, was more than he'd seemed. All the power he'd sensed from Madeleine back in the town common in 1692 now seemed contained in this man standing before him.

With the protections back up for both the property and its people, Solomon was, for the time being, limited in what he could do. He needed time to think. *Ironic*, he thought to himself, *all these years and I still need to buy time.*

"Henry, that was quite the impressive show. Didn't know you had it in you, old boy. It seems you've found a little of the power you enjoyed back in old Salem. But we both know the box is empty, now, don't we?"

"Really?" Henry said. "Because from where I'm standing, and by the look on your face, it seems whatever is in this box is working just fine."

"If that were true, Henry, you would already be using it against me. Wouldn't you?"

"Maybe," Henry said. "But by the same logic, if you could kill us all, right now, we all know you'd do it without batting an eye. Or am I mistaken, Solomon?"

"No. You are not mistaken, Henry. As we can all see, things have taken an unexpected turn. And yes, I expected to be through with my business with the *Foedere In Luna*," Solomon looked at his watch, "about ten minutes ago. But one never goes into one's affairs without making allowances for complications. Thus, I present to you Miss Davis."

Henry focused his attention on Delilah now. She stood with the gun pointed at all of them. Ironically, she was now the most powerful person in the room. Yet, she hadn't just shot them. Why?

"I see you haven't changed a bit, Delilah," Wanda said. "Still hungry for power and prestige. Still chasing the almighty buck. So sad."

Delilah didn't blink. She aimed at Wanda and shot her in the foot.

"You still don't know when to keep your mouth shut, do you, Wanda? That was for stealing my business."

Wanda screamed in pain and dropped to the floor, holding her foot. Archie pulled off his university sweatshirt (thankfully he had a Grateful Dead t-shirt on underneath) and wrapped Wanda's bleeding foot in it. He shot Delilah a wicked look.

Solomon smiled. He was so glad he'd gotten rid of Leonard for his new partner at this moment. Leonard *never* would have acted so decisively in a situation like this.

Delilah next turned her attention to Henry. "So, Henry. Ever decide on buying in Salem?"

"Huh?" It was all Henry could come up with. He was too shocked and angry with Delilah at the moment for anything more.

"Remember our conversation? The one you and I and Leonard had the other day? Near your apartment?"

Henry, irritated, "What about it?"

Delilah tilted her head sideways and to the left, "You don't remember? Think."

She seemed oddly insistent on such a trivial thing. Especially at a time like this. But something about the way she was looking at him caused him to consider the exchange they'd had on Lafayette street. Henry replayed the conversation from the other day in his head ...

... they talked about him possibly buying real estate in Salem. They offered their help. That stupid dog scared the shit out of him, he couldn't forget that. And then she said to him, what was it ... "He really is a sweet dog. I know I sleep well at night, my dreams protected by Herc. And there is nothing more important than that. Wouldn't you agree, Henry?"

He remembered thinking that was strange at the time. 'I sleep well at night, my dreams protected'. He thought it was the "my dreams protected" part that was odd. But the whole fucking conversation left him feeling weird.

A picture formed in his mind. Something about that sentence. Whether it was intuition or training, Henry's mind made a leap. In the medical field, they tended to use acronyms a lot. ER for emergency room, EMT for Emergency Medical Technician, EKG for electrocardiogram. I Sleep Well At Night! THOSE were the words that leaped out in bright, puffy, silver-sparkle letters in Henry's mind. Over the door at the house from the session with Doctor Love. He couldn't identify it as a child, but now, in his adult mind's eye, he could see it! The black bird was a swan! The word etched on the key! The stamp in the Malleus Maleficarum! The box in his hand, right now in front of him!

It was an acronym! And a message! ISWAN!

CHAPTER FORTY-SEVEN

REVELATIONS

HENRY UNDERSTOOD. NOW THE reason Wanda had denied him the knowledge of who his birth mother was came slamming home. If Wanda had disclosed Delilah's identity before this moment, they wouldn't have Solomon trapped in a box like he was right now.

Delilah was the protective white light chasing off the dark figure on the GoPro video! She was the one who wrote the note leading them to the library! She was the one who got them the key and emptied the boxes from Madeleine's grave! She was the one risking her life! All this time he'd just assumed it was Wanda! Delilah was his protector! She was the one who saved all of them by giving up her son! His MOTHER!

And now, Henry had to put on the best acting performance of his life. He realized what was going on now, and how he reacted in this moment meant life or death for all of them.

"What the hell does that have to do with anything right now, Delilah?" Henry asked.

"I just want you to consider the position you're in, Henry. You don't have to die tonight. Neither does Joanne nor the Jerry Garcia-looking guy with the ponytail. *Wanda* caused all the problems here tonight. The only reason I let her live, for the time being, is to offer all of you the chance to leave here alive tonight. I own the real estate firm now. I could offer you any property you'd want within Salem. I could even make you a partner. You and Joanne, if you'd like. Last year alone, we cleared three million in sales. You could become one of us. Become immortal! All the time you'd need to do whatever you want! It beats the alternative, Henry."

Her savvy floored Solomon. He'd never even considered this angle. She was brilliant! He never gave away what he was feeling on the inside. He held position and gladly let her take the reins. He'd chosen well.

Henry made it look as though he were seriously considering her offer. He wasn't sure if Joanne yet understood what was going on here. He had to trust she'd figured it out. Archie probably wouldn't know, but that, too, could be used to their advantage. It was a fine line Henry had to tread now.

"Why should I trust you, Delilah? You just shot one of my friends in the foot. You're holding a gun on all of us now. You've brought Solomon directly into the one place he couldn't get into himself, and for the precise reason of trapping all of us together at the same time in order to kill us. And for what, exactly? So he can go on living forever? So all the *Order Immortalis* can go on living forever?"

"No. That's not what this is about, Henry," Delilah said. "Solomon never wanted things to go this way. I don't know what lies Wanda has been filling your head with. Although, knowing Wanda as I do, I can imagine. Solomon is simply interested in defending what he's created. In being allowed to exist as he's always existed. He wants the constant chase to bring him down to cease. He wants to be left alone!"

Henry took his time. Appearing to actually debate the points Delilah had laid out in his head. He waited a few moments before answering and said, "If that truly is what Solomon wants, and I doubt it, I have a few conditions that have to be met. They are non-negotiable."

Joanne looked at Henry like he'd lost his mind. She said nothing, thankfully. Henry hoped she was doing an incredible job of acting. If the look on her face were genuine, Henry feared he had just lost her for good.

Archie shook his head and looked at the ground. Disappointment and resignation oozed from his posture.

"And what might those be, Henry?" Solomon asked.

"None of us here dies tonight. I don't care what you offer me or Jo or Archie. If Wanda dies, there is no way any of us leaves here alive tonight. I will do whatever is within my power (and as you can see, there is no portal anymore, so it appears I have Madeleine's mojo back) to make sure both of you end up as dead as anyone else you might try to kill here tonight. You walk out of here now, take whatever it is you *think* is a threat with you, do whatever it is you think you have to do to keep things as they are, and leave all of us alone. Especially Wanda. Understood?"

"That seems fair enough, Henry," Solomon said. "But there is one rather colossal problem with your conditions. As we both know, and let's stop pretending otherwise, I possess the item that was contained within the box. Delilah, please show all the item."

Delilah, keeping the gun on everyone, reached her left hand into the satchel she'd slung around her neck and produced a pewter flask. It appeared to be about the size of a liter bottle of vodka. The top of it, however, resembled a vodka bottle in no fashion. The seal was rectangular. It had two sturdy silver bolts that shot through from front to back, and the sides were adorned with latch seals like those you'd find on old-fashioned mason jars. Holding down the latch seals, surrounding the perimeter of the rectangular seal, was gold wire. Opening the flask would be no small feat.

About midway down the middle of the front of the flask—the part facing Henry and his friends—there was a blotch of red wax. It was the wax people in times far past would have sealed a letter with. Under the waxy blotch was the raised shape of what appeared to be some type of label or sign. Unreadable.

"So, what's in the bottle, Solomon?" Henry asked.

"That, my friend, is none of your business. If, however, you and your compatriots wish to leave here tonight with your lives, there is one condition that must be met. And, to quote you, Henry, this is non-negotiable."

"I'm listening," Henry said.

"The item which Delilah holds before you is very important to me. As to the reasons for that, again, it is none of your business. It is my property and its contents are not your concern. But, much like the spells that have kept me out of this establishment, and much like the spells that have kept you all alive, despite my wishes to the contrary, the flask, MY PROPERTY, is also bewitched. I can not lay my hands on it without it causing excruciating pain at the slightest touch. Indeed, it produces pain just to look at it. This is unacceptable. When David buried it with Madeleine, he applied a spell to the object. I'd thought him just a simple hunter, but it appears Madeleine had taught her husband a thing or two about the craft. I need the spell lifted by the one who applied it. Do this, and we can all part. There is obviously no risk to you and the others ... including Wanda, much to my chagrin. As we can all see, the protections on you and the others are again active. I want what is mine, nothing more."

Henry looked at Joanne. She did not return his gaze. Disappointed, she asked, "Is this what you want, Henry?"

"I think it's the only way to go, Jo. Don't you?"

"I think you're selling your soul to the devil. I'll do it, if that's what you want. But this changes things, Henry."

Henry's heart sunk. It was killing him to think he might lose her.

Joanne left Henry's side and made her way slowly toward Delilah. She stopped in front of her, never looking Delilah in the eye, and reached out her hand. It was a display in defeat. Delilah put the flask in Jo's hand and stepped back. Jo closed her eyes and squeezed a tear from them. It wasn't hard to do, she'd been tearing up since Henry had, apparently, given in to Solomon and Delilah. Still holding the flask in her right hand, Jo reached with her left hand and swiped a tear from her cheek. The only way she could remove the spell cast on the flask, being that David cast it, was to use a tear from the eyes of the same soul. She carefully swiped the tear around the perimeter of the flask's top and said, simply, "I remove the binding. So mote it be." She handed the flask to Delilah and made her way back toward Henry. She kept her head forward and down. Jo glanced sideways and to her right, in Henry's direction, and winked. She took position again next to Henry and waited with the rest of them.

"Thank you all for your cooperation tonight," Solomon said. "Delilah, please shoot every one of them. Save Wanda for last, if you don't mind."

Delilah put the flask back in her satchel and made her way over to the members of the *Foedere In Luna*. She pointed the gun at Joanne first, but did not fire. She smiled and moved on to Henry, and did not fire. She bent down in front of Archie and did not fire. Archie did not give her the satisfaction of looking afraid. He stared at her in cold defiance. Kneeling in front of him, Delilah raised the gun slightly above his head and fired. The bullet ricocheted off of a pipe behind the five of them and back in Solomon's direction. One bottle on the bar, behind and to Solomon's right, exploded with the bullet's impact and sprayed its contents onto the floor.

Why would the old bag still have a bar? Solomon thought. She was clean and sober. No matter, she'll be dead in a minute or two.

Five sets of ears within the circle were set to ringing from the blast. Delilah, kneeling and with her back facing Solomon, knowing how he was reacting to her tortuous display, took advantage of the distraction caused by the ricochet and the exploding bottle, and removed the flask from her satchel, handing it to Wanda. She got back up, turned around, and made her way back to Solomon's side. Smiling all the while. Solomon was more than pleased by his new partner.

"And now dear witches, dear warlock, and the good doctor. It's time to say goodbye."

Wanda stood up then, and held the flask out in front of her. "I agree, Solomon. You've been around for way too long." She stripped the gold wire from around the top. She popped the latches on both sides and pushed the now loosened bolts (she'd undone them as Delilah blocked her from view on her way back to Solomon's side) through the top and onto the floor. They made a tinny clanking sound as they bounced several times on the gleaming obsidian surface. To Solomon, it was the loudest sound in the world. She ripped off the rectangular lid and then all hell broke loose.

"Shoot them! Shoot them now!" Solomon bellowed at Delilah.

Delilah whirled toward Solomon and emptied the gun into his belly. She knew this would have no effect. He wouldn't die from gunshot wounds. It just felt so good! This son of a bitch had cost her a life as a mother. She'd given up so much to protect Henry. As the bullets flew, she thought of the day he'd been taken away from her, to live in Maine with his aunt and uncle. She thought of all the times she had to watch him from afar. The tears she'd cry at night after watching him play baseball in Maine. The times in his life that would have been so special between a mother and her son. Birthdays, First Holy Communion, girlfriends and the breakups that inevitably follow, prom night, graduation, and a million other little, special moments she could never, ever share with him. The only time she could even get close to him was when her son dreamed at night. She'd learned a long time ago how to travel the astral plane. She lived her life as a mother there. It was the only way, until today. Every bullet she fired into his miserable, evil body felt like justice. Justice for her, for Henry, for Wanda and Jo and Archie. And justice for the soul trapped in the flask for close to a thousand years.

Solomon was affected by the blasts, just as any mortal might have been, aside from the fact there was no blood where the bullets entered. The powerful handgun sent him reeling backwards into the bar. The bottles rattled on the shelf. Two or three hit the floor and shattered, spilling the clear liquid inside them all over the black floor. Solomon slipped on the remains of those dead glass soldiers and hit the floor hard. Shards impaled his arms and back, and he screamed in pain. But the pain he felt was not only from the glass shards. It was from the holy water covering those shards, seeping through his clothes, and coming into contact with the actual body under the skin. The body of his true nature.

For hundreds of years he'd passed himself off as human. He lied to his followers with promises of wealth and power and immortality. Made them believe they could live forever. Showed them how to extend their lives at the cost of the health and sanity of others. Promised them the world, and he'd delivered. Oh, how he'd delivered! He made countless people wealthy beyond their wildest dreams. Made common men and women into leaders of nations, captains of industry, and trusted servants of religion. He had his fingers in all the right pies. All for the glory of himself! And to show both heaven and hell he could rule in his own domain.

And now, he writhed in pain on the floor. The soul in the flask was now free, causing the disintegration of the flesh Solomon occupied. His true form was now on display for all to see.

For over nine hundred years he'd occupied the body of the fallen soldier. A soul poised on the brink of eternity he'd captured on the battlefield during the Crusades. He'd possessed the man as he lay on the ground, bleeding. The battle had ended, his superiors had counted him for dead. That night, amidst the corpses and the stench from the Battle of Artah—one of the many battles of the Crusades—the demon who now called himself Solomon took advantage of the dark and fled to the woods. He extracted the soul of the soldier and placed it in the flask that, until today, had remained sealed. It was the only way he could maintain the flesh of this body throughout the centuries. Were the soul ever to escape the bonds of the flask, it would seek to move on and grow in spirit in its next incarnation. Being removed prematurely from the body and trapped in the flask, the demon could safely occupy and preserve the flesh it now inhabited.

And now, Henry and Wanda and the rest of the *Foedere In Luna* had defeated him. He'd not thought it possible. And he would never allow the truth of the saying, "Pride goeth before the fall," to enter his mind.

The demon peeled the layers of flesh and clothing from his body. Its exterior now a perfect match for the obsidian floor of the Emporium. Unencumbered by the body of the soldier, the dark entity stretched to its full height. It was massive. Its crimson eyes were set under brow bones that protruded outward. The nostrils at the end of the long, pointy nose flared. Its curved horns tapered down the outside of the brows and framed the face all the way down to the chin and past the end, culminating in two wicked looking spikes. Where there should have been hands, there were three claws on either side—gleaming black daggers. The only way any of the five souls in the middle could even discern its features was by the light from the room reflecting off its skin. Had the lights gone out, the only thing visible would have been its eyes, and the snakelike pupils forming their center.

Henry estimated the fucker had to be at least seven-and-a-half feet tall. He watched as the last of the remains of the poor soul Solomon had inhabited slid from the demon's body and splatted to the floor. It stalked back and forth on two muscular, hair-covered legs. Each with a cloven hoof at the end. It stared at each of the five in turn, as if searching for a weakness. It knew better than attempting to cross the barrier of the outer circle of the room with the pentacle. Even in its enraged state, the foresight of the old witch impressed the dark entity. It could smell the salt sealed into the golden outer ring protecting the inner ring where its enemies stood. What had once been Solomon probed the room, looking for a way to get at them. There was no way into the middle of the room, and no way out.

It focused on Delilah. It roared, "Betrayal!" The dark one paced back and forth. Its claws flexed. Its hideous eyes never strayed from Delilah. "After all I did for you! After all I showed you! This! This is how you repay me!" The last word came out sounding like the guttural echo at the end of a lion's roar.

"How I repay you? As if I owe you a fucking thing!" Delilah roared back. "I had to endure years of watching you cause the suffering of countless people. Watch you suck the life out of others. All so you could keep up the facade of immortality. How many deaths did you cause in the name of "immortality"? How many sick and suffering did you leave behind when you drained them as they slept? Do you know what that does to a person? Do you even care? Well, I know what it does to people. It causes depression, madness, suicide, cancer, and a shit-ton of other problems. I watched good people die just so you could preserve yourself in that poor soul's body. Many of the people who bought your bullshit and joined your pathetic *Order* are dead. Leonard included. The only one who benefited one iota from anything having to do with *The Order* was you. They sold their souls for a lie.

"But you know what, Solomon? I learned. I sat back, and I watched, and I learned. Do you think you're immune from the very things you use to invade the minds of others? Are you so fucking arrogant you think you're untouchable? I know who you are. I saw YOUR dreams. I know what you fear in the deepest, darkest corners of your mind. I know what happens to you if you *fail*. I saw where you *go*. There is no money. There is no power. There is no pleasure, or pain. All the things a pathetic wannabe god values above all else. You know nothing of what it means to live. You know nothing of love or loyalty, except to yourself. You will never know what it means to sacrifice—to risk all that is holy, all you love in the world—so they may go on. You're nothing. And that's what waits for you. And it terrifies you."

The demon stalked back and forth, toeing the line just outside the circle of gold-flaked salt protecting his enemies.

"And what, exactly, have you sacrificed, woman! You're so high and mighty! You talk of love and loyalty. Yet the man you committed to marry is a stain on the windshield of my limousine. And you never batted an eye. When you let me fuck you behind his back, where was your loyalty then? My compliments though, you were a fantastic fuck. When you made the deal—and let us not forget, you did forfeit your soul—where was your loyalty to your longtime friend, Wanda? Please," he mocked. "Enlighten us all, you magnificent martyr!"

Delilah smiled. "Even now, you're nothing but a blind, arrogant fool. I never wanted a thing from you. I was there to watch you, to learn from you. And to *steal* from you."

The dark entity stopped pacing back and forth. Its crimson eyes bored into Delilah's. She met his gaze with defiance.

"That's right, Solomon. Much like you've done to others for centuries, I used you. And the best part ... until a few minutes ago, you knew nothing about it. I admit, I felt some remorse for Leonard. Not a lot. He was almost as evil as you, just a lot dumber. And it tore me up inside, having to pretend to end my relationship with Wanda. I love her more than any friend I've ever had in my life. She's smarter than both of us by a long shot. And the times I had to give my body to you, as disgusted as it makes me feel now—and you suck in bed, by the way—were the times your guard was completely down. It's a funny thing, ecstasy. It's almost exclusively the only time one's mind, demon or otherwise, is only on one thing. And while you were in the middle of it, I took a peek into the places I couldn't go when you were asleep. And I found out one very important truth. Your name. And I know that's not good for you. No, not one bit good for you at all. And one last thing, before you become nothing. You mentioned sacrifice. I know what it is to sacrifice. I gave up the one person in the world who means the most to me. Who I love more than anything in the world. I cried myself to sleep many nights because I had to give up my son."

She saw the look of disbelief on the demon's face. "That's right, Henry is my son. I had to give him up to protect him. To keep you from knowing who he was long enough to get to this night. I knew if you ever saw him before we could protect him, you'd kill him. Wanda knew I'd gotten pregnant when we were both young. It was an accident. At least, that's what we both thought at the time. But she knew who he *used* to be the instant she first met Henry. She felt the spirit of Madeleine within my child. She found me a place outside Salem, away from you and your *Order*. I watched Henry's dreams as a child. When he was about four, the memories of Madeleine entered his dreams. It's funny how children, so open-minded, can recall memories from their past lives. And that's when the danger really started. I told Wanda it was happening, and that's the day we moved him. Thank God my sister and her husband could take him. The rest, as they say, is history."

Joanne was the only one in the room, at that point, who didn't know Delilah was Henry's mother. Her jaw dropped to the floor. If the moment hadn't been so serious, it would have been funny.

"If you know my name, say it," the dark entity growled. "See what happens."

"Once more the fool, Solomon," said Wanda. "If it were that easy, say as in a simple exorcism, we would be done now. We would simply command you to return below and you would be gone. But to say your name is not enough. You've betrayed your master, and you know it. There is no place for you there. And now there is no place for you here. I will cast you into the void, Inanis."

He turned his attention to the pint-sized witch at the mention of his name. She held the flask in her hand. On the floor, at her feet, were shards of the red wax once covering the front of the flask. She'd peeled it from the front while Delilah had engaged the demon. What lay underneath was revealed. A bronze placard with its name etched into it. When Delilah had removed the flask from Madeleine's grave, she'd had it blessed by a priest. It glowed pure white when Wanda held it forth. The entity once named Molonos, then Solomon, and a host of other identities, now knew genuine fear in the form of its own name. It had one trump card left.

"We both know there is only one way this can end, old woman. Step outside the circle and brand me. You know it's the only way." Inanis flicked its shiny, black, forked tongue in Wanda's direction.

Henry grabbed the flask from Wanda's hand and sprinted full speed toward the demon.

"HENRY, NO!" Wanda screamed.

Too late. As the word NO left Wanda's mouth, Henry was already airborne—arm extended, brand out. He was gonna take this fucker out, or die trying.

Inanis stepped back, as far as the holy water behind him would allow, and swatted at Henry's hand in a desperate defensive move. The flask in Henry's outstretched hand came in contact with the claws of the demon. Sparks flew, and the flask bounced on the floor with a metal thonk, thonk, thonk. Henry flew past Inanis and crashed into the base of the bar. More bottles tumbled to the ground and exploded. Holy water flew in a thousand different directions. More than a few of those drops landed on the hair covered legs of Inanis and immediately burned through to the skin. Patches of white light leaked from where the holes in his legs had opened up. The demon screamed. And within that scream was agony and rage, but above all else, fear.

Delilah ran after Henry. Everything seemed like it was moving in slow motion. The satchel fell from her shoulder, she could hear the tinkle of her keys within when it hit the floor. Joanne reached out for Delilah to stop her, grabbing the back of her coat. It barely slowed her down, but the momentum pulled Joanne forward and she lost her balance, tumbling toward the outer ring.

Delilah heard the flask hit the floor and dove after it, gliding on the holy water toward the flask's direction. Archie, watching from his protective stance over Wanda, saw Delilah gliding through the holy water, and had the absurd thought it looked like the world's weirdest slip and slide.

Joanne lost her battle to stay upright and tumbled across the outer ring and into a stack of beanbag chairs in the room's corner.

Delilah reached out and grabbed the flask at the last second, almost sliding by it, and slammed into the wall between where the demon flailed in agony, and where Henry was just now getting to his feet. She scrambled up from the floor, flask in hand, and sprinted full out at the demon with murder on her mind. She was closing fast. Inanis had not seen her coming until the last second. Right before she could sink the brand into the demon's flesh, it flashed its left claw out with inhuman speed. The razor-sharp daggers impaled Delilah, dead-center under the sternum. She sucked in a surprised breath. Her eyes locked with Inanis' eyes. He held her suspended above the floor, as if she were a trophy. Before she slid from the end of his talons, he smiled at her.

Again the flask bounced on the floor. The demon watched as it neared Delilah's son. Henry was unsteady on his feet and slightly dazed from slamming headfirst into the bar. He hadn't noticed the flask as it tumbled toward him, but Inanis had.

Joanne watched in horror as Inanis reached down for the flask, picked it up from the side opposite its name, and headed straight at Henry. She acted on pure instinct. She took advantage of the slippery floor and mimicked Delilah's dive. She knew from the moment she moved her feet what she intended. She'd lost Henry in the life before, when Madeleine was murdered by Solomon's followers. And in that moment, she was David again. Somehow the rage and the anger and the lust for revenge rose within her from that past life, and she channeled it into her next move. There was no fear. There was no hesitation. There was only Henry's life at that moment, and it was all she cared about.

As she slid toward the demon, she seized one of the intact bottles of holy water. She hit the bar with both feet, sprang up behind the demon, jumped on its back, and smashed the bottle directly into its eyes. It stiffened up in agony and bucked her from its back. It flailed wildly, swinging its daggered fingers in all directions. Joanne was still behind it, and off balance, when one claw ripped a gash in her belly. She stumbled backward and fell. Her head hit the floor hard, and she lay in the mess of holy water and glass, bleeding and unconscious.

The demon continued to flail, smashing blindly into anything it could lay its claws on. Glass shattered. It smashed the heavy mahogany bar like it was made from balsa, sending splinters flying in all directions. Beanbag chairs exploded on contact, sending little round styrofoam balls in a thousand directions. It was perfect cover for Henry. He had finally regained his bearings. He made his way quietly toward the flask and picked it up. He took in the scene. His mother lay bleeding on the ground. His soon-to-be wife lay in a twisted heap behind the flailing demon. Wanda and Archie were still safe inside the outer ring. All those he loved were hurt or held captive by this entity. It was time for it to die.

"INANIS!" Henry bellowed, and then he charged.

The blinded demon turned toward Henry's voice. It made for Henry. The two were on a collision course, but only one had sight. Henry launched himself, feet first, at the demon and planted his Adidas squarely in the middle of the dark one's chest. Inanis toppled over backwards and crashed into the wrecked bar. Every remaining bottle of the holy water exploded on impact. Henry had to block his ears as the demon roared in a thousand different voices. White light shot through its body as the holy water ate at its remaining flesh. Henry stood over it and watched as its strength drained by the moment, its body marinating in the holy water. It lay helpless on the ruined bar. Henry knelt down to its left, yanked the demon's head up by one of its horns, and turned it to face him. Although Inanis was blinded, Henry wanted to make sure it knew what was coming.

"Any last words before you become nothing, void boy?"

The demon laughed. "Yes, I may be headed to the void, Henry. But your mother is going with me."

Henry took the flask and slammed it into the forehead of Inanis. The demon spasmed. Its legs and arms shot out and bucked like Henry had hit it with the world's most powerful taser. It screamed obscenities in several languages and cursed all the occupants in the room by name. The flailing and the cursing wound down after a time. Slowly it stopped, gurgled out its last death rattle, and the body was still. Henry stood back and watched as, piece by piece, white light consumed the last of the demon. The essence of Inanis, or Solomon, or Molonos, or the many other names it had gone by, floated toward the ceiling and vanished before reaching it. It was utterly destroyed. Neither above, nor below. Not east. Not west. Not north. Not south. Nowhere.

Chapter Forty-Eight

Bittersweet

Henry got up to check on Joanne. From where he was standing, she didn't look good. There was a lot of blood pooled around her midsection and on the floor underneath. He rolled her over and tapped her lightly on the cheek. "Jo, Jo, ... come on Jo, wake up! Please ..."

She moaned lightly and her eyes fluttered open. "Hey, Band-aid boy. Wouldn't happen to have one on you right now, would ya?"

Henry laughed a little despite the situation. "Still a smart ass, even when you're a bloody mess. Can you get up?"

She unfolded herself slowly from the floor, holding on to his arm for support. Henry helped steady her, walked her over to one of the fallen barstools, righted it, and sat her gently down upon it. He tore away the bottom half of her shirt. "Oh, kinky," she said.

He shook his head, smiling as he inspected her. "Well, it looks like a mostly superficial wound, thank God. Now let me look at your head. I'm more worried about a concussion than ..."

Joanne cut him off. "Henry ..." She pointed.

Henry followed the direction of her finger.

His mother lay on the floor, not moving. He ran over and knelt down next to her. Henry put his cheek right above Delilah's mouth. She was still breathing, barely. Taking great care, he turned her head so it faced the ceiling. He followed the same procedure he'd used on Jo, tapping lightly to bring her back to consciousness. He knew right away, looking at the wound, it was probably fatal. He just wanted to say thank you. And goodbye. "Mom, can you hear me, it's me ... it's Henry."

Nothing.

"Mom? Please, don't leave me yet." He welled up. He couldn't help it when he thought about what she had given up for him, for all of them. The reality hit him in waves. "I love you. I need to tell you something before you go. We're all here for you, Mom. Wanda and Archie and Joanne and me. We all want to say goodbye."

He couldn't believe what he was saying. It was too goddamned much, too goddamned fast.

The others came over to Henry and his mom. Joanne looked at Wanda. No words passed. Both wounded witches knelt, as best they could, on either side of Delilah, and placed their left hands on her shoulders. They closed their eyes and quietly prayed to the power greater than themselves. Delilah's body seemed to steady then. Her breathing, though shallow and bare, became a bit more regular. Her eyelids flickered briefly and then opened. It reminded Henry of the way the bathroom light would come on back at his apartment. He smiled at her through brimming tears and, in a voice thick with sorrow, simply said, "Hi Mom."

"Henry," barely a whisper, "my brave boy. I'm so proud of you."

Tears flowed from his eyes and landed silently on his mother's shattered body.

"I have so much I want to say to you, Mom."

She smiled, "I don't think we have that much time, Henry."

He smiled at her through the tears. "I don't know how to thank you. All you've given up. All you've had to go through, just to keep me alive ... to keep all of us alive. You saved all of us. I don't ... I just wish we could have more time ..."

Delilah reached up with the last of her strength and held her hand to Henry's cheek. "Sleep well at night, Henry. I love you ..."

And she was gone.

Henry sat on the floor cross-legged next to his mom, with his head in his hands, and quietly sobbed. Joanne sat down next to him and rubbed his back to comfort him. It was all she could think to do. Archie and Wanda stood in front of them. Archie had his arm around Wanda's shoulders. Both silently cried.

As Wanda took in the sadness in front of her, her mind took off in a different direction. The flight of her memory landed on a day way back when she was a teenager. A day filled with dread at the thought of going to a party later that night. And not just any party, it was a party with boys! She'd never been to anything more than a sweet-sixteen, and even *that* had been just a few friends. She'd never been Miss Popularity.

Wanda had always felt different—apart from others because of her gifts. Not every young teenage girl wakes up in the middle of the night and gets a visit from a soul who wants you to tell them why they're dead. Some of them don't even know they're dead, but they know you can see them. They know you're the only one who's eye they can catch. The only one who can give them an answer. Any answer would do, they're so desperate for one. Their desperation makes them relentless. They won't let you sleep. They show up when you eat. When you're with friends. At a party. At a funeral. Even when you're using the bathroom. And when you don't really grasp what's happening, when you don't know how to shut it off because you don't even know why it's happening in the first place, it can drive you to the brink. And when your parents don't believe you, when they tell you the person you see in the middle of the night was just a dream, or you're just imagining things, or The Church says there are no such things as ghosts, or maybe you need to see a doctor and take a pill because maybe you're a wee bit touched ... it makes you want to blot things out. So, you're left with few choices: continue on and let it drive you mad, or drink and drug to mute the spiritual gifts you've been given. Wanda had walked through door number two.

This was the place Wanda was at in her life the night her childhood friend DeeDee invited her to the party at the frat-house. DeeDee was the only person in the world who completely understood Wanda. DeeDee saw the same things, too. And was living under almost the same conditions Wanda was, save for one difference—her older sister, Jeannie. And thank God for Jeannie Davis. Jeannie was the only one who understood both of them, and more importantly, believed them. That belief went a long way to keeping both Wanda and Delilah sane. And her boyfriend Dominick was a sweetheart. He would always poke fun at Wanda and Delilah, but playfully, calling them the S-S-Soul Sisters any time the two of them came into a room or showed up together somewhere. The two friends loved it. It was like a secret joke they shared. Dom wasn't a huge believer in things paranormal, but he wasn't an asshole about it either. And they adored him for it.

Wanda had walked over to the Davis house that night after dinner. She remembered all of it so vividly. The smell of the late October air. The cozy silver cast of twilight. The leaves that had given up their battle to remain tree-bound and died in glorious colors, only to be crunched under her feet. And the hopeful anxiety of what the night ahead might hold.

She turned the corner and saw her three friends in the garage. They were quietly talking and laughing when they saw her and waved her over. Dom went and filled a cup for her. When she asked what it was, he'd replied, "the house special." It was his own custom concoction of Mountain Dew and Vodka. He called it "The Dewdriver." He handed Wanda the red, half-filled Solo cup with a smile. Wanda lifted the cup to her lips and took the daintiest of sips. Not bad. She sipped and talked with Jeannie and Dom and DeeDee for the next half hour, and then all four set out for the U. It was less than half a mile from the Davis household.

A strange thing happened for Wanda on that walk to the U. She started to feel happy. Felt like maybe the world wasn't such a horrible place, and maybe, just maybe, this was going to be a good night. Her formerly clumsy mouth wasn't so clumsy anymore, and conversation flowed freely between the four of them. A feeling of well-being she'd *never* felt before seemed to course through her entire being. Things that were on her mind, seemingly 24-7, were easily cast to the wayside. She wasn't worried about her parents or what they thought of her. Ghosts? What ghosts? All was right with the world. And boys? Bring em on! She actually felt a tad horny right now. The dread which had lived squarely within her guts all day long about this party was miraculously supplanted by an alien eagerness to meet new people. And all it took was half a cup full of booze! Problems solved!

All four of them arrived at the frat house with a good buzz. Jeannie and Dom started talking with a couple they were friendly with as soon as they made it through the door. After introducing Wanda and DeeDee to the couple, the older kids pretty much got wrapped up in conversation with them, and left Wanda and DeeDee to their own devices.

The two friends mingled among the others, making conversation here and there. Drinks flowed freely at the party, and neither of the two were without social lubricant for long.

At one point, they found their own little corner of the room to hang out and people-watch. They chitchatted about everything, and nothing in particular—the comfortable banter of two longtime friends. But two pretty girls in a corner at a party don't remain alone for long. Two young freshmen made their way over to Wanda and DeeDee's corner of the world. They introduced themselves and informed the girls they were both psych majors at the U and asked if they'd like to have a drink with them ...

CHAPTER FORTY-NINE
GOOD NIGHT MRS. G

HENRY STOOD UP AND Wanda snapped back to reality, for the time being. There was much to do now. She hated to bring any of it up at a time like this, but there really wasn't much choice. It would be light out soon and the stark reality of the situation was two dead bodies on the grounds of Wanda's Wicca'd Emporium, and no real good explanation why. As if on cue, and to Wanda's eternal gratitude, it was Joanne who spoke first.

"I hate to be the one to say this, Henry, but we have to take your mom from here. And that asshole outside, too. There is no way to explain this to anyone ... well, no explanation anyone would *believe*."

Henry wiped his eyes with his sleeve and nodded. There really wasn't much to argue about. She was right, and he was really in no condition to even think straight. He'd let her take the lead with gratitude.

"I'll be right back," Wanda said. She hobbled her way to the front of the shop and came back with a long cardboard tube in one hand and a bunched up blue painter's tarp in the other. She handed the items to Joanne.

"What are these for?" Jo asked.

"The cardboard tube is a black burial cloth with a gold pentacle embroidered in the middle. It pains me to have DeeDee not receive the proper Wiccan ceremony, but under these circumstances, it's all I can do," Wanda said.

Jo said, "... and I'm assuming the blue thing with paint all over it ... "

"For Leonard. And even *that's* too good for him. But we gotta move him, too," Wanda said.

Henry, without a word, reached out his hand, and Joanne gave him the tube.

He pulled the cloth from the tube and shook it out. Once unfurled, he carefully placed the burial cloth over his mother, and he and Joanne tugged at the sides opposite each other until the pentacle rested perfectly in the center. Henry and Jo then tucked both sides neatly under Delilah and pulled the gold sash tight at each end to seal the cloth.

Archie came over then and nodded at Henry. Both men lifted the body and carried Henry's mom out to the Cadillac that had once belonged to their ancient enemy. They opened the back hatch and laid her down on the left side of the cargo area, leaving room for Leonard's body on the right. Joanne met them at the back of the Caddy with the painter's tarp and the satchel that had belonged to Delilah. Jo laid out the tarp as Henry and Archie peeled Leonard's body from the driver's seat. Most of the blood had dried since

Leonard had shed his mortal coil, but it was still quite a mess to deal with. Archie wretched a few times and almost dropped his end of the body, but he managed. They heaved him in next to Delilah, wrapped him up, and shut the doors. Archie gave them both a hug and went back inside.

"Are you okay, Henry?" Jo asked.

"I'll be alright. Let's get this over with."

"Wanda said the keys to the mortuary would be in Delilah's satchel. We can cremate them there."

Henry nodded. He got into the driver's seat, oblivious of the crud Leonard's body had left behind. Jo got in on the passenger's side. The keys were still on the dash where Solomon's driver had left them. As Henry started the engine of the hearse, the irony struck him that its owner intended a very different payload to be in the cargo space at the end of this night. Shit happens, he thought, and laughed out loud.

Jo looked over at him. "What's funny?"

Henry shook his head. "Meh, I was just thinking about how we were supposed to be the ones in the back of this truck tonight. And the one's supposed to be going into the furnace."

"Yeah, shit happens though," Jo said.

"That was my exact thought, to the word, like two seconds ago."

"Great minds ... " Jo said.

"True, true." Henry smiled. "When all this is over, after tonight, I think we should get married, Jo."

Now it was Jo's turn to laugh.

"What?" Henry asked.

"You know, I've probably thought about the day someone would propose to me a thousand times. I imagined it in a million places ... and not one time did I imagine it would be in a hearse on the way to the morgue. But it's *you*. And the time and the place and the circumstances don't mean jack. The answer is yes. And here's a little secret for you, Henry Trank-Davis. The day you walked into the Cracked Cauldron, we were already married."

Henry gave her thigh a squeeze and held his hand there. Jo slipped her fingers under his hand and laced hers with his. He pulled her hand up and kissed the back of it. He drove on to the morgue, a jumbled mess of joy and sorrow.

)✪(

Archie began cleaning up while Wanda sat in the only corner of the room not festooned with debris. She sat in one of the black beanbag chairs and kept her injured foot raised up on another. The wound wasn't as bad as the bleeding seemed to indicate. She'd been grazed, lost half a nail on her big toe, but otherwise it was fine. It didn't even hurt much. A small price to pay, she thought, compared to Delilah.

Her thoughts turned to Henry. He would have a lot of questions. Some she could answer. Others, in time, would answer themselves. After the cleanup was over, they would all need a day to rest. Clear out the cobwebs, mend the wounds (physical and otherwise), and then all sit down and have a good talk about it.

She waited for Archie to come back from the front of the shop. He had just put the Malleus Maleficarum back in the empty wooden stand in the storefront window. Back in its rightful place, with its rightful owner. It was the last bit of reluctant deception she'd ever have to engage in again, now that it was home. It had been Delilah's idea to put the book in the library. She knew about Chesrule and how they would use him. They'd needed to draw him out. It had worked. Not like they'd expected—the encounter in the library was more risky than they'd imagined. But, in the end, Solomon took the bait and sent his mindless servant after Joanne and then the Tranks. And they'd both paid with their very existence.

"Archie, could you stop for a minute? I need to talk to you about something."

He put down the broom and walked over, pulled up a beanbag chair, and plopped himself down. Archie almost tumbled over the back of it, then righted himself. He never really got the hang of the damned things. And the getting-out-of-them part was the worst.

"What's up?"

"I've been thinking. Could I impose on you to have Henry, Joanne, myself, and Jeannie and Dominik Trank over to your house? I'd like to have a get together, maybe a barbecue in your backyard, so we can talk over everything that's happened. Would you mind? I'll pay for everything, of course. I just think we all need to get together and ... I don't know, see where it all goes from here. I've got a lot on my mind and a lot to tell Henry. And there is something you really need to know about too ... but tonight is definitely not the time."

Archie looked at her warily and said, "You're making me nervous. Is it bad? Do I need to be worried?"

She smiled, gave him a wink, and said, "No worries, it's a good thing, Archie."

)☾✪☽(

By the time Archie and Wanda had left Wanda's Wicca'd Emporium, Henry and Jo stood in front of the furnace at Salem Estate Funeral Home. They'd already disposed of Leonard. Delilah's body lay in front of them on the gurney, awaiting its journey into the flames. Henry hugged Joanne hard. She could feel the fresh tears he'd been crying on her neck, which brought on more of her own. When they released, Henry asked her, "Will you help me put her in?"

She said, "Of course."

Henry bent down and kissed the place on the burial cloth where his mother's head lay underneath. The flames from the furnace turning the tears on his cheeks first orange, then drying them. He said, "Thank you for everything, Mom. Rest in peace. I love you." He stood, looked at Jo, and they both turned and gently pushed Henry's mother into the furnace.

When all was done and the furnace was cold, they left the mortuary and made their way on foot to Henry's apartment. The early morning was cool and dark. The rain had finally stopped. The only snow on the ground was a mile-and-a-half away, outside Wanda's Wicca'd Emporium, and nowhere else in Salem. They walked together through an uncharacteristically quiet Salem Halloween morning. They both knew about the mayhem that would descend on the town later today. It was the same every year.

They climbed the stairs to Henry's second-floor apartment. Henry put the keys in the lock and was about to open it, when the door to the apartment at the end of the hall opened up.

"Another late night for you, Henry?"

It was Mrs. Greenblatt.

"Yes, Mrs. G. But I promise I've been good."

"Oh, I'll bet. Nothing good happens after eleven at night. Nothing."

"Goodnight, Mrs. G."

"Let me know if you see that rotten mutt around here again so I can call animal control. Son of a bitch left a pile of shit in front of my door bigger than the one that dinosaur left in Jurassic Park. Saints alive!"

"I think the owner has that dog back now, Mrs. G. He shouldn't be a problem anymore."

"Oh? And how the hell do you know *that*, Henry Trank?"

"Just a feeling. Call it intuition."

"Bah!" And she slammed the door.

Henry and Jo laughed and went inside. They climbed into bed together and both fell instantly asleep.

Neither remembered a single dream the next morning.

Chapter Fifty

Right Here, Right Now

November second was a cloudless, beautiful day. It was one of those days you counted yourself lucky to get once the calendar turned past the last day of October. After the events of Halloween had taken their toll on everyone, Wanda's suggestion of a day of rest was just what the doctor ordered. Jo was patched up, sore, but otherwise okay. Wanda's toe was bandaged up tight. She had to wear an open-toed sandal on one foot and an orthopedic shoe on the other. She needed a cane to keep her balance. Henry thought she looked like Yoda being discharged from a M*A*S*H unit. He told this to Jo, and they both had a good laugh.

Archie was his usual cheerful self, welcoming everyone with a big hug. Jeannie Trank was bandaged on the identical toe as Wanda, only she was half as lucky. She'd lost half of her big toe to the fangs of Chesrule. Dominick helped her up the driveway and into the backyard of Archie's home. "How the h-h-heck are you Archie?" he said as he shook his hand. Archie clapped him on the shoulder and told him he was good.

Everyone was in a great mood. Talk and laughter flowed freely. Archie had put the speakers in the window, set up the playlist on iTunes (he preferred vinyl but, let's face it, digital was the shit when it came to playlists), and let the tunes rip. Joanne and Henry got up from the table and danced when *'You Shook Me All Night Long'* by AC/DC came up on the list. All the others at the picnic table cheered them on. Two teenage boys were skateboarding along the street when the one in the lead caught sight of Joanne dancing, came to a stop, and was slammed into by his buddy, who was also gawking at Jo. Henry just smiled and thought, 'Yep, and she's gonna be my wife.'

Henry and Jo made their way over to the table when the song was over and sat down. Jo sat across from Archie, Henry across from Wanda, and the Trank's across from each other in the middle. Everyone had eaten. It was time to chill and have a few drinks. Diet Coke for Wanda and Jo. Beers for the guys, and Jeannie was having a Dewdriver Dom had mixed for her.

"Such a nice day," said Wanda. "I'm so happy we could all get together. I've so wanted life to be like this for the longest time. Delilah would have loved this."

Everyone nodded in somber agreement. It was quiet for a time—an unintentional moment of silence for Delilah's passing. Wanda continued, "After the events of the other night in the Emporium, I couldn't help but think about Delilah and I growing up together. We shared so many good times. So many secrets only the very best of friends ever can. Your mother was a gifted woman, Henry. We both grew up misunderstood by most of the people around us. Back then, psychic abilities were not as accepted as they are now. Hell, they're mainstream today. I wish we could have transplanted at least *that* part of our young lives into today. As for the rest, I wouldn't trade a day of it. I didn't have the best childhood in the world, not by a long shot. But I had a best friend, and I had her older sister, Jeannie. The woman you grew up with, Henry, was the only one in both our families who showed us kindness and understanding. But even better, she *believed* us. And Dom did, too. Neither of them thought we were weird or made fun of us. And that meant more to Delilah and I than anyone could possibly know."

Wanda looked at all of them. She knew Henry had forgiven her for having to hold things back from him. Having, at times, to lie straight to his face about so much. He understood, now on such a deeper level than even five days ago, what she'd done was for the good of all of them. To protect them all. She hoped now she would receive the same forgiveness from Jeannie and Dom.

The day of rest she'd recommended for everyone yesterday was more than just a day of rest. It was a day she used to undo some old spells she'd put in place way back in the days they'd had to move Henry north. It was nothing malicious—they would all understand—but it was something that, even though necessary, still left a nasty taste in her mouth. She needed and hoped for their forgiveness. The days of hiding things from the people she loved were over.

"I say all that because I want you, Jeannie and Dom, to know the truth. The entire truth, warts and all. Yesterday, I removed a spell which made the events that have transpired over the last few days possible. Back when you became parents to Henry, I made it so there would be … certain blank spots in your memory. I made it so you would, without a doubt, think you'd adopted Henry. And until you went to sleep last night, that's what you believed. Yesterday, however, I removed those spells. Those blank spots that were there, are no longer. In fact, if I didn't tell you about them, you'd never even know they'd been there. But now, Solomon is gone. I want to live my life being able to look those I love in the eye without feeling ashamed. I'm asking for your forgiveness."

Jeannie and Dom looked at Wanda like she'd lost her mind. None of what she'd said seemed to make any sense to them. And with good reason—the spell had worked. They really had no idea what she was talking about.

"I'm not sure what you mean, Wanda," Jeannie said. "I remember the day I picked up Henry from Delilah like it was yesterday. Dominick does too. We were talking about it on the drive down here. It was painful for all of us. Especially DeeDee. She loved Henry so much, but she understood what was going on and that it was for the good of all. And really, there was no other way. Everyone would be dead if Solomon ever found out about Henry. So, if it makes you feel better, even though I don't see how it's necessary, I forgive you. I believe what you're saying. I just honestly have zero recollection of things being any other way."

For the second time in three days, Wanda felt the weight of all the years of lying (albeit with good cause) slip away. Her soul felt lighter for it. She got up and hobbled over to where Jeannie was sitting and gave her a big hug. She went to the other side of the table and did the same to Dominick. She took her cane and hobbled back to her seat at the table across from Archie.

"And now for you, Archibald. I'm glad you're sitting, cuz this is a big one."

Archie looked at her, left eyebrow raised. "Uh oh."

"You've been warned," she said, smiling. "I told you the other night at the shop it's a good thing. And it is. Joyous, in fact."

"You've got my attention," Archie said.

She had the attention of everyone at the table. It was the middle of the day on a Friday, two days after Halloween in Salem. You could have heard a pin drop in the middle of a grass yard.

Wanda began, "The other night as we stood around my fallen friend, all I could think about was all the wonderful memories we'd shared when we were kids. In particular, my mind went to a night we both went to a party at the U. Now, I realize it's been quite a long time since that day, but I remember it like it was yesterday. I left my house a shy, awkward teenage girl. I met DeeDee, Jeannie, and Dom over at the Davis house in the garage where I got my first taste of the creature. By the time we got to the party, I had a pleasant buzz going. Jeannie and Dom introduced us to some of their friends, and then DeeDee and I made our own way through the crowd. We chatted up a few people here and there, we were both feeling good. I was reveling in my newfound ability to actually talk to strangers, thanks to the liquid courage of alcohol. DeeDee and I both found a quiet corner of the room where we could hang out, watch the crowd and chitchat. And then, out of nowhere, these two handsome freshmen came over to us. They introduced themselves and proudly told us they were both psych majors at the U, and asked if we would like to have a drink with them."

Archie's face lit up instantly. The implication of what Wanda had just revealed to him sent a raw bolt of understanding through his entire being. He'd remembered DeeDee and the night they'd had together. He never knew, however, spell or no spell, her actual name was Delilah, and that she'd ended up pregnant. It was just a one-night stand at a frat house party. He saw where Wanda was going with this now! He understood. Wanda nodded, she'd taken the spell from Archie the day before too. And by the look on his face, she knew begging forgiveness from Archie wasn't necessary.

"The boy I eventually went off with, to his dad's car and wonderful memories of *'Waiting For A Girl Like You,'* was named Bobby Mullins. DeeDee told me, later on that night, her "song to remember" was *'Layla,'* by Derek and the Dominos, and she shared that song with a young man in one of the bedrooms upstairs at the frat house. She thought he was cute and thoughtful, and he really had good taste in music. She said his name was Archie. And he made a joke about it because of his last name. He told her when he got his psych degree one day, everyone would have to call him Doctor Love."

Archie was in tears now. Henry was stunned. He was sitting at the table with his father!

"And you've known it all this time, haven't you, Wanda?" Archie asked. His voice was thick with emotion. He wasn't mad though. He was grinning from ear to ear. He realized the only reason he was sitting at the table now, in this wonderful moment with his son, was because of the careful planning and reluctant dishonesty of his best friend in the world.

Henry was a mix of emotions. Here he sat with his mom and dad, the ones who'd raised him almost his entire life, worried about how this would affect them. Oh, he knew them well enough to know they'd be fine with it, but it was still, for him, uncomfortable. And Dom and Jeannie knew what he was thinking. If there was anything they knew about Henry, it was how loyal he was. It was Dom who sensed the mild discomfort of Henry. He just winked at him and smiled. It was a small gesture, but it meant the world to Henry.

Jeannie got up, went over to Henry and hugged him. "It looks like the family just got a little bit bigger, Henry," Then she went over to Archie and hugged him and said, "So, what do you want for Christmas?" And they all laughed.

Henry got up from the table then and put his hand out to Joanne. She got up ... slowly. She was thinking maybe she should have taken it easy on the dancing (but it's hard not to move your ass to *'You Shook Me All Night Long,'* she thought), when the pain in her midsection gave her a little kick. Maybe a hint of things to come? She ignored it. She knew what Henry was about to tell everyone, and she was ecstatic. Jo took his hand and joined him at the head of the table.

Henry cleared his throat' "It's hard to imagine anything could make this day better than it's already been. I can't believe all that's happened to me, to all of us, in the last five days. But yeah, this day is about to get better." Henry got down on one knee in front of Joanne, in front of the people he cared about the most in the world, and said, "Joanne Andersen, will you marry me?"

In the middle of Henry's father's yard, with the early November sun fading, Joanne smiled down at Henry, a little watery around the eyes. "Well now, this beats the hearse proposal by a mile, Band-aid boy." She started nodding then, because she couldn't find her voice right away, and then, "Yes! From the moment I saw you at the Cauldron, it was always yes."

Archie stood up, excited. "I'll be right back." He ran into the house and sat down at his computer. He found the website he needed, printed out the document, and rushed back outside. He knelt down at the end of the picnic table between where Henry and Joanne now sat. He slapped down the document in front of them.

"What's this?" Joanne asked.

"Read it," said Archie.

Joanne read it aloud, "Commonwealth of Massachusetts, The Trial Court, Probate and Family Court Department. MARRIAGE WITHOUT DELAY. Why, exactly, are you showing us this, Arch?"

Archie grinned from ear to ear. Henry couldn't help but think of the grandfather from Jurassic Park saying, *'We spared no expense.'*

Archie rapped on the document excitedly. "We can do this today! Right now! I'm a justice of the peace!" He looked back and forth at Joanne and Henry. "Whatcha think?"

Henry looked the question at Jo.

She wiggled her eyebrows at Henry. "Let's do it."

And on November 2, 2018, in front of the people they loved the most in the world, Henry and Joanne—David and Madeleine—became one again. Married, three hundred twenty-six years later, by the father Henry never knew he had.

EPILOGUE

AT 3:13 A.M. ON the morning of July 31st, Joanne Trank went into labor. Henry wasn't worried. They had been prepared for this eventuality ever since the day Jo showed him the positive results of the pregnancy test back in January. And being an ER nurse, Henry wasn't about to be caught off-guard. So why was he still so on edge?

He walked Joanne to the door of the apartment, stood her outside, and told her to just breathe.

"No shit, Sherlock," was her reply.

Henry shut and locked the door behind him. "Looks like the balloon's about to pop," said Mrs. Greenblatt from her end of the hall. *Does she ever sleep?*, he thought. Henry ignored her and put his arm behind Jo to support her as they made their way down the one flight of stairs to the street and the warmed-up Camry.

He maneuvered Joanne gently into the passenger's side, shut the door, and hopped in behind the wheel. The streets were empty, and they made it to the hospital in under five minutes.

Seven hours later, Henry had to take a break from the birthing room. Jo had been in labor a long time now. It was proving to be a tough birth and the doctor's were leaning toward performing a C-section if things didn't change.

Standing in the waiting room alone, Henry's thoughts turned to his mother. It was so fucking unfair. He grew sad thinking about all she would miss out on. All the joy of being a grandmother. He couldn't help but be a bit angry at God, or a Higher Power, or whatever kept the wheels of the universe turning. Where was the justice? Where was the fairness? It was at times like this Henry longed for his former ignorance of all things spiritual. But *that* genie was out of the bottle now. He'd seen too much to pretend otherwise.

Their wedding day popped into his head. Even in the midst of all the joy of that day, he carried the sorrow of her absence with him. And even during all the beautiful memories he and Jo had created over the last nine months, there was an undercurrent of loss. Jo sensed it, of course. She was insanely intuitive. More so than he'd ever imagined. And right before he made his way out to the waiting room, she'd told him to call Wanda. So he did.

"Hello?" Wanda answered in a sleep-bleary voice.

"Hi Wanda, it's Henry. Sorry to call you so early."

"Nonsense, honey. It's almost ten-thirty in the morning. I forgot to set my alarm. You did me a favor."

"Jo is in labor. She's having a tough time. She's been in the delivery room for almost seven hours now."

"Oh my God, the poor thing. Do you need me to come down there? I can call Archie right now and he'll come get me."

"No, no. It's not that." Henry wasn't sure what he wanted to say next. And then he realized he was talking to Wanda.

Wanda picked up on the silence. "You're thinking about DeeDee, aren't you?"

"Yes," was all he could think to say.

"What's on your mind, honey?" she asked. "Spill it."

Henry's thoughts carried him back to Halloween. The last words of Inanis rang through his mind. They'd been ringing through his mind since the bastard had spoken them. "There's no other way to say it than just saying it. Inanis said my mother would follow him to the void. She would cease to exist at all, same as him. I can't get it out of my head. Is he right? Is that true?"

Wanda took her time before answering. *Not good*, he thought.

"Henry, the things your mother had to do, the things she had to endure ... I wouldn't wish on my worst enemy, and we both know who *that* was. What I *do* know is Inanis, and those like him—they're liars. Do I know what he said is a lie? No. If I told you otherwise, I'd be just like him. Apart from the bending of the truth I had to, reluctantly, employ to keep us all alive, I would never knowingly and maliciously lie to you, Henry. So the answer is, I don't know."

So much for feeling better, he thought.

Wanda continued, "What I believe though, Henry, is whatever power does indeed pull the strings ... that power, if it's really and truly Divine, could never, ever condemn the selfless acts of a mother trying to protect her son. So, to answer your question, I think he was full of shit. Can I prove it? No. But these things have a way of proving themselves in time. Sometimes quickly, sometimes slowly, but the truth always comes out."

Just then, the nurse from the birthing room came through the door. "Mr. Trank, it's time."

"I gotta go, Wanda. Jo's about to have the baby."

"Oh, wonderful! Get in there! And tell her I love her!"

Henry pocketed his phone and ran into the birthing room just as his child was crowning. Considering how long the process had taken up to this point, the actual birth was a piece of cake. From crown to cord it took just under ten minutes. While the nurse cleaned up their daughter, Henry and Jo had a couple of minutes to themselves.

"How you doing, beautiful?" Henry asked.

"Not bad for having passed a bowling ball, thanks." She looked exhausted but happy.

"How bout you, Henry? You okay? I know you've been thinking about your mom."

He was, once again, blown away by her intuitiveness. He'd never talked much about how he felt after that day at the Emporium. "I'm alright. I just miss her. And I'm sad she won't get to see this. To be a part of it."

Joanne was about to say something more to comfort Henry, but at that moment the nurse came back with their daughter. All wrapped up in a soft, pink blanket and squeaky clean.

Henry looked at Jo, excitement in his eyes. "What do you want to name her?"

Jo took about a nanosecond. "Delilah Wanda Trank."

"I love it!" Henry said. He really did.

Joanne kissed her baby lightly on the head. She was instantly in love. She slid the blanket down a little from Delilah Wanda's shoulders to have a look at her. On the baby's back, right above her left shoulder blade, was a little brown birthmark.

"Henry, look!"

Henry did. It was a little brown birthmark in the shape of a swan.

AFTERWORD

Author's Note

This is my first book. My first time writing fiction of any kind, as a matter of fact. I enjoyed the process a lot, though at times it was challenging, frustrating, and daunting. It was weird for me. In creating characters and the lives around them for this book, I found myself in an unexpected and strange place. I felt responsible for them! I wanted to do them justice. To make them feel real and relatable. I hope I've done that. And as I recently heard another writer mention in a video I watched on YouTube, I had a hard time saying goodbye to them once the book was finished. But I don't think the story is quite done yet. I've included the first chapter of the sequel to "In Your Dreams" starting right after this page, so read on!

Some things that happen to the characters of "In Your Dreams" are actually events that come from experiences in my own life. I'll let you figure out which ones. I hope you enjoyed reading this as much as I enjoyed writing it. And I've already started working on another book. Yep, I got the bug.

I hope you liked it! And, if you have the time, could you please review the book after this page? It would help immensely to spread the word. Thanks! Happy reading!

Rob.

Review link

https://bit.ly/ReviewIYD

Thank you so much!

Swipe on for Chapter 1 of "The Red Witch."

THE RED WITCH

LEAGUE OF THE MOON - BOOK 2

ROBERT SANBORN

Henry watched the moon rise full and bright above the Atlantic Ocean from the seventh-floor hospital room. Its silvery trail danced atop the lazy waves of the dark water. Sunset had arrived only thirty minutes before and now he, Joanne, and little Delilah made their way down through the Salem Hospital, across the parking lot, and into the sultry August night. They were ecstatic. Delilah was healthy, happy, and amazingly *quiet* for a newborn. Both were thinking the same thing at the same time—*probably won't last.*

The trip from the hospital to their apartment on Lafayette Street took five minutes. It was a Sunday night in August in Salem, after all. Not like it would be when the calendar hit October in a couple of months. Salem is the Halloween capital of the world. Every year, thousands from around the globe come to take in "Haunted Happenings," the town's annual month-long Halloween celebration.

Henry pulled the red Toyota Camry up to the curb in front of their apartment. He ran around to the passenger side, opened the door, took the baby from Joanne, and held out his hand. She looked at it, a crooked grin on her face.

"I have a baby and now you're Captain Chivalry?" She shooed his hand away. "I'm okay, Band-Aid boy, just concentrate on getting her into the apartment in one piece."

He loved it when she called him Band-Aid boy. It was her funny pet name for him, inspired by his profession as an ER nurse, and it always made him laugh.

Henry did as instructed and Jo followed behind, carrying two duffel bags full of stuff from the hospital. They entered the lobby, took the elevator up to the second floor, exited, and ran straight into their neighbor, Mrs. Greenblatt. And, again, both had the same thought at the same time. *Does this woman ever sleep?*

"The prodigal son returns! Faith and begorrah!" she said.

"Hi, Mrs. G. How are you?" Henry asked.

"I'm fine, Henry and Mrs. Henry. And I see all those nights I heard the two of you bumpin' uglies has finally paid off! Let me see that little bundle o' joy!"

Henry and Jo exchanged amused glances, and he brought Delilah over to Mrs. Greenblatt. The look of pure joy as she looked over their baby was completely out of place on her usually stern face. And the cooing noises and baby talk she made as she touched Delilah's nose and ran a finger along her cheek ... they just didn't sound right coming from her. To Henry, it was like hearing the sound of a smart car engine coming from a dump truck—just wrong. He smiled anyway.

"Alright, I'll let you two go. It's been so many years since there's been a little one anywhere near a place I call home. Brings back so many wonderful memories."

Henry noticed Mrs. Greenblatt getting misty around the eyes. He didn't want to embarrass her, so he smiled, took his little girl back, and said goodnight.

Jo was already turning the corner and heading toward their apartment. That's when she screamed. Henry knew whatever caused that scream had to be bad. Jo wasn't the type to scare easily. And yeah, it was bad.

Written on the door, in what Henry was pretty sure was not red ink, were three words: *Delilah Is Ours!* And hanging from a spike buried into the eyehole of the door was an effigy that could only be one person. The doll was dressed in a purple cloak, bathed in smears of the blood used to write the message on the door. Its kinky, dirty-blonde hair was a crude match for its human counterpart's. The hanging figure of Wanda Heinze, leader of the *Foedere In Luna* (aka League of the Moon), sent chills down Henry's spine.

"Who in the fuck do these people think they are?" Jo asked.

Well, Henry thought, *she didn't exactly stay scared for long.* He knew his wife pretty well, considering they'd been together for roughly a year. And he knew the dumb bastards who decided they were going to pick a fight with Jo, especially threatening her baby—well, he actually felt a tinge of fear. For them. Joanne Andersen Trank was not one to take a threat lying down. God help them.

Mrs. Greenblatt shuffled around the corner, stopping short when she saw the new decoration on the Tranks' front door.

"What in the hell is that all about, Henry?" asked Mrs. G.

"It's a long story, Mrs. G. But I don't have time at the moment to get into it. Have you seen anyone in the building today that didn't belong here?"

"I've been sleeping most of the afternoon, Henry. And you know me, I don't need a ton of sleep."

Truer words were never spoken, Henry thought.

"You know, I couldn't swear to it, but I have a fuzzy memory of hearing whispers outside my door not long before I fell asleep. But I don't recall actually lying down on my blasted couch. And I wouldn't even *think* about *sleeping* on that lumpy piece o' shite. No, something ain't right. I would have seen or heard whoever did that." She pointed at the door.

Henry believed her. He'd been living in the building for almost a year and a half, and he'd rarely been able to slip by Mrs. Greenblatt unnoticed. He seriously doubted someone who didn't belong here would escape her all-seeing eyes.

Shit just wasn't adding up ... or maybe it was. Solomon Dobson was dead and gone, but the *Order Immortalis,* his group of "Immortal Asshats," as

Wanda called them, were alive and well, and more than likely beyond pissed at the loss of their leader.

Yeah, it didn't take a rocket scientist to figure out who'd done this. But knowing didn't change things. He knew the group responsible for the threat, but that didn't narrow it down to any one person. There was no telling how many members of the group still existed in Salem or around the world.

The apartment building's manager lived off-site. Henry planned to call him as soon as they put Delilah to bed.

Mrs. Greenblatt said her goodnights to Jo and Henry and headed back up the hallway. Henry and Jo slipped inside their door and bolted it from the other side. They put Delilah in her crib and stood over her for a few minutes until she fell asleep. Both parents, though they didn't know it, were thinking the same thing. *I hope they can't get to her in her dreams.* It was how they'd tried to get to Henry when he'd arrived in Salem back in July 2018. The *Order Immortalis* were skilled in traveling the astral plane and using it for whatever ends they deemed necessary. They wouldn't hesitate to invade the dreams of an infant if it meant they could get what they wanted.

Once the baby was asleep, Jo and Henry went into the living room, unpacked, and put away the items from the hospital. With that done, they settled down on the couch. Each with a mug of coffee.

Henry pulled out his cell phone and called the building manager.

"Gino, it's Henry Trank. How are you?"

"I'm good, Henry! How are you, the wife, and the new bambino?"

"We're all good, Gino. Thanks. Hey, listen ..." Henry told him about the mess he'd found on his front door when he came home.

"You gotta be shittin' me!"

"Nope. It's got us all worried. Mrs. G. included."

"Mrs. G. didn't see him? I find that hard to believe!" Gino said.

"So did I. But she said she heard some whispering outside her door before she fell asleep on her couch. There are two things wrong with that statement ..."

"Yeah, I know. You don't have to tell me. I've been the building super for a long time, man. There ain't no way she fell asleep in the middle of the day without some fishy stuff happening, and she would never sleep on that crappy old couch. I believe she calls it the '*lumpy ole piece o' shite*,' or something like that."

Henry asked, "Do you have the video feed available over there, Gino? I would *really* like to see who the hell is threatening us."

"I'm at home right now, Henry. But I can log in from here. Gimme a sec."

Henry waited for a couple of minutes until Gino came back on the line.

"Okay. It's seven twenty-six right now. How long you been home, Henry?"

"Half an hour ... maybe a bit more."

He could hear Gino clicking and typing away over the phone.

"Son of a bitch!"

"What?" Henry asked.

"About 3:13 in the afternoon, there's a guy in a black hoodie. Only it ain't like a regular lookin' hoodie. It kinda goes down to his ankles. The idiot isn't even wearing shoes. He's standing in front of Mrs. G's door; he's pulling out some kinda pouch and putting it on the floor. Looks like he's chanting or praying over it or something. He's opening the pouch and spreading some shit all over the floor right in front of her threshold ... Looks like powder, or salt maybe? He's knocking on the door from his knees, and then he blows on the powder. And now Mrs. G is opening the door."

Henry was getting nervous. This was *not good.*

"She's talking to him, only she ain't acting like Mrs. G.—looks like some kinda zombie or something. Now she's nodding at him and then just shuts the door. Must've been when she went to lie down on the couch that we *both* know she never sleeps on. Hold on, Henry, I gotta switch to the camera aimed at your door."

Henry held. He was getting that nervous feeling in the belly. Jo watched Henry—a mix of concern and anger on her face.

"Okay, Henry, he's reaching into his pocket, he's pulling out a little hammer and now he's bangin' on your door. Looks like he put a big nail right in the eyehole. He's reaching back into the pouch and writing with his finger on your door. Is that blood?"

"Yeah, it's blood, Gino. Keep going."

"I can see what he wrote. You call the cops yet, Henry?"

"If I thought the cops could help us, I would have already called them, Gino."

"Yeah, but ..."

"Trust me, Gino, the cops can't help. But I need to know what's on the rest of the tape. Please, Gino."

"Okay, he looks like he's hangin' something on the spike. It looks like a doll. Now he's reaching into the bag again. He just rubbed blood on the doll. He's closing up the big pouch now. He's turning around to leave and ..."

About ten seconds went by and the line stayed silent.

"Gino, you okay? Gino?"

"Um, Henry. I know why you can't call the cops now."

Henry knew the reason he couldn't call the cops. But he wasn't about to tell Gino why. So, he found it really interesting Gino had figured this out all on his own. He waited. Finally, Gino spoke.

"It's kinda hard to give them a description of the perp when the perp doesn't have a face."

"You mean it's blurred out from the camera?"

"No, the camera works fine. It's 1080p, as a matter of fact. I can see the lint on the guy's hoodie. He doesn't have a face, Henry. It's. Not. There."

Read the rest! Scan the QR Code below!

Contact:

RobertSanborn@robsanbornauthor.com

Website: https://www.robsanbornauthor.com/

Twitter: https://twitter.com/robsanbornauth

Facebook: https://www.facebook.com/robsanbornauthor

Instagram: https://www.instagram.com/robsanborn.author/

TikTok: https://www.tiktok.com/@authorrobertsanborn

FREE Novella "Saving the Witch" with Newsletter Sign-up! Scan QR Code

AUDIOBOOK VERSION

If you'd like to check out the Audiobook Version scan the QR code below.

CONTINUE THE SERIES

The Red Witch: League of the Moon, Book 2

Blood, Magic & Mercy: League of the Moon, Book 3

Printed in Great Britain
by Amazon

19479547R00195